Henrietta Christian Wright

Children's Stories in English Literature from Shakespeare to

Tennyson

Henrietta Christian Wright

Children's Stories in English Literature from Shakespeare to Tennyson

ISBN/EAN: 9783337062040

Printed in Europe, USA, Canada, Australia, Japan

Cover: Foto ©Andreas Hilbeck / pixelio.de

More available books at **www.hansebooks.com**

CHILDREN'S STORIES

IN

ENGLISH LITERATURE

FROM SHAKESPEARE TO TENNYSON

BY

HENRIETTA CHRISTIAN WRIGHT

NEW YORK
CHARLES SCRIBNER'S SONS
1907

TROW DIRECTORY
PRINTING AND BOOKBINDING COMPANY
NEW YORK

CONTENTS.

CHAPTER VI.

CHAPTER VII.

CHAPTER VIII.

CHAPTER IX.

CHAPTER X.

CHAPTER XI

CHAPTER XII.

CHILDREN'S STORIES

IN

ENGLISH LITERATURE

FROM SHAKESPEARE TO TENNYSON

CHAPTER I.

In the year 1564 Stratford-on-Avon, in Warwickshire, England, was a quiet little village
that differed in no way from hundreds of others
scattered over England at that time. In these
little villages the houses were built commonly
of wood, with the upper stories overhanging
the lower, and with windows of lattice work or
horn, as glass was then seldom used except in
the houses of the wealthy, where there could
also be found carved oaken doors and ornamented balconies, and house-fronts covered
with plaster or decorated with panels of oak.
Sometimes the village consisted of one long
straggling street, which began in the open
country and ended perhaps in a moor or bog.
But more often the houses were built around a
large green, in the centre of which were the

may-pole and common well.   There the villagers came in the evening to chat and gossip,
and on holidays they made merry with dancing
and feasting, and the Robin Hood games which
were so popular at that time.

Each cottage had its garden wherein grew
rosemary and fennel and all kinds of herbs, in
closest neighborhood to the roses and daffodils
and violets which were the pride of the cot-
tagers ; and in the fields beyond, the paths led
through scarlet poppies and golden primroses to
the great forests which were then found all
over England.

Quite outside the villages, and often far removed from them, were the manor-houses of
the wealthy squires, the castles of the great
nobles, and the abbeys and cathedrals whose
fine architecture so beautified the country.

But in Stratford itself the beauty consisted
mainly in the prettily kept gardens ; the beautiful river Avon, which wound round the village
on its way to join the Severn ; in the graceful
yew, elm, and lime trees which shaded the cottage roofs ; and in the old church, built possibly

in the days when the Normans were still trying to make the English nation become French, and which may have served as a refuge more than once for some merry band like Robin Hood's.

In one of these cottages, which was richer than many of its neighbors by possessing two stories instead of one, and which had further-more some dormer windows in its roof and a pent-house over its door, was born in 1564 William Shakespeare, whose name stands far above every other in the story of English liter-ature, and whose genius has made the village of Stratford immortal.

Very little is known of Shakespeare's child-hood and boyhood, except that they were spent at Stratford.   But we know that his father was a man of some importance in the village, and that the boy's early days must have been comfort-able and happy.   When he was seven years of age he entered the free grammar-school of the village, where pupils were admitted as soon as they knew how to read.   Here for seven years he learned from books the things that were then taught in the grammar-schools, including no doubt some Latin and Greek and as much English as was considered necessary; for in those days English was thought of little importance, and to be a scholar meant to know certain languages and sciences which the learner would probably never use.

But outside of school Shakespeare learned much, and stored the knowledge well in his heart. He knew all the flowers, plants, and trees which were to be found for miles around in the fields and meadows and woods. He spent hours in poring over the history of Stratford Church, where he had been christened and to which he went regularly every Sunday, and which joined the England of his day with a past that was full of the glorious and stirring history of the English nation. This old church must have told him many stories of other days, and of the time when England knew no such peace and honor as she knew in Shakespeare's time. Not far away was the city of Coventry, where were given at stated times and with great splendor the religious or miracle plays which Shakespeare must have seen many a time.   And a few miles away from Stratford were the great castles of Warwick and Kenilworth, the former of which was rich in memories of the wars of the Roses, when England was a great battle-field from end to end, and which was second in interest only to Kenilworth, where Queen Elizabeth came from time to time with her train of lords and ladies to be entertained by the great Lord Leicester.

And Shakespeare also learned much from the travel which constantly passed through the village, for Stratford was cut into four sections by the two great public highways which ran through the place from the great neighboring cities, and over which went all the travel of that part of the kingdom.   In this way he heard of the great world beyond Stratford.   He learned of those great heroes of the sea, Frobisher, and Hawkins, and Gilbert, and Drake, and followed them in imagination in their voyages across the ocean to the unknown continents and islands of the new world.   And he heard in the same way of the affairs of London, what the Queen and the great nobles were about, and who was famous and who was not, and what was thought to be fine in the sight of London folk, and what they despised as poor and mean.

And the boy learned strange things, too, from the village folk, who believed in all the superstitions of the day. He could tell which plants were used by witches to concoct poisonous broths, and what herbs the village apothecary gathered to dispel evil charms, and why he recommended blood of dragons and oil of scorpions, and powdered mercury for different diseases. He heard also of the alchemists who could turn iron into gold and clay into silver, and who knew the value and use of every precious stone, and could tell why pearls had mystic virtues, and diamonds brought valor to the possessor, and why the topaz could cure madness, and the hyacinth protect from lightning. And, too, at the county fairs where every kind of ware was sold, the boy Shakespeare could see people buying charms to keep off sickness, or bad luck, or to bring happiness and fortune.

Here one could buy love-philters, and croco-
diles' tears, and amulets graven with texts of
scripture, and cabalistic rings, and could hear
strange talk of the wonders produced by the
last eclipse of the sun, such as wars and sick-
nesses, and treason, and could pay an astrolo-
ger to calculate his lucky and unlucky days,
and purchase a charm which would keep at
bay the influence of witches and evil spirits and
wicked fairies, and could even buy, were he
rich enough, the magical fern-seed which would
give to the owner the power of walking invisible among his fellow-men.

Among other things which would be of interest to the youth in Shakespeare's boyhood, may
be counted the royal progresses when Queen
Elizabeth went from palace to palace throughout the country to be entertained by the great
lords of the realm. The Queen on these occa-
sions was always attended by an immense retinue, and the journey was usually made on
horseback. At such times the villages through
which she passed vied with one another to do
her honor. Arches of greenery were erected

for her to pass under, flowers and wreaths were scattered before her, the church bells were rung, and the villagers turned out dressed in holiday attire to welcome the Queen, and to see her brilliant company. The lords and ladies in their beautiful costumes, the horses with their trappings of gold and silver, the trumpeters sounding the approach, the beat of drums, and to crown all, the gracious smile and words of the Queen, were things never to be forgotten.

When Kenilworth was the palace visited, all Stratford was alive with interest, and every villager knew of, and many of them saw, the stately ceremonies of the event, for Queen Elizabeth kept great state always. All the men who served her—chamberlains, cupbearers, carvers, ushers, trumpeters, and grooms—were required to be of fine appearance and manner, and even the smallest service was performed with great ceremony. The bearer of a letter had to deliver it kneeling, and kiss it before placing it in the Queen's hands. When the meals were served, the attendants were required to kneel once or twice after placing the dishes on the table, and if she dined in public she was waited upon by the great lords of the realm. And all these things formed subject of talk around Stratford, and all eyes were turned toward Kenilworth when Elizabeth was there.

Most interesting of all the events connected with her visit were the masks and revels, shows and plays which were given at the castle in her honor. One of the royal progresses to Kenilworth occurred when Shakespeare was about twelve years of age, and very likely the boy was present at the entertainments given there, and watched with eager eyes the scene before him. No expense or trouble was spared to make the masks and interludes as perfect as possible, and lords and ladies of high rank were often the performers. Gods and goddesses of the sea, wood nymphs, fairies, mermaids, and witches flitted before the eyes of the audience, and lakes, seas, groves, castles, gardens, and towers appeared and disappeared as if with magic touch.

There was also given at this time a pageant representing the massacre of the Danes in early

English history, and knights appeared on war-horses, fighting with spears, and on foot, fighting with swords, mimicking a real battle, the performance ending by the defeat of the Danes and the appearance of some English women leading in bands of captives. These plays and interludes were very often acted by children, and there were four companies of these young actors who were especially devoted to the Queen's service. These were called the children of St. Paul's, the children of Westminster, the children of the Chapel, and the children of Windsor, according to the different schools from which they were taken ; and they were in charge of the Master of Revels, whose duty it was to provide their costumes, to rehearse them for the plays, and to attend to the stage properties, which included, among other things, crowns and spangles for angels, sea-horses, devils' eyes, castles, and scenes representing the infernal regions.

Besides these entertainments in honor of the Queen, Shakespeare saw from time to time the companies of regular players, who travelled from London throughout the country, frequently stopping at Stratford, where they gave their performances, as was usual at a time when there were no theatres, in the court-yard of the inn. In this way the boy Shakespeare became familiar with the best plays and players of the day, and this, joined with his visits to Coventry, where the great religious plays were given on the feasts of the Church, must have given him many a glimpse of the life beyond his native village.

Amid such scenes and impressions Shakespeare grew to manhood, and it is easy to trace their influence in his works; and thus we know, that when he speaks of elves and fairies, of spirits, charms, and witchcraft, or when he describes the character of a rustic or the manners of a courtier, he does so from the intimate knowledge he gained of such things in his boyhood.

When Shakespeare was twenty-one he went to London to try his fortunes in that great city, and a very interesting place was the London of his day. The Palace and Abbey of Westminster, the Tower of London, the river Thames, where one could see the tall masts of ships glistening like so many clustered spears, and the wherries plying in every direction, and the flocks of white swans floating, and at night the lights of silken-covered pleasure-boats filled with gayly dressed ladies and gentlemen on their way to some mask or party, enlivening their journey with songs and music. Then there was famous London Bridge and St. Paul's Cathedral, and palaces, and markets, and taverns, and bear-gardens, and long streets full of shops where could be bought cups of gold from Venice, and jewelry of all kinds, and carpets, and silks, and shawls which may have been taken perhaps as plunder from some Spanish ships home-bound from Asia, run down by English sailors. Then, too, there were the daily crowds where could be seen people from all over the world. Knights and courtiers jostling country squires, and scholars and divines touching as they passed the highwayman or thief who had won fame by his clever robberies. Here also were noblemen dressed in velvet and gold from Italy and Spain and France, slaves from Spanish America, sea captains and priests, soldiers and servants, all held by chance or interest within the gray walls which circled London, and whose gates gave welcome to as strange a crowd as could be found in the world.

Into this curious crowd came Shakespeare, quick to see and eager to learn, and before long all these strange sights were as familiar to him as the faces of his own townsfolk; and each one told its story to him so plainly that, as before he had learned the secrets of the fields and woods, so now he learned men and the interests which made up the great world. And he learned these lessons so well, that when he came to write his plays, he made such use of them as no writer ever made before or since; for it is the use of this knowledge of the world, combined with his own genius, that makes Shakespeare the greatest dramatist that has ever lived.

But when Shakespeare first entered London the objects of greatest interest to him were the theatres ; for since his boyhood two or three regular theatres had been opened, though when the first one was built, or rather made out of some dwelling-houses, the mayor of London and other officials complained that a place where such large crowds could come together would surely spread the plague, which was then raging in the city.   And some people even said that the players were the whole cause of the plague, because the acting of plays was a sinful thing.

But when Shakespeare reached London the theatres had been for some years recognized as respectable and proper places of amusement, and persons of all ranks in life visited them daily.   One of the principal theatres was that called Blackfriars, which, like the first one, had been made out of some dwelling-houses, and which took its name from the monastery of Blackfriars near by.   And it was this poor little play-house—lit by candles, and with its floor of earth, and its stage covered with rushes, and with an audience that smoked, laughed, talked, and ate as the play went on—that Shakespeare entered soon after he reached London, and by so doing crowned it with a fame as immortal as that which rests upon Stratford itself.

The company which acted at this theatre had more than once been seen by Shakespeare in his boyhood, as it was one of the regularly licensed companies, and under the protection of the Earl of Leicester; and it is not unlikely that Shakespeare considered himself very lucky in obtaining a place there, though the place was probably a very humble one at first.

The plays that were then most popular were in many cases written by the actors themselves, and as the company at Blackfriars consisted of some of the leading actors of the day, Shakespeare was at once thrown into the society that would best bring out his talents as an actor and playwright. All London then was wild over the plays of Christopher Marlowe, whose genius had first made the English drama seem a picture of real human life. These plays were either full of exciting and splendid scenes from the life of some great Eastern hero, who moved around the stage like a prince in the "Arabian

Nights," or dealt with some trait of human character in such a way that it seemed for the time that the only thing of interest in the world was whether the hero of the play should keep true to his noble nature, or yield to some temptation.

It was in such pictures of character that Marlowe gained the greatest control over his audience, for the struggle between good and evil is one that is constantly going on in men's souls everywhere. Shakespeare frequented the theatres, and acted himself in a small way for a while, perhaps a year or two, and then began to write for the stage himself.

At first he simply joined with some fellow-actor in writing a new play, or in re-writing an old one; but this only continued for a short time, and soon he had begun the series of wonderful plays which stand alone in all literature.

Shakespeare gathered the materials for his plays from many sources, for nearly all the authors of ancient times had been translated into English, and the playwright of the day could choose his plot from many different scenes. In fact, the literature that was open to Shakespeare was as rich and varied as a casket of precious stones, and he made good use of his opportunity. He was familiar with the old writers of Greece and Rome, and knew all the old tales of love and adventure and revenge which filled the pages of Italian writers, and was wise in the old chronicles of England, whose history was as romantic and interesting as a fairy tale. And besides this, he read the tales of those adventurers who had travelled in the far East and told thrilling tales of Arab and Moor and Turk, or excited the imagination by relating the dangers of the Southern Ocean or the Arctic Sea, and the perils among hostile tribes and savage beasts in distant America.

And all this knowledge of books he combined with his knowledge of men, and put both into his plays, and made them so real and true that when people saw them on the stage they forgot that what they saw was acting, and could fancy that they were looking at the real scenes which Shakespeare had in mind when he was writing. And so they laughed over his clowns,

2

and fools, and jesters, and wept over his unhappy kings, and wretched queens, and murdered princes, whose pitiful stories made them think the more tenderly of their own children safe at home. And when the play was over and they came back to everyday life again, it was to declare that this Shakespeare, who also acted in his plays sometimes, was the greatest writer of dramas that had yet appeared, and they crowded the theatre and would listen to no other plays if they might hear his.

Among the plays which Shakespeare put upon the stage of Blackfriars, or that of the Globe Theatre, which was built a few years after he came to London—for his plays were only performed at these two theatres—we find one which takes us back to the time when Chaucer wrote the *Knight's Tale* and gave us the romantic story of the love of the knights Palamon and Arcite for the beautiful Emilie, the sister of Hippolyta, Queen of the Amazons, whom Theseus, Duke of Athens, had married after first taking her prisoner in his war with Thebes.

The old story of Chaucer dealt with a time before elves and fairies had forever left the earth, and when people still believed in fabulous races like the Amazons; and this suggested to Shakespeare the idea of writing a play which should take his English audience back to Athens in the days of the great Theseus, and show them how the great lords and ladies, the common folk, lovers and sweethearts, kings and queens, were duped and made the sport of Oberon, king of the fairies, and his wife Titania, aided by the mischievous Puck. The play is called *A Midsummer Night's Dream*, and most of the scenes are laid at night in a grove near Athens, the favorite haunt of elves and fairies.

This is the story: The beautiful Hermia, daughter of Egeus, had two suitors, Lysander and Demetrius, and she loved Lysander, who seemed to her to have every virtue, and despised Demetrius, who displeased her in every way; and this in itself would not have mattered, but unhappily for Hermia her father heartily liked Demetrius, and heartily disliked Lysander, and thus it was impossible for them to agree as to which of the two Hermia should marry. Now, there was a cruel law in Athens which declared that when a maid refused to marry as her father desired, she should either be made to die a cruel death, or enter a nunnery, and Egeus grew so tired of Hermia's disobedience that at last he resolved to appeal to this law. So, hardly had Theseus returned to Athens with the captive Hippolyta, when there came to him Egeus bringing his wilful daughter, and attended by the two suitors, neither of whom intended to give Hermia up. Theseus listened to the complaint, and tried in vain to persuade Hermia to obey her father and marry Demetrius, and then, not finding it in his heart to punish her for her disobedience, he dismissed them, telling Hermia that he would give her four days to think the matter over before deciding finally what to do with her; for the law of Athens must be carried out, no matter how cruel it might seem. At this Hermia was much dejected, for she had fully resolved never to marry Demetrius, and things would have appeared very dark indeed, had not Lysander managed to console her by proposing that they should run away from Athens, and so get beyond the reach of the cruel law, and thus be happy in spite of it.

This seemed a happy way out of the difficulty, and Hermia agreed to meet Lysander the next night in a grove that was near Athens, in which she had gone maying many a time, and run away with him, and so get beyond her father's anger and the law's injustice. And this plan would have been carried out, and Egeus would never have known what had become of his daughter, but for one thing, and this was the fact that this same Demetrius, whom Hermia despised, was deeply loved by her friend Helena, to whom she told her plan of flight.

Now, Helena loved Demetrius as deeply and truly as Hermia loved Lysander, and she had even a harder lot to bear than her friend ; for while Demetrius had once loved her in return, he now cast her off utterly and would have nothing to do with her, though she tried

in every way to win back his love. And she
was so unhappy that even one kind word from
Demetrius would have been most precious to
her. So she resolved to tell Hermia's plan to
Demetrius, and make him at least think kindly
of her once again, even though it might be the
means of losing him forever. Now, the return
of Theseus to Athens had stirred all the city to
devise means of doing him honor, and all sorts
of entertainments were to take place to celebrate his return and his marriage to Hippolyta.
Among others, a certain number of mechanics
had determined to play the interlude of *Pyramus and Thisbe*, if they could induce Theseus
to see it, thinking that their fine acting would
win them both regard and reward from the
Duke.

And it was their intention to meet in the
grove near Athens and rehearse their parts,
so that they might keep their play a secret;
and, as it happened, the night for their rehearsal was the very one fixed for the meeting
of Hermia and Lysander in the same grove.
And all these plans might have been carried

out, had it not been for an old quarrel between
Oberon and Titania, the king and queen of
fairyland.   The cause of the trouble was a little
Indian boy whom Titania refused to give up
to Oberon, who had taken a fancy to have the
boy in his train, and for a long time the fairy
king and queen had hardly spoken to each
other.   But on the very night that the lovers
and players were to meet in the grove, thence
came also Oberon roving through the moonlit
woods, dull in spirits, and angrier than ever at
Titania, for, try how he would, he could not
get the Indian boy away from her.

And hardly had he entered with his train,
when Titania came also upon the scene, and the
two began quarrelling so fiercely that all the attendant elves and fairies crept into acorn cups
for fear, and trembled as they heard Titania re-
buke Oberon and tell him that the flocks had
died and harvests failed, and the land been
covered with poisonous fogs which brought
diseases to mortals, and that the roses had
been bitten with frost, and summer buds had
bloomed in winter, and in fact the whole course

of nature changed because of his jealousy ; and her words so enraged Oberon that he resolved to humble Titania's pride and get the boy, cost what it might.

And so, as soon as Titania had gone on her way Oberon sent Puck to gather the little flower called *love-in-idleness ;* for he meant with this to work a charm that would bring the proud queen to his will, for the juice of this little flower pressed upon the eyelids of one who was sleeping, would cause the sleeper to fall in love with the first object he should see on awaking, and Oberon declared that whether Titania fell in love with monkey or ape, he would not remove the charm until she gave up her little page to him. But hardly had Puck departed on his errand when Demetrius and Helena came in sight in search of Hermia and Lysander, and Oberon making himself invisible, heard poor Helena's laments; for Demetrius, while willing to take her help, would yet not give her the least kind word, and the fairy king seeing that Helena was young and fair, had his elfin heart touched, and resolved to do her a good service and bring her lover's heart back to her.

And so, when Puck came back, bringing *love-in idleness* with him, he gave him some of it, and told him to anoint the eyes of Demetrius with it, taking care to do it only when the first thing that Demetrius would see after might be the lady Helena. And Puck departed in high glee, for he loved to mix with the affairs of mortals, who all knew it was he who entered their dairies at night and robbed the milk of its cream, and who lurked about in dark corners frightening village maids, and led country lads miles out of their way across bog and brier, all out of pure mischief; or if he chose, would turn unexpectedly up at hard moments and bind sheaves by moonlight, and weave cloth in the dark, so that he might enjoy the amazement of those for whom he had worked.

But this time Puck made a mistake, for roving through the grove he came upon Hermia and Lysander fast asleep, for they had lost their way and had grown too weary to go on, and as Oberon had told him he would know Demetrius by his Athenian dress, he now pressed the juice upon the eyes of Lysander, who also wore the Athenian dress, and thinking his work well done, the mischievous elf flew away to see what Oberon had been about. And so he did not know that as soon as he left, Helena came up, still following Demetrius, who would yet not listen to her, though he knew she was exhausted and could go no farther. And seeing Lysander lying before her, and thinking him dead, Helena called his name again and again until he awoke, when he straightway fell in love with her, and began praising her beauty and sweetness, and at this poor Helena was more grieved than ever, thinking that Lysander was making cruel sport of her because of her unreturned love for Demetrius. And so she fled from him, not seeing Hermia, who awoke the next moment to find her lover gone, and started through the wood to find him, fearing that some evil had happened him.

In the meantime the players had come to the grove for their rehearsal. Bottom, the weaver, Flute, the bellows-mender, Tom Snout, the tinker, Snug, the joiner, Starveling, the tailor, and Peter Quince, all met to play the tragedy of *Pyramus and Thisbe*, two ill-fated lovers who were parted from each other by a cruel father, and who were in the habit of talking to each other through a chink in the wall which separated their houses. The tragedy relates that one night they agreed to meet at Ninus' tomb by moonlight, and that Thisbe coming first, was frightened away by a roaring lion, and fled leaving her mantle on the ground, and that Pyramus, coming to the place soon after, saw the mantle all stained with blood from the lion's wounds, and thought that Thisbe was dead, and so drew sword and killed himself; and hardly had this happened when Thisbe came back— for the lion had run off in the meantime— and seeing Pyramus dead, she stabbed herself with the same sword, and thus ended the play. In the cast the part of Pyramus was given to Bottom, the weaver, who insisted upon an explanation in the prologue, to the effect that he did not really kill himself with a sword, but only made believe, for fear the ladies in the audience would faint. Flute, the bellows-maker, had the part of Thisbe, with the injunction that he should speak in a very small voice, so that he would be thought a real woman. Snug was the lion, being directed to let his nails grow long so that they should hang out like the lion's claws, and to roar as gently as a sucking-dove, or a nightingale, so that the ladies would not be alarmed. Snout was to be spattered with plaster, and hold up his fingers joined in a circle to typify the chink in the wall through which the lovers talked, and another was to have a thorn bush, dog, and lanthorn to represent the moon.

The rehearsal had just begun, and Bottom had said his lines, when as he retired into the brake to wait for his cue, he was seized upon by Puck who had come wandering around in search of whatever mischief he could find, and who fastened upon him an ass's head; and when he next came forward to speak, his strange appearance so frightened the other players that they fled in dismay, and the rehearsal was broken up.

But Bottom, not knowing of his transformation, stayed on and began singing a lively tune, and it was this air which woke Queen Titania, who was sleeping near by, and upon whose eyes Oberon had so spitefully pressed the juice of *love-in-idleness.* And so the poor Queen, being under the charm, had to fall in love with Bottom, as he was the first object her eyes fell upon when waking; so deep was the enchantment that she mistook him for a creature of surpassing loveliness, and commanded Peas-blossom, and Cobweb, and Moth, and the other fairies to attend him wherever he went, and to bring to him dewberries, and figs, and grapes, and honey to eat, and the wings of butterflies "to fan the moonbeams from his sleeping eyes." And no sooner had Puck seen this than away he flew to tell his master that Titania had fallen in love with an ass, at which Oberon rejoiced greatly.

Now, while they stood there along came Hermia and Demetrius, she still looking for Lysander, and he trying in vain to make her listen to his suit. Growing weary at length, he threw himself upon the ground and then Puck learned from Oberon that he had made a mistake, and that he should have anointed the eyes of Demetrius and arranged it so that Helena should be by his side when he awoke. So Oberon sent Puck forth to bring Helena, and he himself pressed the juice of *love-in-idleness* upon Demetrius' eyes, and Demetrius awoke just in time to see Helena enter, followed by Lysander, who was offering her his love.   But Helena would not listen to him, and only rejoiced that Demetrius loved her once more, and after the two men had had some bitter words and were about to lay hands on one another, Puck, who had, by his arts, sent them roaming through the woods, making them lose sight of each other, came to Lysander where he lay asleep quite worn out with fatigue, and removed the fateful charm by applying the juice of another herb, so that when he awoke he would again love Hermia.

Now, in the morning, ere the sun was up, there came Theseus with a hunting party— among them Hermia's father — through the woods, and saw all the lovers asleep on the ground, for they had all drawn near the same place without knowing it, the night before. And Egeus had the huntsmen sound their horns, and at the sound the lovers all started up in amazement. And Theseus and Egeus were in still greater amazement when they heard Demetrius declare that he no longer loved Hermia but Helena, although he knew not what had changed him, for no one dreamed that Oberon and Puck had been busy with the affairs of mortals. But Theseus declared himself satisfied at the new turn of affairs, and said that the lovers should be married at the same time that his own wedding was celebrated.

In the meantime Titania had given the little Indian boy to Oberon, for she had no thought of anyone but Bottom, and Oberon having the boy safe in his possession, removed the charm, brought the queen to her senses, and she forgot Bottom and loved Oberon once more, and went off with him and the other fairies to prepare for Theseus' wedding-night. And Bottom woke to find his ass's head gone—for Puck had taken it off—and went back to

Athens just in time to join his company and play the part of Pyramus before Theseus and Hippolyte and the great company assembled in their honor. And Oberon and Titania and their band were present also, flitting around unseen by mortal eyes, and hearing with amusement how Demetrius and Lysander and Bottom were still in wonder about what took place in the grove on that strange midsummer night, when they had gone to sleep, and waked to find that what had been so real to them the day before had now but the character and substance of a dream.

Another play of Shakespeare was the tragedy of *King Lear*, which was taken from a collection of stories gathered together first, perhaps, by Geoffrey of Monmouth, at the same time that he collected the legends of King Arthur. In Shakespeare's tragedy Lear is a British king who, after reigning successfully for many years, decided in his old age to give up the kingdom to his three daughters, Goneril, Regan, and Cordelia, reserving for himself only the crown and a hundred knights for personal attendants.

As he desired to test the love of his daughters for him, he said that he would give the largest share of the kingdom to the one who loved him the most, and so on an appointed day he called together Goneril and Regan and their husbands, and Cordelia, who was unmarried, and told them of his design and asked each daughter in turn how much she loved him. And Goneril said she loved him beyond all power of speech, and that health, beauty, honor, liberty, and life itself could not compare with her love for him. And for this answer Lear gave her great forests and wide meadows and broad rivers in the rich country which was her dower.

Then Regan spoke and said she loved her father as much as Goneril did, and even more, for she found no other thing in life worth living for but her father only. And to her Lear gave likewise a third of the kingdom, consisting of as rich lands as those he had given to Goneril. But when the old king asked Cordelia how

3

much she loved him, she was silent, for it seemed to her that love was not a thing to be measured or counted by words. And when Lear insisted upon an answer she said that, though she loved and honored him far more than she could tell, yet **she** could not say, as Goneril and Regan did, that she loved nothing else beside; for if she were married, as her sisters were, she should think it right to give some love and honor to her husband. And at this answer Lear fell into a rage and disowned her utterly, and said that from that time she should no more be considered his child, and gave her portion to her sisters; for to him words carried great weight, and Goneril and Regan seemed loving daughters because their words were fair and pleasant to listen to.

Poor Cordelia might have fared badly enough—for the only one at her father's court who spoke a fair word for her was the Duke of Kent, and him the king banished immediately as a punishment for advising him to forgive Cordelia—had it not been that at this time there was a suitor for her hand at court, who loved her for herself alone and was glad to take her for his bride, though she was poor and forsaken and despised, and so he bore her away to become a great queen, for he was the King of France.

But the old king soon found that fair words do not always mean fair deeds, for Goneril and Regan had no love for him in their selfish hearts, and soon began to treat him very cruelly. One thing followed another, and at last Goneril told her steward to treat the king's servants with open disrespect, knowing well that her father would resent it, and when Lear chided her for it she told him that one hundred knights were too many for his service, and that he really needed but fifty. And at this King Lear got into a rage—as she knew he would—and declared he would go to Regan, who could never treat him so. Thereupon, he went to Regan, taking with him his train, and his fool, who still remained faithful to him, and one new attendant who had lately come and who was really Kent, in disguise, whose love and faithfulness could not suffer him to leave the country when he knew the king might need him at any moment.

But when they reached Regan's castle they found no entrance, for hearing that her father was coming, she had gone to the Duke of Gloucester's, a great nobleman of the land, as she wished to show him all the disrespect she could. And when Lear sent the disguised Kent on with letters, she put him in the stocks because he had drawn his sword upon Goneril's servant. Then when Lear arrived and told her how Goneril had treated him, she answered that Goneril was in the right, for he should be willing to dismiss all his knights and let his daughters' servants serve him if they so desired. Just then Goneril herself came in, having travelled thither in great haste, and with these and other unkind words, they showed him that their hearts were both unloving and cruel. Then the old king saw that although he loved these daughters and had given them all he had, yet they had no love for him, and their fair words had meant only a desire to gain the kingdom.

And at this discovery all his love turned to hate and bitterness, and he reproached them so bitterly that it seemed to them all that he was going mad with grief. And he left them and went forth into the wild storm that had begun to rage, and Goneril and Regan commanded the Duke of Gloucester and his servants to make no search for him, and to deny him entrance should he return.

But news of the way in which the old king was treated had reached France, and the King and Cordelia had sent an army to take up Lear's cause, and this army landed at Dover just about the time that Goneril and Regan had cast their father off, and Kent, yet in disguise, knowing this, sent a message to Cordelia to tell her what had happened. But the Duke of Gloucester, in spite of the commands of Goneril and Regan, followed the old king out in the storm, and took him to a place of safety near by, and hearing later that there was a plot against Lear's life, warned his friends to take him straight to Dover, for he had also heard that Cordelia was there. And for this act of loyalty, which was immediately discov, ered, Gloucester was seized, and his eyes put out by order of Goneril and Regan, and he was driven forth into the storm as Lear had been, and his estates were given to his son Edmund, who was as base as Goneril and Regan, and who had persuaded his father that his brother Edgar was a traitor to him, so that the Duke had driven him from his presence, and no longer owned him. But Edgar, disguising himself by feigning madness, still lingered around his home and met his father as he was driven forth helpless and blind, and not letting him know who he was, led him across the stormy moor to a place of safety, reaching Dover at last where Kent and Lear had already arrived. And here there was a great battle fought between the French and the forces of Goneril and Regan, and the French were defeated, and Cordelia and her father were taken prisoners, and Edmund ordered the jailer to strangle Cordelia, and then make it appear that she had killed herself.

Immediately after the battle Edgar and Edmund met in mortal combat, and here Edmund received his death-wound ; but before he breathed his last a messenger entered to say that Goneril and Regan were both dead, for Goneril had poisoned Regan in a fit of jealousy and then stabbed herself, and so all their wicked scheming had done them no good.

And then came in Lear bearing the dead Cordelia in his arms, and the play ends with the death of the old mad king, for this last sorrow had broken his heart.

Another of Shakespeare's plays, called *The Tempest*, is taken from some old tale, which was heard first perhaps in Italy.   This is the story :

Once upon a time there was a duke who reigned over Milan, and who was so wise and kind that he was beloved by his people as though he had been their father, so that the court of Milan was celebrated throughout Italy for its just laws, and the inhabitants of the duchy were envied for having so liberal and wise a prince for their ruler.   But the duke, whose name was Prospero, was much fonder of study than of anything else in the world, and very often, instead of being in the court of justice or in the council chamber, he would be far away in his study, buried deep in some book. The books that he read were of all sorts and kinds. Books of history, philosophy, mathematics, and science, and it was even said that he understood magic and witchcraft. Because of these two last things he was held in great wonder, and the people did not complain because he spent so much time in his study, and left the ruling of the country to his brother Antonio. Thus all was quiet in the land, and Prospero was happy and full of peace, when suddenly all was changed. One night he found himself seized by rough soldiers, who forced him with his little daughter Miranda to leave the castle, and took the two unfortunates down to the sea. They then hurried them in an open boat miles from the shore, and there left them alone in a vessel without sail, mast, or rigging, thinking that thus they would come quickly to their death. For these ruffians were hired by Antonio, who had seized the kingdom while his brother was thinking of nothing but books, and who, by the help of Alonso, the King of Naples, raised such a strong force to defend himself, and promised such rich rewards to those who would help him in the plot, that he carried out his wicked design without much trouble.

But Prospero had one friend, the good Gon-zalo, at court who knew of the design, although he could do nothing to prevent it.   And through his means there were carried aboard the ship some food and water and garments, and also some of the books that Prospero loved so well.   And by fair fortune, it hap-pened that the ship did not go down, but bore them safely to an island far away from the Italian shores, where they found comfort and peace; for on the island there were fresh springs and beautiful flowers, and trees which bore fruits and nuts; and for owner there was none save the monster Caliban, whom Prospero first subdued by the power of witch-craft, and then tried in every kind way to win to goodness. There Prospero and Miranda lived many years, having nothing to annoy them but the wickedness of Caliban, whom Prospero was forced at last to make his slave, and when he did not need him, to confine him in a rock so that he could do no mischief, for Caliban's heart could not be touched by kindness, and he hated Prospero because of his power.

Now, the island was enchanted, and inhabited by spirits of the air, and by deep study of his books of magic Prospero was able at last to command these spirits to do his will, so that although he had landed on the island without a single follower, he soon found one who was willing and able to obey his every wish. This was Ariel, the beautiful chief of the spirits of the air, who before Prospero came had been imprisoned in a pine-tree by Caliban's mother, who was a witch, and who had died leaving Ariel confined for twelve years, as she had no power to let him out. But Prospero had such knowledge of witchcraft that he released Ariel upon his promise to serve him a certain length of time, and for this Ariel and all the spirits of the air gave him cheerful obedience always. By their help and his own powers of magic, Prospero could call up storms and hurricanes, and darken the earth with clouds, and lash the sea into fury; and for him Ariel would fly through the air, or descend into the earth, or dive to the bottom of the ocean, or go with his master on his journeys, when Prospero made himself invisible and floated through the air as if he himself were an air spirit.

Thus Prospero was lord of the whole island and of the inhabitants of the air above, and had no enemy but Caliban, who often had to be punished with cramps and pinches and aching bones ere he would do his duty. Now, it happened after many years—so many in fact that Miranda had grown to womanhood—that the King of Naples gave his daughter in marriage to an African prince, and as he was returning from the wedding with a large company, among whom were Antonio the usurping duke of Milan, the king's son Ferdinand, and the good old Gonzalo, the vessel bearing them passed very near the island where Prospero was living. Prospero, who knew everything by the power of his witchcraft, had knowledge of this and immediately formed a plan by which he might get back his lost dukedom. And first he sent Ariel to raise a furious tempest which would cast the ship on shore and bring all his enemies into his power. So Ariel took on the form of a spirit of flame, and amid the dashing of waves and rush of rain he boarded the ship and darted hither and thither, now flaming on the beak, now on the deck, and again in the cabin, or climbing the masts spread over sail and rigging, till the vessel looked like a great ship of fire, and crew and passengers were alike filled with horror and thought that their last hour had come. Then all the Duke's party leaped in terror from the burning ship, preferring death in the sea rather than to stay amid such terrors. But by the magic of Ariel not one was lost and all reached the island safely, though separated into different parties, for that was what Prospero wished. The sailors who had remained on board were then thrown into an enchanted sleep while the vessel drifted to a safe harbor in a little bay, where the calm waters and the fragrance of dew-laden flowers, and the music of the invisible air-spirits would keep them in peaceful dreaming till Prospero should have accomplished his design.

Then Ariel flew to his master and told him of his success, and was promised his freedom if he would but help Prospero in this last enterprise. In the meantime Prospero called Miranda to him and told her the real story of their lives, and she was amazed to learn that her father was a great duke and she herself of noble birth, for of these things she had never dreamed. She was also glad to know that her father had had good reason for raising the storm, as it had grieved her sadly to watch the burning ship and the unfortunate passengers struggling with the waves; not knowing that Ariel had conducted them safely to land. And having heard this story, Miranda was thrown into an enchanted sleep and did not wake until Ariel again appeared, though visible to Prospero only, leading by magic songs

young Ferdinand, whom he had found sitting on
the shore, alone and disconsolate, mourning for
his father.   And Miranda and Ferdinand immediately fell in love with one another, as Prospero
meant they should, for this was part of his plan.

Then Prospero, with the help of Ariel and the
other air-spirits, led Antonio and his party into
all sorts of queer adventures where they saw
mysterious shapes, heard voices singing in the
air above them, and were continually led from
one delusion to another.   And all this time
graver things were happening, for Sebastian,
brother of the King of Naples, formed a plot
with Antonio to murder Alonso, who was sick
with grief over the loss of his son Ferdinand,
and succeed to the kingdom ; and Caliban, with
the assistance of some of the servants, formed a
plot to murder Prospero.   But Prospero discovered this by the power of his art and laid
charms upon all the plotters, so that nothing
could come of their designs, and then having
tested Ferdinand's love for Miranda by making
him perform many hard tasks, he prepared to
bring the adventure to an end.

So he clothed himself in his magic robes and drew a charmed circle, and into this circle Ariel brought first the King and his friends, who stood there helpless and amazed, looking upon Prospero as they might have looked upon a ghost, and fearing that they were all going mad. And then Prospero told them how they had all been brought to the island by his power and demanded his dukedom back, and Antonio and Alonso were both filled with dread, seeing how their wicked plot had come to an end, and knowing that they were both helpless before the power of Prospero. But Alonso's fear was also mixed with grief at the loss of his son, and Prospero was touched by this grief, and being well pleased that his plan had worked so nicely, he revealed to them Miranda and Ferdinand playing chess together; and when Alonso could believe that it was really his son that he saw, and not one of the island illusions, his joy was beyond words. And then Caliban and the servants were brought into the charmed circle and their plots revealed, and glad enough were they to escape with their lives, for they too saw that nothing could withstand Prospero's magic power.

Then Prospero invited them all to a banquet, and promised them a fair voyage home to Naples, where the marriage of Ferdinand and Miranda should be celebrated. And after this he burned his magic robes, buried his wand, and sunk his magic books deep into the sea, for he had ceased to be king of the enchanted isle and was content to become once more Duke of Milan, and to rule his people and be loved by them as they had loved him before his banishment.

Shakespeare's plays are generally divided for convenience into tragedies, comedies, and historical plays. All of the historical plays, with the exception of three, are based upon facts in English history. They may be enumerated as follows: *King John, Richard II., Henry IV.,* in two parts; *Henry V., Henry VI., Richard III.,* in three parts; *Henry VIII.,* and what are called the three Roman plays, *Coriolanus, Julius Cæsar,* and *Antony and Cleopatra.*

The plays from English history are taken, as a rule, from older plays by the same name written by minor playwrights, or from the old chronicles which describe so minutely and interestingly the affairs of history.   And as these events were transcribed in the main by contemporaries, they are full of life and color, and would thus appeal very strongly to the imagination of Shakespeare.   Hollinshed, Hall, and Fabyan are the chroniclers most often consulted.

The long series presents, with some breaks, a splendid panorama of English history, from the days of John to those of Henry VIII., in which move in stately procession the great historical personages of the Middle Ages in England.   All the great events and important characters—the kings and queens, the knights and barons, the princes and dukes, the soldiers and populace of this time—live again in these plays with the interest of reality.

King John, founded upon an older play of the same name, contains some of the most celebrated of Shakespeare's characters.   It is a story of Norman days (John was the great-great-

4

grandson of the Conqueror), and of the cruel deeds and lawless acts which men committed in those times when kings came to the throne by power and not by right.   John had no right to the throne, as the true heir was Arthur, son of Geoffrey, an elder brother of John.   Arthur's rights were supported by the French King, and Shakespeare has taken the incidents of this war for the throne, and woven them into a play of such interest, that it will forever represent the master in one of his greater moods.   The character of Constance, the mother of Arthur, is one of the most famous in all Shakespeare.   Her pride, and grief, and despair are drawn with Shakespeare's finest touch, while the pitiful story of the little prince is perhaps the most pathetic child-story in Shakespearian art.   Arthur is taken prisoner by John and carried to England, and then because he fears further trouble, John decides upon the death of the boy.   This horrible deed he intrusts to Hubert, Arthur's keeper, instructing him to burn out the child's eyes with red-hot irons.   Hubert goes to the cell to do the deed, and then follows the striking passage in which the heart of the jailer is turned from the crime by the pathetic pleading of Arthur. It is a beautiful picture of depraved manhood kept from utter wicked-ness by the innocent faith of helpless childhood. And so great is the art shown in drawing the picture that it appeals to us not as art but as a faithful representation of nature.

The play ends with the death of John, sup-posedly by poison, and the entrance of his son Henry as his successor, Arthur having been killed by falling from the walls of his prison while trying to escape. The drama has a fine flavor of the old Norman rule ere John had met his barons at Runnymede, and been forced to sign the great charter which heralded in the true liberty of the English nation. As it is also the first written of the historical plays, it marks the dawning of a new epoch in the English drama, which became from that time a means of portraying national interests and affairs as it had never done before.

Richard II. is, in a literary sense, one of the first of the plays, and contains passages of exquisite beauty. It is the story of the rise of the House of Lancaster through the deposition of Richard by Henry, who thereupon became Henry IV.

There are two parts to the story of the latter's reign—*Henry IV., Parts I.* and *II.* The central thought of Henry IV. is the development of the character of the young Prince of Wales, from a mere fun-loving boy into the royal-hearted, knightly Henry V. The famous Falstaff, one of Shakespeare's most celebrated characters, figures in these plays. He is the typical comic character of the stage of Shakespeare's day and was a prime favorite with the crowds which thronged the pit of the Globe and Blackfriars. Falstaff belonged to the masses, and his fat person, and coarse but jolly humor, his fondness for sack, and the merry company he always had around him, delighted the audiences, which saw in him one of their own kind, and recognized the picture as well drawn. His was a humor that could always be understood, because it was English, and his tastes and delights were understood, because they were also

English. This character, therefore, standing for one of the national types, is one of the greatest creations of Shakespearian comedy.

In *Henry V.*, Shakespeare took for his subject the victories of the famous hero king over the French, the last act of the great drama of the hundred years' war which had been waging between England and France. Henry V., the soldier king, was ideally loved by the nation whose glory he had made his own, and his victories at Harfleur and Agincourt were the pride of English history. This story of glory and conquest Shakespeare put into his play and gave to the world an ideal English king, brave, generous, and royal, weaving into the plot besides such a wealth of incident, humor, and romance that it will ever be one of the most popular of the historical plays.

Henry VI., which is in three parts, relates the fall of the House of Lancaster through the defeat of Henry VI. and the death of his only son.

Richard III., one of the finest of the historical plays, opens with the famous soliloquy of Richard upon the old prophecy which said that

the sons of King Edward IV. should be murdered by one whose name began with the letter
G, the initial of Richard's own title as Duke of
Gloster.   In this play one of the darkest chap-
ters of English history is portrayed, that in
which Richard murders successively his brother
Clarence, the Duke of Buckingham, the little
heir to the throne and his brother, and a number of other persons whom he fancied stood in
the way of his advancement.   He gains the
crown through these foul means, but he has
made himself so detested that the people are
glad when the Earl of Richmond claims the
crown and declares war upon Richard.   Richmond was the representative of the Lancastrian
party, as Richard was of that of York, and as
he had married Richard's daughter, the Princess Elizabeth, the two families which had made
the Wars of the Roses famous in England were
in this struggle set against each other for the
last time.   The play ends with the victory of
Richmond, who came to the throne as Henry
VII., and the death of Richard on Bosworth
Field.   It is one of the greatest of Shakespeare's

plays, the dramatic interest being so powerful that we are carried along from scene to scene with almost breathless intensity. The character of Richard is one of the greatest portraits in all literature of wickedness and ability personified.

Henry VIII. is the story of Catharine of Aragon, the first wife of Henry VIII., and the mother of Queen Mary, and of her unhappy divorce from that monarch.

The three Roman plays are taken from Plutarch's "Lives of Distinguished Men of Antiquity." These plays, which picture the severity of the Roman republic in *Coriolanus*, the splendor of the imperial beginnings in *Julius Cæsar*, and the luxury and magnificence of the epoch just following in *Antony and Cleopatra*, also portray every variety of human passion and make the characters of two thousand years ago as real as if they were people of our own time. Of the three, *Antony and Cleopatra* is the most poetic—as it is indeed one of the most poetic of all Shakespeare's plays. *Julius*

Cæsar is a storehouse of political wisdom, full of meaning to the England of Shakespeare's day, as well as to all countries in all times. This play contains the well-known orations of Brutus and Antony over the body of Cæsar, whose assassination by Brutus, Cassius, and other friends of Cæsar forms the climax of the play. These orations produce a dramatic effect which calls back to life that old Roman world as does nothing else in the plot. In the stately and polished arraignment of Brutus, who loved Cæsar well, but Rome more, as in the passionate pleading of Antony, whose love kept faith even with death, we have a backward glance into those far-off days when the eloquence of the orator brought to pass what law or justice might not effect. These orations make the strange power of those old Greek and Roman orators understood, and call up pictures of the crowds which thronged the courts of Athens and Rome to listen to the voices which should depose tyrants or make kings, or inspire deeds of deathless heroism.

The quarrel between Brutus and Cassius, before their defeat by Antony, and the heir of Cæsar, is also one of the striking features of this play, being one of the most famous scenes in the Shakespearian drama.

In his comedies Shakespeare gave full rein to his imagination and fancy, and has left recorded in them some of the most perfect of his works. They are founded upon Italian and French romances as a rule, and show Shakespeare's light and airy humor, and his grace of fancy in striking contrast with his serious vein. In these comedies one feels the joy of life and sees the heart in its sunny moods, with perhaps just enough seriousness intermixed to remind us that it is human life we see and not the picture of a dream. The comedies are: *A Midsummer Night's Dream, The Comedy of Errors, Love's Labor's Lost, The Taming of the Shrew, Two Gentlemen of Verona, All's Well that Ends Well, Much Ado about Nothing, As You Like It, The Merry Wives of Windsor, The Winter's Tale, Measure for Measure, The Tempest, The Merchant of Venice,* and

Twelfth Night; perhaps in this list would also be included *Cymbeline*, a sort of tragi-comedy.

As You Like It is one of the most charming of the comedies, and, next to *A Midsummer Night's Dream* and *The Tempest*, shows, perhaps, Shakespeare's fancy in its lightest mood, though, unlike them, its interest is purely human, with no machinery of fairy, elf, or spirit introduced. It is the story of some lovers whom chance has driven into a forest where already reside a banished duke and his court. The free life of the woods, the out-of-door freshness, the introduction of tree, and rock, and stream as agents in the plot, the poetic rhapsodies of Jacques, the lovers, and the philosophical reflections of the Duke's friend and counsellor, all suggest the pastoral and idyllic life of such an existence as might have been spent by happy shepherds and shepherdesses in Arcadia or some other region of the imagination. It is indeed Arcadia reproduced in the forest of Arden, Arden woods, where grow English flowers, and whose brooks are familiar to English eyes. The lovers hang their love-notes upon the boughs of the oak, and medlar, and hawthorn, names dear to English hearts, and the whole atmosphere of the play is ideally perfect in the portrayal of that mood of fancy which all love to indulge in at times.   In the end, Rosalind, the princess, who roams the forest in the dress of a page, marries the hero, Orlando, and the Duke recovers his inheritance, but this is one of Shakespeare's plays in which the plot seems less important than the poetic translation of an aërial mood, and it is this ideality which makes the play unique among the comedies.

The Merchant of Venice is a play founded upon the promise of a young Venetian to forfeit a pound of his own flesh if he did not pay at a certain time his debt to a Jewish merchant who held his bond to this effect.   There is a love-story interwoven, in which Portia, the heroine, who is in love with Bassanio, a friend of Antonio, saves Antonio's life; for Shylock, the merchant, because he hates the young Christians who borrow money of him and then despise him, has determined to execute his bond, and demands the pound of flesh to be cut

off above Antonio's heart.   Portia enters the
court-room disguised in the gown of a lawyer
as the scene is going on, and by her eloquent
and ingenious pleading, she shows that the
agreement does not provide for shedding one
drop of Antonio's blood, and rescues Antonio,
causing all the property of Shylock to be con-
fiscated and himself banished.   This is one of
the comedies which deals with the deeper emotions of the heart, and the intricate and subtle
intellectual passions are handled with such
masterly skill by Shakespeare that it ranks as
one of his greatest plays.

The Taming of the Shrew is an amusing
story of a lady whose sharp tongue made her
feared by everyone, but who was subdued by
the ingenuity of her husband, who scolded her
so incessantly that she had no chance ever to
say a word back. It has always been one of
the most popular of the comedies, and is among
the most frequently acted.

The Comedy of Errors is founded upon
the comical mistakes and adventures which be-
fall two men and their slaves, who resemble each

other so closely that they are constantly being mistaken for one another.

Much Ado about Nothing relates the love-story of the maid Beatrice and the bachelor Benedict, who, having vowed to hate each other, promptly fell in love when their friends mischievously and deceitfully assured each one privately of the other's love.

And so through all the comedies runs the wide stream of universal sympathy with and understanding of the virtues and faults and foibles of human nature, so skilfully treated and delicately handled that they must forever stand among the best of Shakespeare's productions.

The greatest of Shakespeare's tragedies are *Hamlet*, *King Lear*, *Macbeth*, *Othello*, and *Romeo and Juliet*. *Hamlet*, perhaps the greatest of Shakespeare's plays for its study of the human heart, is founded upon an old Danish story of one of the kings of Denmark, who killed his brother and then married the widowed queen and succeeded to the throne. Hamlet, the son, is visited by the ghost of his father, which reveals the horrible story to him, and the play is the story of Hamlet's vengeance. In with the plot is woven the beautiful love-story of Ophelia and Hamlet with its unhappy ending. Ophelia is one of the most perfectly drawn woman characters in Shakespeare's works.

The play of *Hamlet* contains a philosophy of life. In it the feelings of the heart are brought out and marshalled before the eyes like the actors on a stage. We see the weakness of Hamlet's character contrasted with his intellectual greatness, just as we might see one character in a play standing before another. Thus we are made to feel that it is not the ambition of the king, nor the wickedness of the queen, nor the treachery of friends which leads to the final catastrophe, but Hamlet's own irresolute spirit, which could never rise to the proper height, and which constantly wavered and drew back at critical moments. It is this marvellous portrayal of the mingled strength and weakness of the soul that makes Hamlet one of the most perfect and human creations in all literature.

The tragedy of *Macbeth*, taken from Hollinshed's chronicles, is founded upon one of those dark tales of murder which fill the pages of early Scottish history. Macbeth, thane of Glammis and Cawdor, is excited by the prophecy of three witches to murder Duncan, the king, and usurp the crown. His courage, however, would have failed him at the last moment had not Lady Macbeth urged him on to the deed. He murders Duncan at night, and Lady Macbeth throws suspicion upon the two servants of the king by placing their bloody daggers (with which Macbeth had done the deed) beside them as they slept. Macbeth is crowned, and all goes well for a time. Then suspicions arise. Lady Macbeth walks in her sleep and is watched by her attendants, who see her washing her hands as if trying to wipe out blood-stains. Macbeth himself sees ghosts and has visions of the crimes he has committed, but is comforted by a prophecy to the effect that no harm shall reach him till Birnamwood, the distant forest, shall come to his palace at Dunsinane. But the trouble forms, enemies rise, an army is formed against the usurping king headed by Malcolm, son of Duncan. The soldiers advance to Dunsinane Castle bearing boughs from Birnamwood upon their shoulders, and thus fulfil the prophecy, and Macbeth, after more than one bloody deed, dies at last by the hand of Macduff, one of Malcolm's captains.

In *Macbeth*, Shakespeare has made a powerful study of the effect of conscience upon conduct. This play is remarkable from the fact that the downfall of Lady Macbeth and her husband is due to no outside influence or circumstance, but comes solely from within. As in *Hamlet* we see two emotions of the heart placed opposite and warring one with the other. And this unseen war of conscience with crime is the one agent which leads to the downfall of the murderers. If Lady Macbeth had been entirely wicked, her husband might have lived and died king of Scotland. But no one is entirely wicked. Behind the ambition which plotted the murder stood the conscience which guarded the soul, and which might not be slain as kings are slain. It was this conscience, more terrible than swords of foes, which turned and betrayed her, and delivered her into the hands of her enemies—

another instance of the masterly insight of Shakespeare into the human soul and the springs of human action.

In the play of *Othello*, Shakespeare has painted one of the darkest pictures in all his tragedies. The plot was taken from an Italian novel, a popular story of Shakespeare's day. *Romeo and Juliet*, also taken from Italian source, is, perhaps, next to *Hamlet*, the most popular of the tragedies. It is the story of the two young lovers, Romeo and Juliet, whose love was crossed by a fate so unkind that all lovers who hear their story must weep for them. These two lovers each represented the great houses of Capulet and Montague, which had been at bitter feud for years, and from this fact they knew that their cause was hopeless, as the heads of the families would rather have seen their children dead than united in marriage.

Juliet, in order to prevent a marriage with a young nobleman whom her father had chosen, takes a sleeping potion which makes her appear as if dead, and she is interred in the tomb of the Capulets on what was to have been her

5

wedding-day. Romeo, who had been banished for killing a follower of the Capulets, hears of Juliet's burial, and procuring a poison, goes to the tomb to die by her side. He takes the drug and Juliet wakes to find him dead, and in the despair of love kills herself with his dagger.

This tale of old Verona was made by Shakespeare to live again with new life in this powerful drama, which is now the most famous love-story in the world. It is full of beauty, pathos, and strength, and ranks among the great masterpieces of the poet.

Thus we see from a study of the different plays of Shakespeare that there is no passion of the heart that he has not touched, and that he represents in his works the life of man in whatever society or condition. It is this human interest which invests his pages with a charm that can never die, and which, combined with his poetic genius, places him at the head of all other writers.

Shakespeare always considered Stratford his home, and bought there an estate where he visited his family from time to time. When he had accumulated a sufficient fortune he sold his interest in the Globe Theatre and retired to Stratford to spend the rest of his life. There he died four years later, on the anniversary of his fifty-second birthday, and was buried in the little parish church so closely connected with his first childish memories of the outside world.

Outside of his plays he is known as the author of a few other poems and songs and more than a hundred sonnets possessed of exquisite beauty, but it is his great dramas which have won for Shakespeare the fame which has placed his name far above and beyond any other in the history of the world.

Shakespeare's friend and contemporary, Ben Jonson, was, next to Marlowe, the most popular of the playwrights who formed the group of which Shakespeare himself was the head. Jonson's plays were, in nearly every sense, comedies based upon the affairs and manners of the day and particularly of London life. He introduced all kinds of odd characters into his dramas, and made them ridiculous by setting their oddities against one another, or gave the play a humorous cast by bringing in some absurd or extravagant whim of the moment as the centre spring of the plot.   His best known plays are : *Every Man in his Humor, Every Man out of his Humor, Bartholomew Fair, The Alchemist, Volpone,* and *The Silent Woman,* an unfinished drama of great beauty, called *The Sad Shepherd,* and the tragedy, *Catiline.* Jonson was also the author of many beautiful masques which were given at the court entertainments, among which may be mentioned *The Masque of Oberon, The Masque of Queens,* and *The Paris Anniversary.* Besides his dramas, Jonson wrote many songs which have become famous, and which place him high among English lyrical poets. These songs occur in his masques and also in his collected poems, called *Forest and Underwoods.*

CHAPTER II.

While Shakespeare was a lad wandering among the lanes and fields of Stratford, and learning the wisdom of nature from the lips of nature herself, another boy, two or three years older, was wandering through the streets of London, or visiting the court, and learning the ways of the world and the wisdom of men from the crowds that thronged what was then perhaps the most interesting city in the world.

This was Francis Bacon, son of Nicholas Bacon, Lord Keeper of the Great Seal, and a man of influence at court. The boy was born at York House, so called because it had been formerly the dwelling of the Archbishop of York, and, outside of the royal palaces, it was considered one of the finest mansions in London.

His mother, who was a daughter of Sir Anthony Cook, tutor to Queen Elizabeth's brother, Edward VI., had studied in the evening the same lessons that the young prince learned in the morning, and was considered a woman of fine education in those days, when all ladies of high birth read Greek and Latin poetry, and studied grave questions of philosophy and religion. She was Bacon's first teacher, and it was well for him that besides a knowledge of books she also possessed a strong, earnest character, so that from the beginning his great talent was well directed by this wise and loving friend. But learning from books was but a small part of his early education. At his father's house gathered all the great and learned men of the day. Thither came the great statesmen and lords of the realm, who discussed grave matters of state, and the part that England was to play in the history of the world. And close beside them could be seen those famous men whose names were ringing all over Europe, because they were the champions of Protestantism, the new religion which England fostered, and for which so many thousands had lately laid down their lives on the battle-fields of the Netherlands. And there also were to be found great men of science, who were studying the secret laws of nature, and men of adventure who had carried the English flag into hitherto unknown regions of the earth, and men of letters whose works were to be a glory to England forever; and in such company as this, both in his father's house and in the homes of his young playmates, Bacon learned those lessons which can never be taught from books, and which give to the learner knowledge of men and the world.

Bacon was also frequently present at those grand entertainments which Elizabeth loved to give and take part in, and he no doubt saw many a time the same representations of the miracle plays and masques which charmed the soul of the boy Shakespeare away in quiet Stratford. Only there was this difference, that while Shakespeare went to Kenilworth an unknown and uninvited visitor, taking only such cheer as was given to the humble village folk,

Bacon visited the court and the houses of the nobility as a welcome guest, the pet of the Queen, who called him her little Lord Keeper, a favorite among the sons of nobles, respected by the great men who honored his father, and the idol of the fashionable ladies, who admired his beauty and wit.

Thus from the beginning the world was a wide place to Bacon, and he began early to think about those questions which were being discussed by the great men of the times, and to take an interest in those great events which were happening. For England was then passing through one of the most important periods of her history. The Protestants of the Netherlands were looking to her for help in the struggle for freedom from the tyranny of their King, Philip II. of Spain ; great companies were being formed for the purpose of colonizing America ; the English navy was just beginning that career of greatness which made the flag of England feared in every sea, and above all, the English people themselves were divided into two parties, one of which was loyal to Elizabeth and

Protestantism, while the other favored the Catholic Church, and was continually plotting to bring the Queen of Scots to the throne. It was a time for wise thought, careful plans, and great action, for no one could guess the answer to any of the difficult questions that the English nation was then called upon to solve, and every thoughtful man could not but feel the importance of the hour.

But besides these great political questions, other subjects were then demanding attention. Problems in natural science that no man had been able to unravel were now being studied out, and as each question was answered it seemed to lead the way to still greater discoveries, so that the world of science appeared like a fairy land, the gates to which were being unbarred one after another, so that all who would might enter in and share its wonders. And all these things Bacon heard discussed day after day, and they were as familiar to him as the legends of the elves and fairies who inhabited the woods and dales of Warwickshire were to the boy Shakespeare.

When a boy has such surroundings as these
he becomes thoughtful, and when he hears continually great questions discussed by great men,
from many points of view, he also gains the
habit of thinking independently, and learns that
the wisest man is he who studies and thinks for
himself. Therefore Bacon, when very young,
began to ponder over the questions that few
of his companions troubled themselves about,
even in that age when boys took up the re-
sponsibilities of life very early, and when every
great man was still a young man.

This early training showed its influence upon
Bacon, who was gifted with an inquiring mind,
and who was continually trying to find out
causes. There is a story told that, in his tenth
year, he left off playing with his companions one
day to find out the reason of an echo which
came from a vault near the playground; and
when he was only twelve he was thinking upon
the laws which govern the imagination. He
entered Cambridge at thirteen, and remained at
the University three years, during which time
he made few friends among the professors,

as he thought them too willing to follow what was accepted as truth, without seeking to discover whether it were really truth or not. He said that his fellow-students were shut up in little cells and spun cobwebs, instead of living in the light and seeking knowledge for themselves. And he compared the university to a becalmed ship, which only moved by the breath which came from the outside.

In these college days Bacon planned a university which should be a true help and guide to earnest students, and this plan he put in writing many years after. Also at this time there came to him a hint of that system of philosophy which was to make his name immortal. And so, although his college training was of little direct use to Bacon, and he might have spent the time more profitably in private study, yet the very defects that he found led in time to the publication of his own great work, which was meant to remedy the evils that existed. He left Cambridge without taking a degree, and went to Paris under charge of the English Ambassador, as his father wished him to enter political life.

After four years spent on the Continent he returned to England and began the study of law, and from this time on the history of Bacon is closely connected with the history of English politics and English literature. His political life began in the House of Commons, and extended up to his sixtieth year, when he occupied the position of Lord High Chancellor, and held the title of Viscount St. Albans. But during this long period his work for literature and science was unceasing, and so important that his fame as a philosopher and writer will endure long after the memory of his political career shall have faded away.

Bacon's first important publication was a volume of essays written in English, and treating of almost every subject that is of interest to man. And it is in this volume that he shows his great knowledge of human nature, and his wide sympathy with human life. These essays include thoughts on character, truth, riches, fame, right living, friendship, love, and death, besides a variety of other subjects, not the least important being the essays on the building of houses and the making of gardens, which show so plainly the writer's interest in the things of common life, and his love and sympathy with the works of nature.

But the great desire of Bacon's life was to found a system of philosophy which would give to the world a better method of acquiring truth and knowledge than then existed. This thought had come to him dimly in his college days, and when he was twenty-five he made a sketch of a great work which should revolutionize the accepted methods of acquiring knowledge, and lead mankind into truer ways of thought, and throughout his long political career this idea never left him. It followed him everywhere, and at all times he cherished it as his chief joy, and in the excitement of political life found this work his greatest comfort and refreshment.

Up to this time the whole world of learned men had implicitly followed the doctrines of Aristotle, the Greek philosopher who lived

about 300 B.C., and whose great mind had bestowed some new gift upon every branch of
knowledge.   The system of Aristotle was based
upon the method of first laying down some law
in regard to any subject or operation of nature,
and then gathering together all the facts possible to prove that the law was true.   Thus, in
studying the cause of sound, Aristotle claimed
that sound was governed by certain laws, and
then gathered facts to prove this statement.
This is called the Deductive method of reasoning, because the mind goes from the general
law down to a particular fact or number of facts
for proof.   This method had been used in the
schools for centuries, and was considered the
only true way of arriving at a knowledge
either of the laws of nature, or of any other
department of learning.

But to Bacon this method of reasoning
seemed false, and he believed that he could
find the key to the interpretation of nature by
exactly the opposite means—that is, by studying first the operations of nature and upon a
knowledge of these building the laws which

seem to govern the universe. This method of
first collecting facts and from these establishing
a law, is called the Inductive method, or often
the Baconian Method, after its originator.
And this system of Bacon was so new and
startling that it came upon the world of learning with as great a shock as the discovery of
the new world by Columbus. By this method
every operation of nature was to be studied,
and experiment after experiment made and
proved before any conclusion could be proclaimed.

This method had really been followed many
and many a time by the earnest workers for science, for the old alchemists and other students
of nature had spent long lives in experimenting,
and had arrived at some clear knowledge of
many of the laws of nature. But these men
were not great philosophers, and were, sometimes only learned in one direction. They
were often regarded by their fellow-men as men
who were striving to reach some unscalable
height, and more than once they were only rewarded by seeing their work scorned, and by

being themselves accused of witchcraft and sympathy with the spirits of evil.

But Bacon changed all this. In a day of great minds his was one of the greatest, and his voice was the voice of authority. He proclaimed the new gospel which made the crucible of the alchemist and the scales of the philosopher the *open sesame* to the undiscovered realms of nature, and made experiment the magic wand which placed the wonders of the world at the feet of the careful student. His philosophy, in fact, taught men not to make laws, but to find truth, and this is the greatest thing that any man can teach.

This alone was the true philosopher's stone which could turn all things to gold, and with it men learned to find great laws of nature revealed in the tint of the rose or the wings of the butterfly, or the stones that they trod over daily.

Thus the world of nature was thrown open to all, and even a child might enter in and learn its mysteries.

Bacon planned a great work which should

set forth his system, but only a part of it was ever finished.

This work, written in Latin, was to have been called the *Instauratio Magna*, or Great Institution of True Philosophy, and was to consist of separate books which should contain, among other things, a summary of all knowledge then existing, a complete explanation of Bacon's new methods of discovering truth, a record of facts and experiments in the different branches of knowledge, and a summary of the results obtained by the Inductive method.

The most important part of this work was the second book, called the *Novum Organum*, in which Bacon lays down the principles of his new method, and it is this on which his fame as a philosopher rests, for it was the proclamation of the Inductive method which placed him among the great discoverers of the world. Indeed, Bacon himself was content with the glory of having given this great idea to the race, and was well satisfied to leave the work of proving its value to others. In this respect he says of himself: "I sound the clarion, but I enter not into the battle," and the succeeding ages have shown that this trumpet call led indeed to glorious conquest.

The idea of a model college, which should be an ideal institution of learning, had followed Bacon from his own college days, and one of the most interesting of his works is a romance called *The New Atlantis* in which he draws a picture of what a university should be.

This is the story: A ship, sailing from Peru to China, was sent by contrary winds far out of its course, and for many days was driven helplessly through the waters of an unknown sea. The provisions gave out and despair settled upon all hearts, for the sailors well knew that, even if the wind changed, they should all starve long before they had time to reach their destination, and that no other ship would ever flash its white sails upon the gray horizon that shut them in, for these waters had never been explored, and no chart of them existed.

And so they gave themselves up to despair and prayed that God would either deliver them out of their trouble or permit them to die speedily, for no human help seemed near. But as the ship still drifted on through strange waters and under strange skies, they saw one day, toward evening, a sight which gladdened all hearts and brought hope to the most despairing. Far away on the edge of the horizon they saw where the clouds seemed to darken and hold their shape, and by this they dared hope that land was near, and so all night they steered the ship toward that place. When the day dawned they saw that their hope had not been in vain, for an unknown land lay before them with its shores covered with trees, and a little sailing brought them into a good harbor which they perceived to be the port of a fair city, and so they made all the more haste to land.

But before they could leave the ship a crowd of people appeared warning them off with gestures, and presently a small boat carrying eight persons came up to the ship, and one who appeared to be the leader came on board and presented a scroll of yellow parchment on which was written, in Greek and Hebrew and Latin and Spanish, an order forbidding the strangers to land, and ordering them to leave the coast in sixteen days; yet offering help if they were in any need through sickness or other trouble. The chief man of the ship's company wrote an answer in Spanish, declaring that unless they were permitted to land many of their sick would die, and when this reply was carried to the land another boat came back bearing one of the officers of the city, who signed to them to send some one to meet him. And so they sent their chief man in a boat which was allowed to come only within six yards of the other, and then the visitor from the city stood up, and in a loud voice asked if the ship's company were Christians. And when he received answer that they were, he said that if they would swear that they were not pirates, nor had shed blood within forty days, they might land. And as everyone could take this oath in sincerity, they were told that they would be allowed to enter the city.

In a short time after this they were permitted

to go on shore, and were given a shelter in the Stranger's House, a mansion devoted to the use of all strangers who might come to the land. The weary voyagers here received the best care and attention from the servants appointed to the management of the house, and the sick were so carefully nursed, and treated with such excellent remedies that in a few days every one was well. And then, the people of the city, seeing that their visitors meant them no harm and were grateful for all the kindness they received, did everything in their power to make the days pass pleasantly. For these people were very hospitable, and delighted in entertaining strangers, and showing them their beautiful city, with its fine mansions and fair streets and gardens, and the visitors did not wonder when their entertainers told them strangers who came to that city never wanted to return to their own homes again.

But what puzzled the visitors very much was, that although this island was quite unknown to the rest of the world, and no one had ever heard its name, yet the rest of the world seemed to be very well known to the people of the island. They could talk about all the different places of Europe and Asia and Africa, could speak the languages of many countries, and knew all the latest inventions in mechanics, and all the latest discoveries in science, besides being familiar with the history of many persons famous throughout the world. Another thing that was also puzzling was the fact that none of the inhabitants of the city could be persuaded to accept the slightest payment for the services they performed for their guests. If one were pressed to accept money he would answer that it was considered the highest crime for any one to be twice paid for the same service, and that each citizen was expected by the city to be kind to strangers, that being the law of the land, to provide for which there was a special fund set aside. Therefore no one would receive any gift, though the visitors offered them gold and velvet and jewels, and other things of value.

But all this was understood when the governor of the city explained their peculiar customs one day to the chief men of the ship's company.

He said that about three thousand years before, this island, which was called Bensalem, was renowned for its commerce, and had in its service fifteen hundred strong ships which sailed to every port of the world, carrying merchandise and bringing back the products of other nations. That then the ships of China and Egypt, Phœnicia and other Eastern nations, came regularly to their harbors, bringing gold and jewels and merchandise of every kind, and carrying also as passengers men from Persia and Arabia and Chaldea, who had heard of the fame of Bensalem, and had come to look upon its glories.   And that, furthermore, there traded with them the people of that great country Atlantis, which lay to the west, and which was famous for its magnificent temples and palaces and cities, and also the people of Peru and Mexico, two other proud and mighty kingdoms. And he said that these latter nations were so great that they determined to conquer all the rest of the world.   So a great expedition was sent eastward across the Atlantic, and through the Mediterranean Sea, to conquer the nations

of Europe, but what happened to it no one in
Atlantis ever knew, for not one man returned
from that voyage. The manner of their death,
or what nation held them captive, was never
told, and it was only known that their ships
had passed like a flight of birds across the gray
bars of the horizon never to return again.

At the same time an expedition was sent to
conquer Bensalem, and this likewise came to
an unfruitful end, for the King of Bensalem was
a mighty warrior, and he made a cunning plot
by which all the ships and men fell into his
hands before a blow could be struck, and then
being merciful as well as mighty, he allowed the
captives to return home again upon their oath
that they would never again bear arms against
him. And so neither of the two expeditions
conquered the world, or any part of it.

But because the people of Atlantis had not
been content with their own greatness and
wealth, and had sought to harm other nations,
vengeance overtook them, and a great deluge
fell upon the land, and all the mountains poured
down their swollen streams into the valleys,

till not a place of safety remained, so that nothing escaped save a few beasts and birds, and
some wild races of men who fled to the caves in
the mountains. This flood lay over the land
so long that, when the waters dried up, the
land was desolate everywhere, and not a trace
remained of all its glory. The few people who
were left were forced to clothe themselves with
skins of beasts, or to migrate to the warm valleys and wander naked, for they had no ma-
terial or skill for making clothing. And so
Atlantis passed away from the memory of man,
for no ships left her shores, and all knowledge
of this great country was lost to Europe and
the rest of the world excepting Bensalem alone.
But the ports of Bensalem still remained open
to strangers for centuries, and ships came
thither from all the countries of the East, so
that knowledge of the island was spread
abroad, and some account of it crept into the
histories that were written by the ancient nations. And traditions of its greatness were
handed down from one generation to another
long after those nations had ceased to visit it.

For their voyages ceased after a time, owing to the fact that the old nations fell into decay, and new nations sprung up to take their places, and all this brought about wars and conquests and occupations enough at home. Then fewer voyages were undertaken, and gradually all commerce with Bensalem ceased, and navigation declined, and men only went on short voyages in familiar waters, carried in ships that were worked by oars, and that were not strong enough to brave the rough waves of the outer ocean. And in time, too, the ships of Bensalem ceased to visit other nations, and the reason of this is as follows :

About a thousand years after the destruction of Atlantis a ruler of great power came to the throne of Bensalem, and being wise and thoughtful, he pondered constantly on the best means of bringing greater happiness and prosperity to the kingdom. But this seemed hard to accomplish, as throughout the length and breadth of the land there were peace and plenty everywhere, and not one subject had cause to complain of his lot.

Then the king, who was learned in the history of all the nations of the world, thought that since he could bring no greater happiness to his country than that which already existed, he would at least try to make that happiness enduring, so that when he passed away he could leave behind him a promise of perpetual prosperity. He therefore ordained certain laws which forbade any stranger to land upon the coasts of the island, and which also forbade the people of Bensalem to go abroad, for he believed that all the troubles which vexed the nations of the old world came from intercourse with strangers.

But in order that the people of the island should not become utterly indifferent to the welfare of others, he ordered that all ships coming to their coast should be received for a few days, if help of any kind was needed. And if the ship's company wished, they could also be allowed to make the island their home, on condition that they would never ask to return to their own country. Besides ordaining these laws, this wise king did another thing which kept his memory ever before the people, and this was the erection of a great temple of learning, called Solomon's House, in which knowledge of every kind was taught. The teachers of this college were allowed from time to time to visit other countries for the purpose of studying and bringing back with them any new knowledge which might come to the world. These voyages were conducted with such secrecy, and under such disguise, that the presence of the visitors was never suspected in the different countries which they visited, and so the memory of Bensalem passed almost entirely away, though its own people were kept familiar with all the progress of the world. And this was the reason why the island was not down upon any maps or charts then used, and why the people of the ship had been led to think that they had come to some land unknown to the rest of the world.

The governor of the city furthermore told them how the country had been converted to Christianity. He said that one dark night the people saw a great pillar of light shining far

out at sea, upon the top of which blazed a large
cross. The whole population of that part of
the coast was soon gathered on the beach
watching this strange sight, and several of the
chief men rowed out in boats to see what it
might mean. But as they neared the light a
strange feeling bound them so they could not
move, and they were therefore forced to remain
in the boats at some distance from it. And at
this, one of the men present, who was a member of Solomon's House, fell upon his face and
prayed that God would deign to reveal what
this thing might mean. And presently he
found that his boat was able to move, and he
approached the column of light, but as he came
nearer, the pillar and cross broke up into thousands and thousands of stars, which floated
away and were lost in the space of heaven, and
there was nothing left but a small cedar chest,
out of one end of which a green branch of palm
was growing. This ark floated toward him of
its own will, and he received it into his boat,
and opening it found therein the books of the
New Testament which had been committed to

the sea by one of the apostles, in order that the message of Christ might be carried to distant lands. And so the members of Solomon's House read the book, and finding in it a message of love and peace to mankind, they accepted its story, and called themselves Christians from that day.

This history of Bensalem interested the visitors very much, and they were glad to accept the invitation of the governor of the city and visit the House of Solomon and see for themselves some of the wonders that it held. And they found that this college excelled all other colleges that had ever been seen or heard of in ancient or modern times.

It not only had great buildings especially devoted to study, but it had resources such as no other seat of learning had ever possessed. It had great lakes and rivers under its control, both of salt and fresh water, for the study of the fish and water-fowl that inhabited them. It had artificial wells and fountains tinctured with medicines for the cure and study of disease, and great houses where artificial rain, snow, hail, and ice were produced. There were also certain rooms, called chambers of health, where the air was laden with those perfumes and odors of plants that were considered preservative to the health. Then there were great orchards and gardens wherein grew every kind of tree or shrub or flower known to the whole earth. There were parks and enclosures for birds and beasts, both of those kinds that had their home in the island and those that had been brought from the various parts of the world.

There were factories where paper, linen, silks, velvets, dyes and stuffs of every kind were manufactured. There were houses for studying light and heat and motion, and so far advanced were they in their knowledge of these subjects that they could bring light from dark objects, make artificial rainbows, produce colors, shadows, and figures of things that were far off or not in sight, and make things that were near by appear at a great distance or vanish utterly before the eyes of the spectator. In the house of sound there were bells and rings and instruments of all kinds for producing strange sounds. All the voices and notes of beasts and birds were exactly imitated by some instruments, while others gave forth echoes and sounds of the human voice, sometimes making the voice shriller and sometimes deeper. There were also trumpets and pipes to carry sound from one place to another.

There was besides, a house of precious stones where were kept great stores of gems, and numbers of fossils and minerals, and these were used for study, and were not considered a part of the wealth of the kingdom. There was also a house devoted to the study of motion. Here were machines for flying, and boats and ships that could sail under water, and swimming girdles, and images of men, beasts, birds, fishes, serpents, and other animals, which were worked by machinery and imitated exactly the motions of the thing each represented ; there were here also all kinds of engines of war, and compositions of gunpowder, and curious powder that was unquenchable and could burn in water, and fireworks of all kinds.

There was also a house for the study of mathematics, geometry, and astronomy, furnished with the most perfect instruments.

And there was a house of deceit, where all manner of juggling was taught, together with tricks of various kinds, so that it would be impossible for anyone educated in that house ever to be imposed upon.

There were besides, great towers built upon high mountains, for the purpose of studying the wind and atmosphere and stars, so that the people would know whether to expect tempests, earthquakes, plagues, comets, drought, and other calamities, and could be taught how to prepare against them. There were also deep mines and caves where one could study the interior of the earth, and where new metals were produced by laws of chemistry not known to the Eastern world. And, in fact, there were separate houses for the study of every possible art or science, not the least interesting being a gallery of invention where were samples of every art known to the world, and which was adorned with busts of all the great inventors, such as the inventor of music, the inventor of letters, the inventor of printing, and so on.

The visitors were lost in amazement at the resources and wealth of this wonderful college, and when they thought of the wisdom of these people and their wealth and power, which they used only for good, they could well believe the assertion that of all the ships which had ever visited this land not one ever returned, and out of all the many strangers who had come there since the proclamation of the law against aliens, only thirteen had ever gone back to their own land.

Bacon did not finish the New Atlantis, and we can only guess what the end might have been, but the part that he has left gives us a clear idea of what he thought a state should be, and of his broad views of education.

This dream of an ideal commonwealth where all men were brothers and each one was given a fair chance in life, shows that Bacon, like other great philosophers, did not think such a thing an impossibility and had faith in the good that the future might bring to mankind. Bacon died in 1626 from the effects of a cold caught while trying the effect of snow to arrest decay in the dead bodies of animals. He was buried at St. Albans in the church of St. Michael's.

CHAPTER III.

MILTON—SEVENTEENTH CENTURY.

England throughout the greater part of the seventeenth century was a vast field of war on which were fought some of the greatest battles in history. Sometimes these battles were fought by armed men, as when the troops of Charles I. met the troops of Cromwell and both struggled for victory. And in this struggle the people finally triumphed and established civil and religious liberty in the land.

But more often the battles of this period were fought without any weapons, and the conflict was not between man and man—Royalist against Puritan—but between man and his own conscience. The Puritan spirit, which looked upon this world as a passing show, had permeated every thoughtful mind, and men everywhere were thinking of spiritual things, and

wondering whether the Puritans were right in
saying that the glory of this world, which would
fade away, was nothing in comparison to the
glory of noble living and the conquest of evil in
the soul. This question held the hearts of the
people as nothing had ever held them before,
and it was a question that each one must answer for himself. And so the battles fought on
these battle-fields were silent ones, and whether
one were victorious or not, none could tell save
the victor or vanquished himself. Men turned
from the things of daily life to ponder upon the
mysteries of the spiritual life, and gain and
honor here seemed to sink into insignificance,
and each man was engaged in following what
he considered the right rather than in achieving
worldly success. And this warfare left its mark.
The children of these people grew up in homes
where spiritual things were talked of continually, and where a good life was considered the
one important thing. Even their very names,
such as Patience, Honor, and Hope, had a spiritual meaning, and they were taught that life
meant only a conflict between good and evil, in

which each one must fight as a brave soldier on the side of righteousness.

Throughout this great world of puritanism the Bible was the one book that was read and discussed, and was in fact a part of the daily life of the household. To the Puritan child the sight of the Bible was as familiar as his own father's face, and in fact often one seemed inseparable from the other; and he was taught that this wonderful book, with its stories of prophets and saints and martyrs, and its visions of heavenly beauty, was the only guide which could lead him safely through this life and fit him for the life beyond. And from the time they could remember they were used to seeing their fathers and brothers go forth in round hat and doublet to fight the king, with sword and Bible as their companions.

This puritanism took deep hold of the middle and lower classes, and though it was often unwise in its actions and uncharitable in its judgment, yet it still was the vital force which so moulded the character of the age that the English race became forever its debtor, while English literature received from it two books which stand alone in the world of literature.

The first of these books, *Paradise Lost*, dealt with the Paradise which man had lost through his sin, and was a vision of the Eden wherein the heart of man was as pure as the heart of a little child. The second book took up the story of man laden with sin and sorrow, and showed him on his journey through this world to the heavenly kingdom, wherein he should find his lost inheritance awaiting him. This book was called *Pilgrim's Progress*, and was published three years after the publication of *Paradise Lost*.

The author of *Paradise Lost* was John Milton, a Puritan of the middle class. The author of *Pilgrim's Progress* was John Bunyan, the son of a tinker and a tinker himself by trade.

Milton, like Chaucer, Spenser, and Bacon, was born in London, and the first memories of his childhood were connected with the sights and sounds of a great city. But the London of Milton's early years was not quite the one familiar to the young eyes of Bacon, for the family of Milton belonged to the middle class, and the future poet's surroundings were very different from those of the son of the lord keeper.

The father of Milton was a scrivener, a man who drew up wills, leases, and other legal documents, and who carried on his business either in a plain little shop, or at the homes of his patrons. A scrivener would never be seen at court or in the houses of the nobility unless sent for to pursue his calling, and the manner of his life was far removed from that of the great world of the court.

In those days the life of the middle class was simple and wholesome. Tradesmen, merchants, mechanics, brewers, and all men engaged in business were included in this class, and as each trade formed a guild or corporation which was always rich and powerful, the members were highly respected, and represented a certain influence in all questions of the day.

This class lived, as a rule, in the streets that were devoted to business, and their families occupied the rooms at the back or over the shop.

The master's apprentices always formed part of the family, sharing the meals and having equal privileges in many respects with the children, and it was no uncommon thing for an apprentice to succeed to his master's business and marry one of the daughters of the house.

Bread Street near Cheapside was one of the principal business streets of the city at that time, and was occupied almost entirely by wealthy merchants. The houses were substantial and often handsome, standing with gable end toward the street and bearing over their doors the arms which stood for their calling, many of these being very fantastic and gorgeous, as each man's shop was known to the business world only by the sign or emblem over the door. Thus one shop was known as the Silver Shield, because that was the sign of the silver-smith who carried on his business therein, and another would be known as the Golden Arrow, because of the sign which told that the master was a dealer in weapons of warfare. In Bread Street there was a row of houses all adorned with the showy arms of the goldsmith's guild and the figures of

wood-men riding on monstrous beasts, because
the builder had been a goldsmith by the name
of Woodman, and not far away from this spot
Milton was born, in 1608, in a comfortable house
having over its doors the device of an eagle
with spread wings, which probably stood for the
arms of the corporation of scriveners to which
Milton's father belonged.

But whatever its origin, the sign was used to
denote that in that house dwelt a scrivener having the King's authority for the prosecution of
his business. And, as in many other cases, the
house in time gave its name to the immediate
locality, and the little court at the upper end of
which it stood came to be known as Black
Spread Eagle Court, a name that stuck to it
long after merchants had ceased to depend
upon the signs over their doors for identification
and houses were properly numbered. The
London of those days was much given to shows
and pageants of all kinds in which the merchants and mechanics took a prominent part,
and besides these there were the many holidays
in which the master and his family would leave

the town and spend the day in the country, taking with them certain of the apprentices so that all might share in the pleasant time.

Thus there was mutual respect and good feeling among this class, who represented perhaps the truest way of living in a time when between very rich and very poor there was an almost impassable gulf. Into this commonwealth of the middle class Milton was born, amid fortunate surroundings for a poet, for this class was in close touch with the outside world, and Bread Street itself was in the heart of London and represented all the business life of that great city. Here were shops of merchants whose ships were sailing the waters of the Mediterranean, the Indian Ocean, and the South Sea, and displayed in their windows were the silks and velvets and carpets which they had imported from those far-off places. Here daily could be met ship-masters who had fought with pirates and captured Spanish freebooters, and had seen with their own eyes the wonders of those great cities of the New World whose temples blazed with gold and jewels and whose treasure-houses contained inexhaustible wealth taken from their native mines.

Here too were the celebrated inns for the accommodation of the carriers who traversed England from end to end carrying merchandise and passengers, and for the use of travellers who had come to visit London on business or pleasure or curiosity ; while near at hand were the two parish churches of All Hallows and Bow Church, whose famous bells were destined to ring out many a strange story in future years.

But perhaps the object of most interest of all in this neighborhood was that famous tavern, called The Mermaid, where Shakespeare and Ben Jonson and other celebrities used to meet and make merry. This inn was famous even then, for it was toward the latter part of Shake-speare's life that Milton was born, and the child must have listened many a time to the stories told of the great poets whose names were known all over England, and whose plays thousands thronged daily to see.

These, then, were the associations of Milton's childhood—the prosperous business life of a great city, whose thrifty merchants visited his father's house and with whose children he played ; the atmosphere of foreign lands clinging to the bronzed merchantmen and sailors who passed his door daily; the vision of the great pageants for which London was famous, when he and others of his companions looked wonderingly on to see the King and great nobles and lords of the realm passing by; and not least, the murmur of the name and fame of Shakespeare, who must have passed the house of the Spread Eagle many a time, and was no doubt seen more than once by the child with the wonderful eyes and auburn hair, whose beauty was a proverb among his friends.

Milton's home was an ideal one in many ways. His father was a man of fine character and deep thought, and his mother, whom he tenderly loved, was celebrated in the neighborhood for her kindness and generosity. The family was well to do, for the scrivener had brought to his business much sagacity and cleverness, and the children were carefully bred and nurtured. And this home-life, so wholesome and happy, was, besides, made beautiful by the sympathy which existed between the parents and children, and which made all the affairs of the family common. The father was a musician, as well as a man of education, and was not unknown to the musical world of London. He had composed the music for many of the psalms and hymns used in the services of the church, and from time to time had published, in connection with other poets, several madrigals and poems.

Thus, from his infancy, Milton was familiar with the group of artists who gathered in his father's house from time to time, and sang and practised to the accompaniment of the organ and other musical instruments which graced the house in Bread Street; and as he inherited his father's taste for music, he very early took a share in these performances. His father also taught him the organ, upon which he became a skilful player, and well acquainted with the best music of his time.

The father also noticed early that the boy had a natural fondness and aptitude for learning of all kinds, and that he had inherited the gift of writing verse, for as early as his tenth year the young Milton, who was looked upon as a prodigy by his brother and sister, had begun to write poetry and had made amazing progress in his studies. In his twelfth year he entered St. Paul's Grammar School, not far away from Bread Street, and from this time on his passion for study increased daily. He devoured his text-books as another child would devour fairy-stories, and it was no uncommon thing for him to sit up till twelve o'clock at night studying—a practice for which he paid dearly in later years. But his will seems to have been law in the household, as his father not only allowed him to sit up till midnight to study, but ordered the maid to wait attendance upon him in case he should need anything for his comfort. The time thus spent was so well used, as far as learning from books was concerned, that in five years he entered Cambridge possessing a good knowledge of Latin and Greek, some amount of French, Italian, and Hebrew, and a familiarity with the works of Spenser, Shakespeare, and other English poets.

He was also known as a pupil who at fifteen had written very fair verse.

At Cambridge Milton remained seven years, passing, for the most part, an uneventful life there, though in England even then was beginning that great struggle between the Crown and the people, the one demanding absolute obedience, and the other absolute freedom in matters of religion ; and this struggle from the first made a deep impression upon Milton.   Already he knew the discontent and unrest of the people, for his father was a Puritan, and in his twelfth year, the year he entered St. Paul's, the Pilgrims had sailed away from England to find in the New World a place where they might worship God in their own way, freed from the tyranny of a bigoted king.   Already he knew too that the faith that he had been reared in had had more than one martyr, and that it must have many more before peace would come.

But for all this dark threatening, the trouble only touched Milton in his college days as a shadow passing by, and he was to see many happy years before it actually reached him.   It was during his college days, however, that he seriously decided to give his life to literature, though from his childhood his father had desired him to be a man of letters. And there is not recorded in the history of any other great poet such a solemn dedication of his life to a great work as we see in Milton's. To him it seemed that the poet, like the knight of old, had a holy mission to fulfil, and that mission was to teach men the beauty and sacredness of life, and to make them so love truth that they would follow nothing else. And as the knight, before he received the accolade, had to learn to be noble in thought, brave in act, and pure in heart, so he thought that the poet must prepare himself for his work by noble living so that he might be worthy to record the deeds of great heroes who had lived purely and died gloriously, and being the servant of righteousness, be able to lead others in the same paths.

It was about this time, and with these thoughts in his mind, that Milton first dreamed of writing a great poem which should so lift men's souls to higher planes that they would not will-

ingly let it die.   Only he thought then that the
poem would relate the deeds of Arthur or some
other great English knight and hero whose
name still shone with splendor through the mists
of many centuries; but in this respect his dream
did not come true.   It was also during his college days that he wrote some short poems in
English, which first foreshadowed his coming
glory as a poet, one of these, *The Ode on the
Nativity ; or, Birth of Christ,* being sometimes
called the finest ode in the English language.

He left Cambridge in 1632 and went to live
with his father, who had bought a place in the
country, and there Milton spent the next seven
years of his life, learning of nature the things
that the country-born learn in childhood, and
becoming familiar with the wealth of meadow
and pasture land, of blossoming orchards and
old forests, and pleasant river banks.   Milton
took in this beauty with the poet's own gift, and
made it a part of his soul, so that in reading
his poems one can see the spring skies, the
clouds of blossoms, the floods of sunlight, the
creeping shadows, and the misty twilight, and

hear the nightingale singing in the dusk. During this time Milton wrote six poems, which are so full of the soul and feeling of nature, and so perfect and true in expression, that they could be as readily understood by a child, or one who was unlearned, as by the greatest scholar, for they are pictures of things familiar and beautiful with the grace of daily life and thus appeal to all. These are *L'Allegro*, a poem illustrative of joy; *Il Penseroso*, a poem illustrative of melancholy; two masques, and *Lycidas*, a poem written on the death of his friend, Edward King.

With the last of these poems his country life came to an end, and a short time after he left England for a tour on the Continent. There he stayed two years, making friends wherever he went, and was received into the society of the most famous people of the day. While there he paid a visit to Galileo, then old and in prison for teaching his pupils that the earth moved around the sun, while all the famous churchmen of the day denied this truth, and no doubt the memory of this visit must have come to Milton many a time in later years when he himself suffered persecution and imprisonment for the sake of the truth.

His stay abroad was cut short by news he received from home, for England was then in the midst of many troubles. The King, Charles I., was trying to force the English and Scotch Puritans into accepting religious views which differed widely from those that the Puritans held, and as Charles was tyrannical and determined to assert his kingly powers, and the Puritans were obstinate and would have thought it a deadly sin to make the smallest concession, there was no hope of a peaceful ending to the quarrel.

Charles was supported by the nobles, clergy, and the upper class generally, and the Puritans, who in themselves represented the powerful middle class, had the support of many of the most earnest thinkers of the day, who saw that religious liberty was the corner-stone of civil liberty, and that England never could be called a nation of free people so long as it suffered itself to be led by the arbitrary will of a king. Milton heard of these troubles and came back

to England to take his part in the conflict, saying that he thought it disgraceful to be travelling abroad for pleasure while his fellow-coun-
trymen were fighting for liberty ; and from the
moment of his return his voice was heard continually speaking for the cause of the Puritans.

The trouble grew. The King and the Puritans took up arms against each other, and England felt all the horrors of civil war and that
state of doubt when no man could tell whether
even his own brother was true to him or not.

For nearly nine years there was open warfare between the King and the Puritans, and
during this time Milton's pen was ever busy in
the Puritan cause. His tracts on religious and
civil liberty, the freedom of the press, and like
subjects were of priceless value to the Puritans.
When in the end the Puritans triumphed, and
Charles was beheaded and the Commonwealth
proclaimed, Milton was made Latin Secretary
to the State, and for ten years longer he wrote
pamphlet after pamphlet defending the rights of
the people. In this war with old beliefs he became known throughout Europe as a powerful

thinker and as a man whose honor and patriot-
ism were beyond reproach.   Even his bitterest
enemies respected always the purity of his motives and the honesty of his life.

But this time of political triumph was one of
bitter personal grief for Milton, for in 1652 his
eyes, which had always troubled him, failed
utterly and he became blind.

But the Commonwealth came to an end and
Charles II. was placed upon the throne.   He
issued a pardon to all who had taken part in
the late rebellion, excepting only those who
were immediately connected with the death of
his father, and among this latter number Milton
was included.   The evil days touched Milton at
last, and he was judged guilty of regicide—the
murder of a king—and was sentenced to imprisonment while waiting the final decision.   At
this time some of the pamphlets he had written
were burned by the hangman, and what fortune
he had once possessed was lost.   Thus, at fifty
we see him poor, blind, and in prison, and the
cause for which he had given all, in appearance
hopelessly lost.

But through the influence of a personal friend, Milton regained his liberty, and then finding a home in a quiet street, he set himself seriously to the work that he had had it in his heart to do since his college days; this was the writing of an epic poem which should celebrate the deeds of some great hero. He had long since decided not to found his work upon the story of King Arthur, or of any historical hero, but to choose rather for his theme some subject taken from the Bible. And after much thought he selected the story of the creation of the world, and the expulsion of man from the Garden of Eden. This poem was to be called *Paradise Lost.* He drew up a rough draft of this work very soon after his return to England from the Continent, but it was not till twenty years later that he found the leisure to write it.

It was then, during the latter part of his life, that he wrote the great poem which has made his name immortal, and which stands among the grand epics of the world. And it was during the days when the beauty of this world was sealed to his eyes forever that he saw those wonderful visions of earth and heaven which are to be found in *Paradise Lost* alone.

The poem was indited by many different hands, as Milton was dependent entirely upon the services of others; sometimes one of his daughters, sometimes a friend, often a paid secretary, performed the office of amanuensis, but the work went on steadily and harmoniously to the end, and when it was published placed Milton at once among the great poets of the world, and gave to English literature an epic poem.

Milton by his choice of subject joined the England of his time with those far-off days when Caedmon sang the first English songs in Whitby choir. It is worthy of remembrance that that first note of melody which deepened at last into the deathless music of Shakespeare, should have kept throughout its divine sweetness and purity, and that Milton, the last great poet whose life touched Shakespeare's, should have so crowned and glorified the whole.

The story of *Paradise Lost* is as follows :

Far back in the dawn of time, before the earth or man was created, the angels of God wandered through the ways of heaven as pure as the light and happy in their utter ignorance of sin. For them the trees of Paradise bore golden fruits and the flowers shed perfume and the rivers wound in beauty through the green meadows, and in the midst of these blissful abodes the angels were ever joyous, for they knew not what change meant and any knowledge of pain had never been theirs.

But a change came, for one of the great angels, named Lucifer, because of his splendid beauty, took to his heart one day a thought that grew there like a poisonous weed and drove all happiness away from him, so that he shunned the company of his companions and the looks of his friend, the great archangel Michael, who kept the gates of heaven.

The thought grew stronger and stronger, until it was like a great shadow, barring out the light, so that heaven ceased to be beautiful; and it also stood like a drawn sword between the angel and his friend, and kept them apart, though the archangel Michael knew not the reason. This thought, which dimmed for Lucifer the brightness of heaven, and blighted the flowers, and made the fruit seem as ashes in his mouth, was the knowledge that throughout the length and breadth of heaven the angels gave homage and adoration to God alone, and that no one else could claim their worship.

Lucifer brooded long over this, and knowing his own strength and power, grew jealous of the greatness of God; and he formed at last a project so daring and awful that he dared not even think of it except when alone, and the knowledge of it brought even fear to him who had never known fear before. But by long familiarity the thought came to seem less fearful, and at last, very slowly, Lucifer let first one and then another see what was in his mind; and some shuddered and were afraid, and others admired and reverenced him the more, for he was one of the highest of the angels, and one whose friendship was deemed an honor by the lesser angels.

As the knowledge of this project spread among the angelic hosts, it turned the hearts of many away from their loyalty to God, un-

til at last one-third of the angels had promised to aid and support Lucifer in his mighty
undertaking; for he had determined to over-
throw the power of God and either rule in heav-
en himself, or at least share the sovereignty;
for he was weary of obedience and had stood
so high in favor that he had come to think himself equal with the Creator.

Among the multitudes that promised him
allegiance were many of those great angels
whose beauty and wisdom were the glory of
heaven, and as Lucifer numbered over his vast
army he felt that victory must be his, and that
he should be able to reward his faithful friends
with power such as had never been theirs before.

But to the Archangel Michael he breathed no
word of his design, knowing that angel to be as
incorruptible as truth itself; only, as the time
for his revolt came nearer, he went less and less
into the presence of Michael, whose glance alone
seemed to pierce the soul of Lucifer and make
his fair hopes fade like blighted flowers.

So the time came, and one day the music of

heaven was drowned by sounds never heard there before, for Lucifer, the shining one, had drawn his vast host into battle array, and their white wings and glistening shields lighted the wide space in which they stood till it seemed as if all the glory of paradise was gathered there. And, in response to this dread challenge, came Michael the Archangel, leading the loyal legions of heaven, the numberless forces crowding close around him whose majesty was beyond the majesty of all other angels, and whose power was invincible, and the dreadful combat began.

But though the forces of Lucifer were of the angelic host and he, himself, was one of the princes of heaven, they could not win the victory; for Michael fought with the sword of God and his followers were beyond the power of failure, having never known either fear or sin. Battle after battle was lost to Lucifer and he was at last conquered, and with his legions was cast down from the heights of heaven, and fell through deep spaces of darkness till he reached the shores of hell, which was thereafter to be his eternal abode, bearing with him, out of the conflict which was to have ended so gloriously, only bitter defeat and unending disgrace. And on those shores of darkness he and his armies lay for a long time stunned, unconscious even of defeat.

For nine days and nights they lay there, at the end of which time his power came again to the vanquished leader, who was to be known no longer as Lucifer, the shining one, but who was called thereafter Satan, the enemy of God. And he rose and summoned his legions back to consciousness, and called his great chieftains to a council to decide what next to do, for though vanquished he had not yet given up hope.

The fallen angels sprang readily to their master's bidding, for his old authority still held them under its spell, and from the dark storehouses of hell they gathered gold and silver and precious stones, and built therewith a stately and beautiful palace from whose arched roof rows of starry lamps shed their light upon the throne, beneath which blazed countless jewels; and thither came Satan and his great ministers to deliberate what to do.

Some advised another battle, being unwilling to believe that their cause was forever lost, and some advised submission, feeling how vain it was to fight against heaven; and at last Satan himself proposed that they should accept their defeat, and instead of trying to conquer heaven, which could not be conquered, set about seeking some means of revenge; for though they never again could win back their lost glory, they could at least war continually with whatever God loved. Then Beelzebub, next to his master, chief of the fallen princes, recalled to their minds the old tradition that had long existed in heaven, that God intended to create a new race of beings, equal to but different from the angels, and that for their use he was also to create a place called paradise, which should partake of the divine beauty of heaven and be a fitting home for the pure beings who were to dwell therein. And he urged them to win their revenge by tempting this race to rebellion against God even as they had rebelled, so that the work of God might be marred and the beings that he created in love become his enemies and haters.

This last suggestion was accepted by the powers of hell, for Satan did not doubt his ability to tempt the new race to rebellion against God, as he still possessed the majestic power and wisdom which had been his when he roamed through heaven, the peer of the archangels and the favored of God. But now the lost beauty of heaven appeared hateful to him and only that which was evil seemed desirable, for his soul had lost its angel nature, and its whiteness was marred with shadows as dark as those which lay over the borders of hell.

Then the council having come to an end, Satan started forth to see if he could find the new world and its dwellers, not knowing whether they had yet been created. He travelled through the wide spaces of darkness borne on his mighty wings, and felt neither fear nor fatigue till he reached the boundaries of hell and came to its nine portals of brass and iron and rock, and heeded not the fire-encircled shapes which guarded them, and forced Death, its warder, to unbar the gates.

Traversing the outer regions, he saw at

last a gleam of light, and drew nearer until he saw the walls of heaven gleaming down upon him, and attached to it by golden chains, the shining sphere which held the new-created universe. Then he quickly winged his way through the regions of the stars, and came at last to the sun in splendor above them all; then he alighted and saw standing near him an angel shape, whose hair was of the color of the sun, and upon whose brow blazed a crown of many precious stones, and whose wings hung motionless as if he waited some command. Although the face of the angel was turned away, Satan knew him to be Uriel, one of the seven great angels who stand nearest the throne of God, and are ever his chosen messengers. And because he knew that this holy angel would not hold converse with such as he, Satan changed himself speedily into another shape, and stood there with flowing curls crowned with gold, and with wings of myriad colored plumes, smiling in youthful grace, and begged the angel to tell him in which of the shining orbs beneath them dwelt the new race of man, or whether all those spheres were his homes at different times, for he would fain look upon this great work of God.

Uriel, who knew not deceit, nor could detect it in others, pointed out the earth shining far beneath, and told Satan that that was the home that God had made for man; and with this answer Satan took his leave, and sped through the starry spheres till he came to the new earth, and alighted there and took his way onward till he came to Eden, the beautiful garden wherein dwelt the new race. There he saw the trees hanging with blossom and fruit, and the herbs with their perfumed buds, and the many colored flowers, and clear streams and shady walks, and in the midst the tree of life, taller than any other tree, and bearing rich stores of golden fruit; and next to it the tree of the knowledge of good and evil, whose fruit no one might touch. And this view so enchanted Satan that he knew beyond doubt that man must also be found in that garden, and he spread his wings and passed the walls and took his flight to the tree of life, and sheltered himself in its spreading branches so that none might see him.

Then looking down, he saw the new creatures that God had made, and found that they were as fair as the angels themselves, while around them played other living creatures which had been created for their use, and which joined in their play and shared their food ; for there was no such thing known as fear or hatred.

As Satan looked down and saw Adam and Eve walking through this fair garden, where grew every kind of delicious food, and where the lion played with the lamb and the tiger sported with the fawn, he was filled with hatred of the goodness of God, and he resolved to change this abode of peace to one of ruin and despair, if he could. Then he quickly came down from his high place, and changing his form constantly into the shapes of the different beasts who played around them, he came at last to the noble pair, and heard them praise the beauty of the garden and their happy lot therein, and heard also that of all the delights of the garden, one alone was denied them, and that was the fruit of the tree of knowledge, which had been forbidden them by God.

And hearing this, Satan resolved to make this command the means of their ruin, and to excite in them such a wish for this fruit that they would eat it at all hazards. And having determined thus, he left them for the time.

Now, the great angel Uriel had watched Satan as he winged his way earthward, and seeing that he cast looks full of evil around him as he entered paradise, Uriel feared that he meant harm to the dwellers therein. So he hastened to the Archangel Gabriel, who kept guard at the gates, and bade him search the garden for the intruder; and Gabriel sent the two angels Ithuriel and Zephon to search the garden and find any stranger who might be therein. And Ithuriel found Satan where he was hidden and touched him with his shining spear, and bade him arise and follow him, not knowing who he was, for his form was marred and his beauty was dimmed, and the glory of angelhood vanished from him; and Ithuriel was

filled with wonder when Satan made himself
known, so greatly had he changed.

Then he was brought into the presence of
Gabriel, yet feared him not till Gabriel threatened him with chains and torture if he went
not away ; and so Satan returned to hell for the
time, though he held his purpose still firm in
his mind. And in the morning God sent the
great angel Raphael down from heaven to warn
Adam that an enemy would try and make him
break his faith, and to warn him to be steadfast.
And Raphael, with his six wings of rainbow
hue that shed perfume as he went, sped
through the ways of heaven, whose hosts all
bowed in reverence as he passed, and came to
paradise and warned Adam of his peril, praying
him above all things to touch not the tree of
knowledge. Then Raphael related to him the
strange story of the war in heaven, and how
Satan and his legions had been cast out forever more, and God had created a new race
to fill their places in his love. And after relating these marvels, and warning them again
to keep their faith, Raphael spread his wings

and soared heavenward and was lost to their view.

So Adam and Eve dwelt in security in the garden, and the tree of knowledge hung its golden fruits above their heads and they looked upon it with no wish to eat thereof, it being their chief joy to obey the commands of God. And for seven days and nights Satan hovered near the earth but dared not enter paradise, because of the presence of the angelic guardians and the eyes of Uriel, whose glances saw all things.

But on the eighth night he returned at midnight, and hovering near the garden, wondered if he might enter in safety, for the darkness hid him and he knew that daylight would soon reveal his presence if he tarried longer. Then fearing to pass the boundaries in a shape that could be seen, for he knew not what hosts of angels kept the ward, he plunged into the river which flowed just outside of paradise and part of whose waters, coursing underground, rose again in a fountain near the tree of life. And from this fountain Satan rose in the form of a mist, and viewing all the different beasts which were sleeping around him, he entered at last the body of a sleeping serpent, knowing that in this disguise his presence would not be suspected.

During the hours of the next morning, as Eve was walking amid the roses of the garden, she saw a serpent of wondrous beauty approaching, not crawling on the ground in the man· ner of other serpents, but walking erect. And her wonder at this soon changed to greater wonder still, for as the serpent drew near he began to speak, and the tones of his voice were sweet and pleasing, and his speech was such as that used by Adam and Eve themselves.

But the serpent pretended not to see her wonder and began talking to her of her beauty, and when she asked him from whence he had obtained his gift of speech, he answered that he too had been created, like the other serpents and beasts of the field, to be the slaves of Adam and Eve, and that at first, like his fellows, he had been content to grovel on the ground. But, he said, coming one day to a certain tree, he was seized with a desire to eat of the red and golden fruit that hung there; so he wound himself up the trunk till he reached the high branches on which the fruit hung so temptingly, and gathering a goodly store he ate greedily, much envied by the other beasts who stood watching him below. And from that hour the gift of speech had been his and knowledge of all things, so that he was equal to the angels in wisdom and knew many of the secrets of the Creator.

Then Eve was desirous to see this wonderful tree and begged the serpent to lead her to it, but when they came near it she saw that it was the tree of knowledge, and she confessed that she dared not eat of its fruit, for God had commanded them neither to eat or touch it, saying that if they disobeyed him death would follow. But the serpent answered her with such cunning words that she could find no reply to them, telling her that this command she had received had been given to the beasts also, but that he had eaten of this tree, and instead of hurt he had received knowledge and the power of speech, and that death even could not harm him. And at last, after much persuasion, Eve came to believe that God had forbidden them the fruit of this tree because he feared that they should come to wisdom like his own; then she ceased to fear death, seeing that the serpent had only grown in beauty and power since he had eaten of the tree; so she plucked the golden fruit and ate it greedily, and seeing this the serpent slunk back into the thicket, for his work was accomplished.

But to Eve there came not the happiness she had expected, for although the taste of the fruit pleased her she could not utterly believe the words of the serpent, and she began to fear that death might after all come to her. And then she decided to tempt Adam too to eat the fruit, so that if she were to die he might also die, for she dreaded the thought of bearing her punishment alone. So she bore the fruit to Adam and confessed that she had eaten of it, and Adam was lost in sorrow and amazement, but yet, at her persuasion, he ate also, choosing death with her, if death should come, because of his great love for her.

But instead of happiness and joy, their dis-obedience brought to Adam and Eve something that they had never known before, and that was fear, which came and dwelt in their hearts as it had dwelt in the hearts of the angels who rebelled against God. Then the beauty of Eden was dimmed for them, and they wandered through its bowers with shrinking souls, fearing constantly lest some evil thing might happen.

And all the angel hosts which had guarded the gates of paradise flew back to heaven, for their mission was over since Satan had entered the place and tempted man to his ruin; so that there was left in paradise no creature of heavenly birth. And in the twilight Adam and Eve heard the voice of God calling to them, and they hid themselves in the dusk of the trees, for they were seized with bitter fear. But they could not free themselves from the presence of the Creator, and to him at last they confessed their sin, knowing that he knew it and that all disguise would be vain. Then they learned that instead of blessing, the fruit had brought woe and eternal sorrow, for even as they had disobeyed, so now they must suffer the consequences; for God said that from that day all the heavenly influences which made the earth so beautiful should be destroyed, since man himself had snapped the golden cord which bound him to heaven, and had chosen rather to obey the voice of Satan, the enemy of God. And thereafter the earth should yield fruits to man only in return for toil and care, and the beasts that had been created for his service should become his enemies, filled with the hatred of all mankind because their master had chosen evil rather than good; for the influence of Satan in paradise had been like a blighting breath which crept into all created things, and imbued them with its own power for evil, which was doubly potent because Adam and Eve had been warned against it and yet had sinned.

This was the sentence which God pronounced as he talked with them in the twilight; and its weight pressed all the more heavily because they knew that they had had the choice of better things, but choosing evil, had shut themselves out from the heavenly beauty and had brought, not only to themselves alone but to all the earth, the blight and shadow of evil.

Then God sent the great angel Michael to

drive Adam and Eve forth from paradise, so that they might seek a home elsewhere, and Michael, attended by the chief archangels, came down to earth and bade the two transgressors prepare to leave the beautiful garden which had been their home.   But, in pity for their grief, he first showed Adam a vision of future ages in which the race of man, purified by sorrow and through the mission of Christ, the divine Son, should regain those blissful abodes and find the lost paradise of their first parents freed from trace of evil, and beautiful as in its first beauty, and that they should dwell therein peacefully, with all power of sin destroyed.

And with this hope in their hearts Adam and Eve went forth from Eden, and the archangel closed the shining gates behind them, and set on either side of the gates the awful four-faced cherubim, whose eyes looked toward the four corners of the earth, and whose wings were many-hued, and shadowed them like a rainbow ; and over the gates he placed a fiery sword whose flames shot out on every side.   And having thus finished his work, he sped heavenward and entered the presence of God, while Adam and Eve still wandered homeless, look· ing for an abiding place, and the cherubim kept watch over the barred gates.

Paradise Lost was published in 1667, when Milton was fifty-nine years old, although it had been finished for two years.   Before its publica· tion he had written a second part, called *Para- dise Regained*—which connected the story of Eden with the story of the temptation of Christ by Satan, as related in the New Testament. This poem, which is much shorter than *Para- adise Lost*, showed Satan still warring with goodness, because goodness was loved of God, and in it we see the figure of Satan shorn of its beauty and majesty, which it has lost in its long conflict against God, and are shown the fallen angel with his strength gone, and only cunning and malice left to him as weapons.   Against these the soul of Christ stands firm, and with this last lost battle Satan acknowledges his own defeat, the bitterest grief that he has felt since the day that he had been driven from heaven.

Paradise Regained was published in 1671, in the same volume with another poem called *Samson Agonistes*—Samson the Wrestler—a tragedy having for its subject the Samson of the Bible.

This tragedy shows, by its great power and pathos, that Milton's strength had not declined, and that the great epic, which had been living in his heart for thirty years, had not driven out that love for tragedy which he had felt in early life, when it was yet a question with him whether the work he was to write should take on the dramatic or epic form.

This tragedy, which takes up the life of Samson after he has become blind, has been compared by some with the tragedy of Milton's own life, which throughout had been full of many sorrows. Samson, in his blindness and strength, seeming to typify Milton in his blindness and strength, doing his greatest work after life had laid her crown of sorrow upon him. But whether this comparison be true or not, we know this, which is better still, that Milton himself crowned his great work with a life still greater ; that in the midst of tyranny he was the champion of liberty ; that through many private sorrows he kept his soul serene and pure ; and that in prosperity and adversity alike he bore himself like those stainless knights of old, who he had said in early years should be the poet's ideal, and thus gained the life victory which comes only to him who is worthy.

CHAPTER IV.

JOHN BUNYAN—SEVENTEENTH CENTURY.

John Bunyan was born in the village of
Elstow in 1628, twenty years after the birth of
Milton. Elstow was a pretty little hamlet, sit-
uated in what are called the English midlands,
a low country where bogs and fens abound, and
where the streams run slowly and linger by the
sides of the fields, as if they found the quiet
pleasant after their rush from the hill districts.

The village of Elstow was not far from Bedford, the chief town of Bedfordshire, and the
main street of which was the highway to London; and Bedfordshire was puritan, and furnished many recruits for Cromwell's army. In
fact, the great dukes of Bedford and Kent were
among the chief supporters of the puritan cause,
and throughout the whole history of puritanism
Bedfordshire played an important part.

The father of Bunyan was a tinker, and wandered from village to village carrying his tools with him, and following his calling contentedly with no thoughts of greater things in his mind. As a boy, Bunyan often accompanied his father on these trips through the different villages, whose people were for the most part poor but kindly disposed, and where the different affairs of the village, the county, and the state were discussed from house to house, and thus an interest and connection kept up with the great world. Thus, though Bunyan was born of parents who were very poor in this world's goods, his childhood was not touched by that meanness which makes up a life of poverty in a great city; for if the family of the tinker was poor, no one else in Elstow was very rich, and in the affairs and interests of the village life, one voice was of almost as great importance as another.

So, as Bunyan passed through the pretty streets of Elstow, whose quaint cottages, with overhanging upper stories and dormer windows, may yet be seen, or as he took his way to the village green and joined in the May-day festivals, fairs, market-day happenings, and public rejoicings of every kind, he went as one entitled to respect and the equal of many there, even though his father pursued one of the humblest of callings, and one in which gypsies, vagrants, and even beggars, were often found.

And this, perhaps, was not only because the village life of Elstow was simple in itself, but because Bunyan early showed his great strength and originality of character; so that wherever he went people were impressed by him, even though they often censured his actions. For in this village life Bunyan was always a leader, and his companions were always willing to trust to him to lead them into all kinds of mischief. Sometimes the mischief was harmless and resulted only in fun, sometimes it was more serious, and the mischief-makers put themselves in danger of the law. Whichever way it was, Bunyan was at the head of it, for even in his boyhood days people acknowledged and yielded to his strange power of compelling others to his own way of thinking.

Poor as his parents were, they sent him for some time to a little school where he learned to read and write, though he learned little else; and in speaking of his education Bunyan says he knew neither Aristotle nor Plato, but was brought up in a very mean condition among the poorest people, his father's house being of that rank which was despised by all the families of the land. But this cannot be taken as literally true, for though the calling of a tinker was often considered disreputable, yet Bunyan's own family was respectable, and his ancestors had been known in Elstow for generations.

Going back to Elstow, then, two hundred years ago, we should see the boy Bunyan, big-bodied and bright-eyed, and clad in homespun, going to and from the village school, playing with his companions among the fields, visiting the village green on Fair days, and looking curiously at the wares displayed there, listening to the mountebanks and jugglers who practised their arts there, standing in Bedford watching the procession of travellers on its way to London, and attending on Sundays the little church to which his mother went regularly, and in which he had been christened.

We should see him also in one of those strange moods, which often seized him, when in the midst of a game he would suddenly cease playing, and stand, with his eyes fixed and staring, as if he were looking on strange sights. For this healthy, mischief-loving lad had, even in childhood, the singular experiences which belong to those natures that are gifted beyond their fellows. Whether in school or at home, or wandering through the lanes with his father, the fit would come upon him, and all the scenes about him would fade away, and it would seem as if he were living another life in another world far away from this. But these day dreams into which he fell troubled him much less than the dreams that came to him in the darkness of the night, and which played such an important part in his early life ; for these latter dreams influenced his mind and affected his conduct even in childhood, and it is possible to think that they had much to do with the character of his later life.

These dreams were always sombre and terrifying, and Bunyan often awoke from them filled with horror that could not be dispelled, for the dream, in whatever form it came, always appeared to threaten him with dread punishment for wrong-doing. Sometimes, after a day of healthy work and play, he would go to bed with his mind filled with the peace of healthy nature, and would wake horrified by an awful vision of the end of the world and the wrath of God, who had refused him entrance to heaven. Sometimes falling asleep, and hearing only the rustle of the trees and the murmur of the little stream outside the cottage, he would awake with shrieks and groans sounding in his ears, and horrible noises echoing back from some dream of the infernal regions. Wherever he went, or whatever he did, made no difference, he could not escape from his dreams, which followed him and stood waiting to turn his nights into horror.

Thus even in childhood he was known as the dreamer, and there is no doubt that these vivid and terrifying experiences left such an impression upon the mind of Bunyan, that we can trace to them many of those striking and wonderful descriptions of mental anguish which distinguish the *Pilgrim's Progress*, and make it seem like an actual experience.

These dreams had their source, no doubt, in very natural circumstances. Bunyan was gifted with great imaginative power, and had, besides, that intense sympathy which made it easy for him to imagine the feelings of others. He had also a very tender conscience, and evil doing by him was always followed by quick and bitter remorse. The preachers of that day loved to dwell upon the consequences of sin and the punishments that followed the sinner, and in their sermons they drew terrifying pictures of the punishment of the wicked after death. Sunday after Sunday Bunyan would enter the little church at Elstow, whose gray walls shut out the beautiful world of nature, and there listen to the gloomy and harrowing Puritan sermons, which dwelt only on the wrath of God and the terrors of the law, and took no heed of the gospel of love and forgiveness.

Thus it is easy to see how an imaginative child, listening to one of these discourses, would go home with his mind filled with terrifying images, and his soul shaken with horror of the dreadful fate that was surely to overtake him; and then would come the dreams of the night and the waking visions, in which he suffered such anguish that it left an impression which never passed away.

Speaking of this time Bunyan says, that often when at work or play, there would come a voice from above threatening him with torment unless he changed his life and left all the joys of this world behind him, and he adds that often at such times his heart would rise in rebellion and he would shut the voice out, refuse to listen, and would hope rather that if there were devils in hell, then he might become one also, so that he could torment others instead of being himself continually tormented.

This strange struggle went on in his soul constantly, and was no doubt due to the condition of the times when men who called themselves religious thought they must turn away from all the pleasures of this life and find comfort only in thinking of heaven. This Bunyan could not do, for this world seemed to him a beautiful and kindly place wherein one could find much comfort and enjoyment. But as this belief was directly contrary to the doctrines which he heard preached constantly, he was always being drawn first one way and then another, fearing pleasure and yet not wishing to give it up utterly; and this conflict was all the harder because he was naturally of a deeply religious nature. Therefore, the Puritanism of the day was like a whip from which he could never escape, for no preacher of those days ever showed to his followers any picture of a human soul which could find reason for the beauty of this life or see any charm in the glory of the world of nature; but the pictures were always dark and repelling, and made religion seem a thing of gloom.

Bunyan has left us a picture of his life in a book called *Grace Abounding*, and though this work is called an autobiography, it is strange to see how little of his outside life has a place in it. It is really a picture of the soul, and shows us that strange war which he fought with himself continually. This book is unique in its power of making us see the actual struggle that went on in Bunyan's soul, and reading its pages we seem to have before us real battle-fields and actual victories and defeats. In this strange story we are thrilled with those awful words which sound like a trumpet-call, and which over and over again break in upon his peaceful hours. Then, as he starts in fear, we watch him as he meets the call with words of mockery or promises of amendment, or hopeless resignation to a fate which he may not avert; and as we read all seems as real to us as to him. He tells us that once, as he was walking through the street, he suddenly saw, in a vision, a high mountain on the sunny slopes of which all his friends and acquaintances wandered up and down, refreshing themselves in the beautiful sunlight, while he himself stood below shivering in the cold and surrounded with frost and snow and dark clouds; and that as he tried to pass to his friends he could not, for between stood a great wall compassing every side of the mountain, and through this wall he could find no passage. But as he was wandering in despair he came at last to a narrow gap, and although it seemed hardly possible that he could push his way through this, yet, by great effort, he finally succeeded, and so he came into the company of his friends and was comforted. And this vision, he said, revealed to him that by great striving even he might enter the kingdom of heaven.

Another time he tells us that once, as he was praying, Satan stood beside him and told him to cease praying, for he was the chief of sinners and for him there was no forgiveness. And still again, he would have a vision of himself walking through this world peacefully and happily, because of some great hope that had been given him.

Such scenes as these make up the strange story of *Grace Abounding*, and they take us back to other stories of the doubts and fears of the human soul and the battle of good with evil, and we feel the great power of the book, knowing that it deals with the one subject that must ever interest mankind, and that here too, as in the

Vision of the old poet Langlande, or in the mystic legends of the knights who followed the Holy Grail, the same picture is before us—the vision of the soul trying, with burdened wings, to strive after ever loftier and purer heights.

This unrest and unhappiness followed Bunyan on through his early manhood, and in *Grace Abounding* we still read of his later doubts and fears in regard to the spiritual world, though there is hardly a line to tell us what part he was playing in the work-a-day world around him. It was at this time that he married and began housekeeping in one of the poorest cottages of Elstow, earning his living by means of his trade. But in the record he has left us he does not speak of poverty or ambition or success from a worldly point of view; to him the little cottage with the forge attached to it was a place good enough to work and sleep in, and the rest of his life meant that strange existence within himself which went on regardless of the world outside. Even the most harmless pleasures often, at this time, seemed to him wicked, and he either shut himself off from them entirely, or gave himself up to them utterly, as hope or despair ruled him. At one time he would spend the whole of Sunday in sport and games, and another time would find him so convinced that he was the chief of sinners, that he would refuse to go into the belfry and ring the bells for church, saying that he was unfit for such an office. This last was a great denial to him, for he loved to join the other ringers and send the music of the bells pealing across the fields and lanes of Elstow, and in one of these despairing moods he would steal to the belfry tower and stand looking on, while the bells rang out their sweet message, and feel that he was forever shut out from all that was good and beautiful.

But this wretched state passed at last, and Bunyan came into ways of peace, and as his was one of those earnest natures in which doing meant everything, as soon as he felt comfort in his own soul he began to preach to others. And because of the strange experience of his life and his natural eloquence, he soon became one of the most popular of preachers, and his fame spread abroad, even to London, whither he went more than once. During these visits to London he preached to large congregations, and many people of all ranks in life came eagerly to hear him. But this period of his life was also one of great trial outwardly; for during these years of earnest work, Bunyan suffered cruelly from the injustice and bigotry which still pursued the Puritan faith, after the fall of the Puritan power and the crowning of Charles II. There was, in Bunyan's case, no reason for persecution, except from a religious point of view, as he was a man of mean position in life, and but for his religion, his name would never have been heard beyond Bedford.

But because he preached the Puritan doctrines he was considered an enemy to the state, and, in 1660, he was imprisoned in the county jail of Bedford and held there for twelve years, because he would not promise to give up what he considered his life's work. During this time his family suffered the greatest poverty and Bunyan suffered with them, not knowing how to provide bread for the wife and little children, one of whom was blind. Some work he could do, though it brought little money, and while making shoe-laces, and doing other such work as could be done in prisons, his mind was full of sorrow, knowing that through him his family must suffer hunger and all the hardships of the poor, while he could do nothing to help them.

Bunyan's friends made many efforts to obtain his release, but year after year passed away, leaving him still in prison, and even when, after twelve years, he was freed, his liberty was again taken from him, and he was made a prisoner for conscience's sake. But this latter imprisonment lasted less than two years, and at the end of that time he was a free man once more, with the liberty of going whither he would and preaching whatever doctrines seemed best to him.

With this liberty came to him also some of that great fame which soon crowned him, for during his prison life he had written many books, which had been widely read by all classes of people. These books preached the Puritan faith as persistently and eloquently as Bunyan's own lips had preached it; and thus, in spite of his weary imprisonment, his great missions had still been carried on. But the great book of all, the book which brought him his immortal fame, was not published until after his release. In fact, there is some doubt as to whether the entire work was finished in prison, but we know that the greater part was written there, and that it was completed immediately after his release, if not before, so that it belongs to this period of his life, whether the actual words were written down then or not.

This book he called *Pilgrim's Progress*, saying that it portrayed the journey of the human soul from this life to the heavenly kingdom. It is thus an allegory, and the genius of Bunyan made it the greatest allegory that has ever been written, both because it dealt with a subject of interest to all mankind, and because as a literary work it stands on a level with the great masterpieces of the world.

The book is written under the form of a dream, and with his strange power Bunyan takes us with him to the world of sleep, and makes it so real to us that only the waking

seems odd and unreal. The book was published in 1678 by Nathaniel Ponder, a London
bookseller, who had already suffered the pen-
alty of the law for publishing Puritan tracts and
pamphlets. It was a little brown book bearing
on the cover only the title and the date of publication. It was printed on yellowish paper and
from new Dutch type, and the title-page, as
well as the rest of the book, was adorned with
many of those fanciful and unique characters
which soon after passed into disuse. There is
an introduction in verse, which Bunyan called
An Apology, in which he gives his reasons for
writing the story, and to which his name is attached. And at the end of the book there is another bit of verse called *The Conclusion*. The
dream itself, which ends with the word *Finis*,
occupies two hundred and thirty pages, which
are wide-margined and clear in type. Perhaps
of all the great books of the world *Pilgrim's
Progress* is the smallest, as its first appearance
may have been the humblest, for outside the
initial letter, a capital A on a spray of flowers,
there is no attempt at decorations, and it is evi-

dent that Nathaniel Ponder thought only of doing his work honestly and with as little show as possible.

But this humble little book, written in such language as was used by the middle-class countrymen, was soon perceived to be a wonder, and took its rank in the world of literature by the side of Milton's splendid epic, for, like that, it was possessed by a genius such as the world seldom sees. It was read eagerly by all classes, it was accorded a high place by scholars, and the author was looked upon as one of the world's favored ones.

Bunyan's life, after the publication of *Pilgrim's Progress*, was one of constant and earnest work. It was during this time that he made those visits to London which gave him such fame as a preacher. He also published other books rich in thought and powerful in their effect upon the minds of the day, of which the chief is *The Holy War*, like *Pilgrim's Progress*, an allegory, in which the celestial and infernal armies contend for the possession of the town of "Mansoul." But his great work was *Pilgrim's Progress,* and it is this book which gives him his place in English literature. It has been read since then in every quarter of the world, and has been translated into seventy different dialects.

Bunyan died, in 1688, in London, and was buried in Bunhill Fields, one of the great burial places near London.

The story of *Pilgrim's Progress* is as follows:

Bunyan says that as he walked through the wilderness of the world he came to a den where he laid himself down to sleep, and as he slept he dreamed a dream. The den was the prison at Bedford in which he was confined, and the dream was the vision of *Pilgrim's Progress,* in which he saw the hero Christian standing before him clothed in rags, and bearing upon his back a heavy burden. And in his hand there was an open book which he read continually, weeping all the while, for from this book he learned that the city in which he dwelt, and which had always seemed to him a fair and beautiful place, was doomed to be de-

11

stroyed soon with fire, and that all the inhabitants who remained there would be burned in the flames.

But while Christian thus wept, not knowing whither to go to escape this fate, there came a stranger to him and asked him why he wept. And when Christian told him, the stranger comforted him by telling him of a beautiful city which had been built as a refuge for all those who wished to leave the doomed city of destruction. Then he showed him a bright light shining across the wide plain, and told Christian that close beside the light stood a wicket gate, and the gate-keeper would tell him the way to the beautiful country if he wished to go. He also gave him a parchment roll containing many directions about the way. And at this Christian was greatly comforted, and started immediately toward the wicket gate, nor would he go back, though his friends and neighbors tried hard to persuade him. Then one of his friends joined him across the plain and said that he too would leave the City of Destruction. But as they were thus walking together, they fell all at once

into a miry slough called the Slough of De-
spond, because many who fell therein became
discouraged and would not go any further.
And in this place Christian's companion left
him, and the Pilgrim went on his way alone,
struggling hard to cross the miry ground, and
weighed down by the burden on his back.
And he became almost discouraged himself,
and might have turned back also had not one
named Help come to his assistance and showed
him the way out of the slough. And then
Christian perceived a curious thing, and one
that comforted him greatly, which was that the
King of the Celestial City, knowing how hard
was the way thither, and how full of difficulties and dangers, had set certain of his servants in different places in the road to guard
and help the poor pilgrims travelling along it.
Help was one of these, and it was well for
Christian that he came at the right moment
to help him out of his trouble, for he was un-
used to travel, and the City of Destruction was
a place where one thought of pleasure only,
and where lessons of endurance and fortitude

were seldom learned. Then Christian went on his way and came at last to the wicket gate, over which was written, *Knock and it shall be opened unto you.* He knocked cheerily, and presently the porter came and opened the gate, and on hearing Christian's story showed him a narrow path leading straight from the gate, and told him that that was the road to the Celestial City, and that by keeping to it he would be in no danger of losing his way. For this road, he said, was distinguished from all others by being straight and narrow, never turning either to the right or the left, or joining itself to any other road. The porter also told Christian that a little distance beyond stood the House of the Interpreter, built by the King of the Celestial City, where he could learn many things useful for his journey. So Christian left him and went on his way, following the little narrow path, though he could go but slowly, owing to the burden upon his back, till he came to the house of which the porter had spoken. And when someone came to open the door in answer to his knocking, Christian perceived that this

was the most wonderful house he had ever
seen ; for it was full of pictures of pilgrims
on their way to the Celestial City. Some
pictures showed them happy and prosperous,
and others showed them discouraged and fearful, and from these pictures he gained many a
hint for his own journey. The Interpreter
also showed him other strange things. In one
room he saw two children sitting, one weeping
and full of anger, and the other silent and full
of peace ; and the name of the one was Passion,
and the name of the other Patience ; and the
Interpreter said that Passion wept because
he could not have all the pleasures of life
brought to him at once, and Patience was calm
because he was willing to wait, knowing that
whatever he was worthy of would come to him
at last. Christian saw that from this he was
to learn a lesson of patience, because when
all the treasures which Passion desired were
brought to him, he squandered them at once
and presently had nothing left but rags, nor
could hope for anything more, while Patience
still could look forward to a reward that would

be his when he had at last earned it faithfully.

And many other things the Interpreter
showed him, among them being a stately palace, upon the roof of which walked many people dressed in garments of gold. Before the
palace doors stood many persons desirous of
getting in, but fearing the men in armor who
kept guard. So no one tried to pass the men
till one man came, braver than the others, who
rushed upon the armed men and, after a fierce
fight, entered the palace victoriously, and was
welcomed by those who walked upon the
house-top, and was given a garment of gold.
And this Christian saw was a picture of the opposition which a pilgrim must meet on his way
to the Celestial City, and that if he would win
his way he must boldly attack all enemies, and
know neither fear nor faint-heartedness.

With such thoughts in his mind Christian
left the House of the Interpreter and went
on his way. As he went slowly along stoop-
ing under his heavy burden, he came to a
place where the path made a little ascent,

and looking to the higher ground above him
he saw a cross standing; and as he came
up to the cross his burden suddenly loosed
itself from his back and rolled away from him,
and tumbled at last into a pit beneath the cross.
And at this Christian was much rejoiced,
though it did not seem strange to him, for the
cross was the symbol of the king of that country whither he was going, and by its means
many were able to overcome difficulties that
might otherwise have overwhelmed them.

As he stood looking at the cross, there came
to him three shining ones who said *Peace be
to thee*, for they were also the servants of the
king; and with this they stripped him of his
rags and clothed him in fair garments, and gave
him a roll of parchment sealed with the king's
seal, telling him to keep this safely, for no one
would be admitted to the Celestial City who
possessed not one of these rolls. Then they
left him, and Christian went on with a light
heart and a light foot, for his burden lay behind
him in the pit, and the shining ones had given
him words of good cheer and blessed hope.

As he went he saw other persons also travelling in the same direction, and some were
asleep by the wayside and were bound with fetters, and some were travelling outside the narrow path, and told Christian that they had not
even entered by means of the Wicket Gate; and
when he tried to free them of their fetters, or
persuade them to journey to the Celestial City
by the way the king had directed, they only
laughed at him, so he had his trouble for
nothing. But some of them still journeyed
near him until they came to a great hill called
the Hill of Difficulty, up which the narrow path
led directly to the steepest part. And here
Christian lost his companions, for they would
have none of the narrow path, but took another road which led around the side of the
hill, and Christian found he must go on his way
alone. But this did not trouble him, as ever
since the burden had dropped off his back he
had felt brave-hearted and fresh; and so after
taking a refreshing drink from the little spring
which welled up at the foot of the hill, he took
his way up the steep slopes, singing as he

went, though the way was rough with stones, and there was not even a shrub or tree by which he might help himself along the way; for he knew that however difficult at first, the little path would lead him at last to the beautiful country on which his heart was fixed. When he had gone half-way up the hill, he saw something that encouraged him greatly; right before him stood a little arbor, green with running vines, and pleasant with flowers and songs of birds; and here Christian was glad to rest, as the arbor had been built by the king of the Celestial City for the rest and comfort of weary pilgrims. But as Christian sat there thinking over the events of his journey, and gathering strength for the remainder of the hill, the quiet and beauty of the place lulled him to sleep, and he slept many hours, while the day sped on till the sun began sinking in the west; then a warning voice sounded in his ears, and he woke from his slumbers with a start, and went on his way without thought of further rest, till he came to the top of the hill. And he was glad at this, for he dreaded the perils of the night in such a lonely place. But as he went along he saw two men running toward him with faces full of fear; and when they came up to him they told him that a little way beyond stood two lions in the path, whose roaring had frightened them back, though, like him, they were pilgrims on their way to the Celestial City. Then as Christian could not persuade them to turn back, he had to go on his way alone. Being much troubled by thought of the lions, he put his hand in his bosom to take out the parchment roll which the shining ones had told him to read when he felt downcast or fearful, but found to his distress, that the roll was gone, for he had lost it while he slept. As he could not enter the Celestial City without the roll, there was nothing for him to do but turn back; so Christian retreated his way step by step, searching everywhere eagerly; but he saw nothing of the roll, and came back at last to the green arbor where he had slept, and there he sat down and wept, for his heart was heavy with fear and sorrow. But as he sat there weeping, he chanced to look down under the seat, and there he saw his precious roll lying unharmed, and with great joy he snatched it up and put it safe in his bosom, and began his second journey up the hill, being now more fearful than ever of the strange way; for before he had arrived at the top the sun went down, and the twilight settled over the land; and the twilight gave place to the night, and Christian found himself alone upon the hill with darkness around him, and his heart filled with fearful thoughts of the lions in the pathway beyond.

Still he went on as bravely as he might and reached the top at last, and followed the narrow path till he saw before him a stately dwelling, which stood by the highway side, called The Palace Beautiful. Christian pressed on, hoping to find shelter there for the night; but as he came nearer, he saw the way guarded by the two fierce lions, whose roars were frightful to hear. And at this sight Christian stood still, for his heart failed him utterly. But as he stood there, the porter called to him from the lodge to come on, as the lions were chained; and at this Christian took heart and went on.

though he had to pass right between the lions, which gnashed their teeth at him and tried in vain to reach him; and then he was admitted to the Palace Beautiful, for this also belonged to the king, and was for the use of all pilgrims.

After Christian had told the inmates of the palace something of his journey, and had been refreshed with food and wine, he was taken to a chamber called Peace, where he lay down and slept till the day broke.

Here Christian stayed two days and was showed all the wonders of the house; and of these there were many, as it contained mementoes of all the great pilgrims who had passed that way to the Celestial City since the beginning of the world. They showed him also from the housetops a view of a mountainous land far away in the south, and which was beautiful with woods, vineyards, flowers, fruits, springs, and fountains, and told him that that was Immanuel's land, through which he would pass on his way, and that the mountains were called the Delectable Mountains, from whose summit could be seen even the gates of the Celestial City.

Then they took him to the armory and dressed him in complete armor, and gave him weapons to defend himself from the enemies he might meet; and so, with many words of comfort and counsel, they let him go.

It was well for Christian that he had this rest and comfort, for just beyond he came to the Valley of Humiliation, wherein dwelt the foul fiend Apollyon, who passed his life in warring against all pilgrims. And when Christian saw this monster, who was clad in scales and had wings like a dragon, and from whose mouth came forth smoke and fire, he was right glad that he had on his staunch breast-plate and heavy helmet; for he saw that unless he turned back, he must fight his way through. At first Apollyon tried to persuade Christian to leave his pilgrimage and serve him, and promised him great rewards if he would do so. But when he found that Christian would not listen to these offers, his rage knew no bounds, and he challenged him to deadly combat, feeling sure that the pilgrim would be easily vanquished. So Christian stood still and awaited the attack, knowing now that he must fight his way through the Valley or turn back. First Apollyon threw one of his fiery darts at him, but Christian quickly raised his shield, so that the dart glanced off; then Christian drew his sword and advanced toward Apollyon, who threw one dart after another, till the pilgrim was wounded in his head, and hands, and feet, and grew faint with the loss of blood before he had given Apollyon one blow. Then though his heart was still brave, he had to fall back a little, and Apollyon, seeing this, closed in upon him and gave him such a blow, that Christian fell to the ground and his sword flew from out his hand, and he gave himself up to death, feeling that his hour had come; for Apollyon followed one blow with another, all the while uttering such hideous yells and shrieks, that the valley echoed with them from end to end. But just as Christian had given up all hope, he reached out his hand suddenly and touched his good sword again, and gathering together all his strength, he struck Apollyon one last blow. This thrust came upon Apollyon so unexpectedly that he had no time to defend himself, while the sword bit so fiercely, that he had to shrink back in spite of himself; and with this Christian gathered up hope and prepared for another blow. But Apollyon had received a deadly wound, and such faintness spread through all his body, that he could do nothing but spread his great wings and soar out of reach, and the victory was with Christian.

As he lay there weak and helpless, he saw a hand above his head holding some leaves from the tree of life, which heals all manner of hurts, and these leaves Christian took and applied to his wounds and was healed immediately, so that he went on his journey.

But this dread valley only led to another called the Valley of the Shadow of Death, and which also abounded in dangers of every kind, though there was no Apollyon to bar the way. This valley was as dark as night, and in it were deserts and pits and bogs and ditches, and therein dwelt hobgoblins and satyrs and dragons; but the narrow path, on one side of which was a deep ditch and on the other a bottomless bog, led directly through the valley, and through these dangers Christian must pass if he would reach the Celestial City.

So he called courage to his heart and began the perilous journey, though because of the darkness and the pitfalls, he could go but slowly, and knew not at what moment he might step aside or fall into one of the traps and snares which the dwellers of the valley had set for all travellers. But at last he passed safely through, though the cries and shrieks of the dragons sounded so dismally in his ears, that he thought he should die from very fright; and when the end of the valley was reached he saw the day breaking, and looking back, was glad that he had made the passage in the night, when most of the hideous sights were hidden from him; for the daylight showed him things so terrible that he felt sure his heart would have failed him, had he tried to pass them. So he left the valley, at the end of which had dwelt two giants in olden time, and where yet lay the bones and ashes of the pilgrims they had put to death, and came out once more into sunlight and safety.

And now something happened which brought him great happiness and cheer, for just before him he saw another pilgrim walking in the narrow path, and when he came up to him he found it was one of his own neighbors, who had also left the city of Destruction through fear of the fate that was to come upon it, and who was now on his way to the Celestial City. Christian saw that he would now have a companion for his journey, and his heart grew light indeed, and he and Faithful went on very happily together. And as they presently entered a vast wilderness, they found much comfort in passing the time by telling each other their various adventures since they had left home.

Beyond the wilderness lay the town of Vanity, where there was a great fair held throughout the year, and as the narrow path led directly through this fair, Christian and Faithful could not help seeing the merchandise exhibited and the crowds which came there daily to buy.

12

Now, the governors of this fair, one of whom was Apollyon himself, were bitter enemies of the king of the Celestial City, and they had set up the fair in the narrow path, so that all pil·grims would have to pass through its streets, hoping thus to entice them to linger in the town and buy the wares of Vanity Fair, and thus bring their pilgrimage to an end. Many a pilgrim had fallen a victim to the designs of the governors, for in this fair were displayed silver and gold and precious stones, and all manner of things to be desired, all offered at such a price that even the poorest could buy; and by tempting pilgrims with these wares Apollyon gained many subjects, and thus exulted over the king of the Celestial City, whom he hated.

Now, as Christian and Faithful entered the fair all the people stopped buying and looked at them, for it was seen at once that they were strangers in the town, being dressed in such garments as were never worn in Vanity Fair. And those who were near by pressed nearer, and those who were farther away came closer, and there was so much commotion and excitement

that soon everyone knew that something unusual had happened. Christian and Faithful paid
no attention to this hubbub and tried to go on
their way quietly; but at this the crowd grew
more excited than ever, and the merchants offered their wares, and the lookers-on pressed
around the more eagerly to see what the
strangers would buy; and when it was found that
the pilgrims would neither buy nor linger at the
booths, all the people of the fair took it as an in-
sult to themselves, and they raised such cries of
disdain and anger that the lord of the fair sent
in haste to see what was the matter.

Then they told him that two unknown men
had entered the fair dressed in strange garments, and speaking a language hardly to be
understood, and that they had created a disturb-
ance by their disorderly conduct. And at this
the lord of the fair ordered Christian and Faithful to be put in a large iron cage as a punishment for disturbing the peace, and before they
could defend themselves the pilgrims were
seized and put in the cage, where they were
left many days, while all the inhabitants of the

town crowded around them daily and reviled them, and treated them as if they had been wild beasts.

But Christian and Faithful answered nothing back, and were so quiet and patient under all their misfortune, that some of the people of the fair began to wonder if the pilgrims were really such bad men as they had been represented to be ; and so gradually there gathered around the cage a few who sympathized with the prisoners, and who would have been glad to set them free. This so offended the chief men of the fair that they hated Christian and Faithful more than ever, and accused them of enticing others to their own evil ways ; and so the pilgrims were taken out of the cage and beaten and put in irons, and were led in chains up and down the fair so that every one might look upon them, while the governors threatened a like fate to all who sympathized with them.

But this only won the pilgrims still more friends, for many now perceived that the strangers were unjustly treated ; and at last the lord of the fair ordered the pilgrims to be brought to trial for disturbing the peace of the town and deluding the people of the fair; for Christian and Faithful had talked continually since their imprisonment of the joys of the Celestial City, and many had expressed a desire to go thither. So the trial was called and the pilgrims were questioned by the judges, who tried in vain to frighten them into submission, and at last Faithful was judged guilty of death, though some mercy was shown to Christian, who was sent back to jail for a time.

Then Faithful was brought out for punishment, and was beaten and stoned and cut with knives, and then burned. But by the help of one of the townspeople, Christian was able to elude his keepers and escape out of the town in the darkness. And with him went also Hopeful, who had helped him escape, and the people of Vanity Fair never saw either of them again. At first they could go but slowly, for Christian was worn with his imprisonment; but after a few days they came to a beautiful river which flowed close by the side of the narrow path, and on the banks of the river grew many trees whose leaves could heal all kinds of sickness, and whose fruits were both delicious and strengthening; and thus Christian found remedies for his wounds, and refreshment for his spirits, for the water of the river soothed all who drank of it.

There were also pleasant meadows on either side of the river, green all the year round and beautified with lilies, and in these meadows the pilgrims slept many nights, till Christian was cured of his wounds and had recovered his strength.

And as they went on their way they were glad to find that the rivers till followed the narrow path, and so for a while the journeying was most pleasant.   But they came to a place at last where the path turned aside from the river and led over stony places, and at this Christian was much discouraged, for his feet were yet tender and the stones hurt him cruelly.   But they dared not leave the narrow path, though the ground became rougher and rougher, so that Christian groaned continually with pain.

A little way beyond the path took its way

by the side of another meadow which seemed
to them as fresh and beautiful as the first, and
on the other side of the fence a little path led
right beside their own, and in the fence was
set a stile so that whoever wished might enter the meadow at his will. And Christian,
seeing that the soft grass would make easy
walking for his feet, persuaded Hopeful to leave
the narrow path and walk in the meadow for a
while.

As they passed over the stile they saw just
before them a man walking in the same path,
and when they called to him to know who he
was, he told them he was a pilgrim on his
way to the Celestial City ; and then Christian
and Hopeful felt sure that they had not done
wrong in leaving the narrow path. So they
went on pleasantly enough till the night came,
when the darkness grew so thick that the man
who went before lost his way and fell into a deep
pit, and Christian and Hopeful heard him groan
in great agony. But when they called to him
they received no answer, excepting cries of pain,
and then they stood still in fear, not knowing

what was before them. And while they waited
it began to lighten and thunder and rain, and
the rain fell in such torrents that the whole
meadow seemed suddenly like a river. Then
they feared to stand still and thought it best to
try and get back to the stile, but this they could
not accomplish, for they lost their way continually, and were forced at last to take shelter under some bushes; and being very weary, they
fell asleep.

Now, this meadow was owned by a grim
giant, whose name was Despair, and who lived
in a gloomy castle near by. At daybreak, as
this giant came walking through the meadow,
he espied Christian and Hopeful fast asleep,
and awoke them, and told them they were his
prisoners, because he had caught them tres-
passing on his grounds. Then he led them
away to Doubting Castle, and confined them
in a dungeon far underneath the ground; and
here they lay for three days and nights without anything to eat, and in utter darkness,
expecting every moment that Giant Despair
would enter and make away with them. And

so bitter was their despair that they gave up all hope of reaching the Celestial City.

But about midnight of the third night, Christian suddenly gave a great start and sprang to his feet with joy, for he remembered that he had a key in his bosom called Promise, which would unlock the doors of Doubting Castle and let them out. Then he and Hopeful set to work carefully and quietly to unlock the door of their cell, and found to their great joy that the key fitted the lock perfectly. Then they stole cautiously into the corridor and unlocked one door after another, until at last they reached the outer door; and here their hearts gave way, for the key would not turn in the lock. But after much trial and pushing this lock too finally yielded, and the door swung open; but the hinges were so rusty from disuse, and the door was so heavy, that the noise of the opening awoke Giant Despair, and suspecting that the pilgrims had escaped, he rushed in great haste after them. They were fortunate enough, however, to elude him, and got out into the air and safe across the meadow and over the stile into the narrow path. And then, seeing how much danger the meadow path held for pilgrims, they set up a stone before the stile and wrote on it an inscription, warning all pilgrims that the way across that meadow led to the castle of Giant Despair; and by this means they saved the lives of many who came after them.

Glad enough were they then to keep to the narrow path, for the stones were better than the walls of Doubting Castle, and the grim voice of Giant Despair. And after a while the path grew less stony, and entered a pleasant countryside, where they had a view of fair distant mountains, and as they drew nearer they found that these were the Delectable Mountains, about which Christian had been told at the Palace Beautiful; and at this they were greatly rejoiced, for they were sure of a warm welcome.

These mountains, which lay always in the sunshine, abounded in pleasant things: there were orchards, and vineyards, and gardens, and fountains, and beautiful rivers; and the shepherds who lived there were servants of the

king of the Celestial City, and found their chief
pleasure in showing kindness to the pilgrims
who were continually passing through their
country. Here Christian and Hopeful remained
for a day or two, and the shepherds showed
them wonderful things from the top of the
mountains. Among other sights they saw afar
off in the valley a place of tombs, where blind
men were walking up and down; and the shepherds said that these men were prisoners of
Giant Despair, whom he had captured as he
had captured Christian and Hopeful, and that it
was his custom, after keeping his captives in
the dungeon for a while, to put out their eyes
and set them among the tombs to wander up
and down till they died.

They saw also many dangerous places that
lay before them on their journey, and the
shepherds showed them how to avoid these
dangers, and gave them a note of the way so
they might pass them by unharmed. And, last
of all, the pilgrims had a view of the gates of
the Celestial City, which shone dimly through
the distance, and with this they were forced

to say farewell to the shepherds and go on
their way. So they passed down the mountain side into the king's highway again, and
as they went on they saw other men in the
guise of pilgrims walking in the narrow path,
with whom they talked about their journey.
Some of these travellers Christian and Hopeful saw were honest pilgrims like themselves,
and others were only going that way because of some selfish end they had in view;
and presently these latter came to a place
where their pilgrim robes fell off, and they
were forced to leave the narrow path, and were
cast out from the company of all good men.
And amid such experiences Christian and his
companion passed over a large part of their way,
and came at last to a certain country which
seemed to them a beautiful and restful place;
for the air had in it a quality which was so
soothing that it made one feel that sleep was
the best thing in the world. Then Hopeful,
being very weary, proposed that they should
lie down there and sleep a while; and Christian
would have consented, had he not suddenly re-

membered that this country was one of the sights he had seen from the Delectable Mountains, and that the shepherds had warned them that it was enchanted ground, and whoever slept there would never wake again. And when he heard this Hopeful started to his feet wide awake, and he and Christian hurried over the enchanted ground as fast as they could, telling each other stories of the Celestial City and talking of many things to keep from falling asleep; so they came safely at last to the end of the ground where even the flowers seemed to sleep, and the trees all nodded drowsily.

Just beyond the enchanted ground they entered the Land of Beulah, where the sun shone ever as it did on the Delectable Mountains. Here the air was sweet and pleasant, and flowers grew everywhere, and the birds sang continually. And everywhere the pilgrims met people clothed in shining garments, walking up and down, and talking about the beauty of the heavenly country; for the Land of Beulah lay close beside the Celestial City, and Christian and Hopeful could even see the city plainly, for it was built of gold and shone like the sun. In this land were orchards, and vineyards, and gardens kept by the king's gardener, and beautiful arbors, where weary pilgrims might refresh themselves with sleep; and journeying through this beautiful country they came at last in sight of the gates of the city, and knew that their long pilgrimage was nearly at an end.

But between the Land of Beulah and the Celestial City flowed a deep river across which there was no bridge, and when they saw this river Christian and Hopeful stood still in fear, not knowing what to do. While they stood thus, there came to them two shining ones whose raiment shone like gold, and whose faces were illumined with the light of the city, and they told the pilgrims that unless the river was passed over, the gates could not be reached, as there was no other way thither.

And at this Christian and Hopeful were filled with dismay, and stood for a time unable to speak. But at last they gathered up courage, and knowing that other pilgrims had made the passage of the river, they entered the water; the cold waves came up close to their heads and the rough billows dashed them hither and thither, and Christian began to lose courage from the fright, and he would have sunk beneath the waters, had not Hopeful kept his head above the waves and comforted him with cheering words. Christian also saw visions of hobgoblins and evil spirits, and heard dreadful noises such as he had heard in his fight with Apollyon. But by Hopeful's aid the dreadful passage was at last made and they came to the other side, where stood the two shining ones ready to receive them. The shining ones led them up to the gates, telling them all the while of the great joys that awaited them; and as they came to the gates they were met by a great host of the dwellers of the heavenly city who came out to meet them, singing songs of welcome. Then Christian and Hopeful gave their rolls to the warder of the gates, who sent them to the king, and when he had read them the king commanded the gates to be opened. Then Christian and Hopeful entered the gates, and were immediately clothed in shining raiment and were crowned with crowns of gold, and had golden harps given them so that they might join in the hymns of thanksgiving.   And then all the bells of the city rang for joy as they were led into the presence of the king.   And so their long journey came to an end, and they found the Celestial City at last fair as they had hoped, and received their reward for all the troubles and dangers of the way.

CHAPTER V.

THE ESSAY AND THE POETRY OF THE EIGHTEENTH CENTURY.

In English literature the seventeenth century is joined to the eighteenth by four writers whose names occupy high places in the history of letters. These men were all born during the lifetime of Milton and Bunyan, and their lives also touched those writers who belong entirely to the eighteenth century, so that they form an unbroken link between the two periods. But although these men lived during the same literary period, their writings are so different in character, purpose, and style that each one may be said to have marked an epoch in literature. Unlike the seventeenth century, when the Puritan idea influenced the thoughts of the greatest minds, this period is remarkable for the widely different characters of the men

13

who were its representatives. It was also remarkable as the birth-time of some new forms of literature.

The four men who distinguished the early part of the eighteenth century were Daniel Defoe, the founder of the English novel; Jonathan Swift, the greatest satirist of modern times; Joseph Addison, one of the creators of the essay, and John Dryden, the most popular poet since the sixteenth century.

The essay was in the eighteenth century made so popular by the two writers, Steele and Addison, who also brought it to such perfection that it is generally considered to date from that time.

The essay of those days was a paper upon any subject which the writer thought would interest his readers, and appeared always in a little journal that was published daily, tri-weekly, or weekly, and which held beside the essay some general news and advertisements.

The first of these journals from which the modern essay dates was called the *Tatler*, and appeared in 1709, ten years before the publica-

tion of the first English novel.   The *Tatler*
was founded by Steele, but soon after its appearance Addison joined with Steele in its production, and from this time on the two men
worked together, sometimes one contributing
the chief paper and sometimes the other.

Coming in between the decline of the theatre and the birth of the novel, gave the *Tatler*
an instant success, for society at that time was
depending greatly for itself upon amusement,
and the amusements were not always successful or satisfactory.   People often grew weary
of entertainment, though the life of England at
that time was more purely social than it has
ever been since.   There were clubs everywhere
and of all kinds, and these, with the coffee-
houses, where the men of the day met to talk,
and the tea-tables, where the women met to
gossip, were the great bonds of social union.
It was an age of talk, and people found nothing
too high or too low, too serious or too flippant,
to talk about.   And besides this, fashionable
society had come to regard learning and literature as old-fashioned accomplishments, and

fops and fine ladies even boasted their ignorance of books and their lack of education.

Steele and Addison set themselves to better
this state of things, and the way they chose was
such a pleasant one that people found their
taste improving and a love for good literature
growing, without even suspecting that they
themselves had not brought it about.

This was done by making the *Tatler*, and the
Spectator—the journal which succeeded it—so
bright, chatty, witty, and amusing, that reading
it at the club or tea-table seemed like listening
to a good story told by one of the members,
with the exception that the story was more interesting and better told than those they had
been accustomed to. The charm was also
heightened by the illusion which was kept up
in regard to the journal itself, for the *Spectator*
was represented as being the mouth-piece of a
fashionable club. To this imaginary club belonged Sir Andrew Freeport, the wealthy and
important merchant; Captain Sentry, the brave
and dashing soldier; Will Honeycomb, the
fashionable man about town; and Sir Roger de

Coverley, the old-fashioned country gentleman, whose true courtesy, genial humor, and gracious charity, were the types of that fine old school of elegance which it was the fashion to deride.   To the club also belonged Mr. Spectator himself, who is always known as the short-faced gentleman, good-humored and observing, but of less importance than the others.

The experiences, adventures, conversations, and reflections of this imaginary club became a daily delight to fashionable London.   The *Spectator* was read at the clubs, in the coffee-houses, and at the tea-table; it became the fashion, and not to read it was a sign of being out of the fashionable world; and everyone, no matter what his tastes, could find something to his liking.   Sometimes one of the imaginary members would visit the opera, or the play, and the *Spectator* would contain a paper so full of humor and fine observation, yet so full also of suggestion for a higher kind of play, that the reader would begin to criticise what he had before admired, and to talk himself of the degeneration of the drama.   Again, there would be a paper on some great poet, as for instance, Milton, and the reader finding himself addressed as if he were familiar with this great poet, had to admit an interest or lose his standing of comradeship with the now popular imaginary club. And so on ; no matter what was the subject of the essay, the reader gradually found his tastes grow finer, his judgment improving, and a love for good literature springing up in him. For above and beyond everything else, the essays of the *Tatler*, the *Spectator*, and the *Guardian* were remarkable for the purity and elegance of their language, and this influence in an age of frivolity and bad taste, was priceless as a means of elevating the tone of society, as well as of incalculable benefit in reviving a taste for good literature.

This, then, was the mission of the essay, a mission that it fulfilled at a time when preaching would not have been listened to, and when any other great work of literature would have failed because of the lack of an audience capable of understanding it. But because Addison and Steele were men who understood and mingled with other men, and who spoke to them in their own tongue, they were able to establish first a feeling of comradeship, next to raise the tone of society, and lastly to create a love for good literature ; and so their work was a noble one even above and beyond the fact that the essays themselves, from a purely literary point of view, rank with the masterpieces of English fiction and criticism.

The eighteenth century produced no great poet like Chaucer or Spenser or Milton, and it is chiefly noted, not for the excellence of its poets, but for the work it did for poetry.

John Dryden, who knew Milton, connected the poetry of the seventeenth century with that of the eighteenth century, and was one of the first poets who wrote for the stage after the fall of the Puritan power, when the theatres were again allowed to be opened. For twenty years no theatres had been open in England, and the charm of the Elizabethan drama was unknown to the generation which had grown accustomed to Puritan gloom and severity of thought. But when the Stuarts came back to the throne the theatres were again opened, and a demand for plays began; and as England was very tired of Puritan dreariness, it welcomed eagerly the gay and frivolous pleasures which Charles II. introduced, and which were the foundation of a new drama. All the playwrights immediately began to write such plays as would please the court and the gay ladies and lords who were the king's intimate friends, and all the comedies of this period are marred by the immorality of the times.

Dryden was regularly paid to write three plays a year for the king, and produced a number of comedies and tragedies which, though satisfying the taste of the day, lack skill in drawing a character and in picturing the emotions of the heart, two qualities which may not be absent from great dramas. He was a man of great ability, and possessed one of the finest minds in the whole range of English literature, but in his dramas he is clever rather than great, and although many of his sentences and lines compare worthily with the Shakesperean school, the plays as a whole cannot be placed with the best dramatic literature, even though redeemed in some cases by a style whose force, vigor, and majesty took in his own day the place of inspiration and genius.

Besides his dramas, Dryden wrote a number of long poems on satirical and religious subjects. He also translated into English verse some of the Latin writers. Among these translations was one of Virgil which, as a translation, is considered one of the best in English poetry. Besides this, he produced a series of poems which he called fables, but which were in reality a set of stories from old French and Italian poets introduced in a new dress. Many of them were the same as those which Chaucer used as foundations for his immortal poems, and in some cases Dryden simply modernized the old English of Chaucer into the speech of his time. These fables are among the best poems that he wrote.

But his greatest work as a poet is found in the single poem on music which was written in honor of St. Cecilia's Day, and was called

Alexander's Feast. This poem has inspiration, melody, and exquisite perfection of form. It is one of the great lyrics of English literature, and it is safe to say that it will be remembered when all the rest of his poetry is forgotten; for the poetry of Dryden, though polished and magnificent in style, full of countless beauties and the production of one of the greatest men of his age, yet lacks the creative power which distinguishes the greatest poets.

But yet his work for English poetry was great and original, and of service to his age, for this century, which was the century of style in writing, left also its impress on the verse, which it refined and polished, and made beautiful in a sense that it had never known before. This period is sometimes called the age of the correct poets, because whoever wrote verse was guided by certain rules of composition which had never been so rigorously followed before. It was, in fact, an age in which English poetry brought forth few great works, but in which workmen learned to polish and beautify and enhance the value of poetry, as the lapidary learns to polish and perfect the beauty of the diamond.   This work of perfecting had for its two great apostles Dryden, whose prose essays on poetry are so valuable that he is called the first critic who raised criticism to an art, and his disciple Alexander Pope, who was born twelve years before Dryden's death.

Pope's greatest contributions to English literature were a translation of Homer, a philosophical poem called *An Essay on Man*, an exquisite little burlesque called the *Rape of the Lock*, in which the stealing of a lock of hair is made the subject of a poem resembling in form one of the great epics, a long satirical poem called *The Dunciad*, in which the poet ridicules many of the prominent writers of the day, and an immense number of fragmentary poems in the shape of essays, epistles, pastorals, elegies, and other forms.   Like Dryden, Pope is one of the great figures of the eighteenth century, though he is considered by many as a great man of letters rather than a great poet.   There is one thing which distinguishes him above every other writer of the century, and that is his immense popularity, which began with his first publications, followed him through life, and for fifty years after made him the criterion for all who pursued poetry as an art.

Dryden and Pope thus created what is called the classical school of poetry, the poetry which depends upon form rather than inspiration for its power, and which, with the development of history, the essay, and the novel, was the great work which the eighteenth century accomplished for literature.

But the latter part of this period saw the birth of a new school of poetry even while the classic school was still in power, and a new group of men arose who dreamed, not of producing a polished bit of verse which should be beyond the criticism of artists, but who desired rather to interpret nature, or to find some treasure of poetic thought in an old-time ballad, or to speak a word whose pathos would touch the heart because it came from the heart.

This was the beginning of what is called sometimes the Romantic, and sometimes the

Naturalistic, school of poetry, because its disci-
ples set themselves in opposition to the classical school, and cared for romance, sentiment,
and the interpretation of nature rather than for
form.

This school had many followers, for the poets
of the eighteenth century are very numerous,
and many fine poems of this class were produced.   The greatest of the group are James
Thompson, whose great poem called the *Sea-
sons*, is a description of nature in every season of the English year; William Collins, celebrated for his Odes; Thomas Gray, whose
Elegy in a Country Churchyard is considered
the finest elegy in the English language; William Cowper, the poet of domestic life whose
greatest poem, the *Task*, celebrates the joys
of home; Young, the author of the celebrated
poem *Night Thoughts*, or *Meditations on Life,
Death, and Immortality;* and Thomas Chatterton, who died before he was eighteen, but
who left behind him a number of poems of such
great promise that there is no doubt that if he
had lived he would have become one of the

great poets of the world. Besides these there were numbers of other poets who wrote dramas and lyric poetry, the age between Dryden and Chatterton producing in all nearly thirty writers in verse.

The last of the eighteenth century poets is Robert Burns, the greatest genius that Scotland has ever seen, and one of the greatest song-writers of the world. There is no greater contrast possible than that between the lives of the other poets of the eighteenth century and that of Burns. Almost without an exception they were all men who had the advantages of education and of association with other writers; they were all also familiar with the world, and with that literature which formed the guide for writers of those times. To all these things Burns was a stranger. He was the son of a Scotch peasant who was so poor that he did not even own the miserable thatch-roofed cottage which sheltered his family, and all the education which the boy had in his young days was received in a little parish school, which he went to for a few years while he was growing big enough to help his father with the work of the farm. But this peasant lad, born in the lowliest rank of life, had come into the world with a gift that belongs to very few, the poet's gift, but which enables him who has it to call the whole world his kingdom, and makes him brother to the greatest men that have ever lived.

Very early in life the child discovered that this gift was his, and his young days were enriched with those subtle impressions and understandings of nature which only the poetic mind can receive. All the world around him held wonderful meanings, and its beauty taught him lessons which books and masters could never have taught. So he grew up in the school of Nature, nurtured by her until his soul had absorbed many of her secrets and knew her moods, and felt that some of her wisdom and sympathy and tenderness had become his. With this early training it is not strange that Burns should be able to touch the heart and sympathies of his readers, for what he gave them came from his own heart, and was due to his subtle but powerful sympathy with all life and all forms of nature. And his sweetest and strongest poems are those in which he transcribes this wide and universal sympathy, for they sing those emotions which govern every heart, and to which every soul must respond. In these poems he is like an artist who places in a city window a picture of some shaded fern-draped brook, which runs its quiet course far away from the noise and glare of crowded streets, and which takes those who see it back to long-forgotten days, so that they hear again the songs of wild birds in the woods, and smell the wild flowers by brook-sides and in green meadows. Thus the picture becomes a memory, or reminiscence of life, and it is this quality of reminiscence which so distinguishes the poetry of Burns. He sings, and his hearers feel again the emotions that they felt in the great moments of life, and they are held, not by any new charm, but by an old and familiar one sweet with the memories of days that can never come again.

It is this power of transcription which makes the great lyric poet, the poet who sings songs. And in this way it is as high as the creative power which enables the great dramatist to write dramas that are placed among the immortal works of the world. In fact the lyric poet who chooses his subjects from the every-day world around him reaches perhaps a larger audience than any other kind of poet, for he endows with grace things that to the world at large appear commonplace, and sees beauty in what to careless eyes seems without charm ; thus he becomes a teacher, teaching those who know nothing of books the eternal glory of the world around them.

Among the most famous of the shorter poems of Burns are his *Lines to a Mountain Daisy*, the one *To a Mouse on Turning up her Nest with a Plough*, the love song, *Ae Fond Kiss and then we Sever*, his patriotic poem, *Scots wha hae wi' Wallace Bled*, and that lament for the past, *The Banks of Bonny Doon*. But indeed all his poetry is so full of the truest pathos, tenderness, humor, and deep feeling that it is hard to decide where the greatest merit lies.

14

CHAPTER VI.

THE BIRTH OF THE NOVEL—EIGHTEENTH CENTURY.

English literature began with the stories that the old bards and minstrels used to chant and sing in the halls of the great chiefs or at the firesides of the peasantry, in the beginning of the nation's history. And for centuries after, popular literature, the literature of the people, was thrown into the form of a tale or romance, so that if we look at English letters from the earliest times down to the sixteenth century, we shall see that it is always a story in some form or another which fascinated the nation at large, though books on history or religion might claim the attention of the scholar.

Whether it were Beowulf, King Arthur, Robin Hood, Sir John Mandeville, the Canterbury Pilgrims, or the Adventures of the Red

Cross Knight, depended upon the date and history of the time, but the book for the people must be a story-book.

Spenser was the last of the great romance writers who threw their stories into the form of poetry, for with the exception of the legends of King Arthur and the tales of Mandeville, nearly all the stories were written in verse. A little before, and during, the lifetime of Spenser, the love of this form of literature seemed to grow less, so that for nearly a hundred years after the publication of *The Faery Queene* no story of any importance was written in England with the exception of Bacon's *Atlantis*, which belongs to the same period as *The Faery Queene* itself. This was because the genius of the great English writers was during this time engaged in developing and perfecting the English drama, and all the great works then produced were thrown into the dramatic form. Ever since the twelfth century, when the miracle and mystery plays fascinated the heart of the English people, the drama had been slowly growing to the height it reached in the time of

Shakespeare, whose genius, with that of Marlowe, Ben Johnson, and their friends and successors, made the English nation a nation of play-lovers and theatre-goers.

This love for the drama held strong for a hundred years, and then only relaxed because the works of the great dramatists had been put aside to make room for plays which had so little merit that they soon wearied the better class, and were chiefly patronized by those who cared rather for pantomime and nonsense than the true drama.

And it was just at this time, when the people swung back into their old habit of reading stories instead of going to see them played, that one of the greatest stories in the English language was written; and the fact that it was written in prose and was a pure fiction, a thing designed to please and amuse only, has given the author the position of founder of the English novel. This great book was *Robinson Crusoe*, which was first given to the world in 1719.

Daniel De Foe, the author of *Robinson Crusoe*, was born in London in 1661, and was the son of a butcher. His father was a Dissenter, as those Protestants are called in England who do not belong to the English Church, and for this reason De Foe could not be educated at any school under the jurisdiction of the Church, but was sent to one of those seminaries which the Dissenters founded to supply the place of the Church schools and colleges. At this school, at Stoke Newington, De Foe laid the foundation of a good education which served him well in after-life; and either at school or later on, he must have been at some time a diligent scholar, as he knew Greek, Latin, Spanish, Italian, and French, besides being well versed in history, astronomy, and various other branches of study.

His father intended him to be a preacher, but De Foe did not feel called to the ministry, and after he left school he was engaged for some years in business. But business could not satisfy such a mind as his, which was interested in literature, religion, and politics more than in anything else, and as his thinking was of an earnest and original kind, it followed naturally that after a time he began to put his thoughts into words printed and open to all who would read. He first came into notice as a writer of political pamphlets and religious tracts, and for ten years edited a tri-weekly paper which was partly political and partly literary in its aims. He also had office under the government for a time. But his career was from the first one of ups and downs. He would prosper a while financially, to lose suddenly all his money and find himself in debt. At one time he was in favor with the king, at another he was imprisoned two years on a charge of disloyalty. He once wrote a pamphlet which sentenced him to the pillory, because it championed the cause of the Dissenters ; and yet this very disgrace showed him his power with the people, for multitudes of his friends stood around the pillory for the three days of his punishment, covered it with flowers, and drank his health. And so it continued through his long career, during which he produced so many tracts, pamphlets, and papers of every kind that even a list of them would fill pages. But although

De Foe won for himself a place as a brilliant political writer, his claim to one of the greatest places in English literature was not made till he was nearly sixty years of age.

And this claim was not based upon his power as a political writer, or as a defender of any religious sect, but upon his gift of story-telling, a gift so great that it has placed him among the geniuses of the world. The time in which he lived was celebrated for those marvellous adventures on land and sea which filled the ears of people with stories of pirates, freebooters, and fights between men-of-war of different nations, for each country had its own cruisers out on the high seas, and England, France, and Spain were jealous of the enterprises and ambitions of one another.

The Spanish ships were not allowed to touch at English ports, and English vessels on the sea were sure of one thing only when they engaged a Spanish enemy, that they must either conquer or spend the rest of their lives in working as slaves in the mines of Spanish America. Still the spirit of enterprise could

not be crushed, and long voyages were continually undertaken to remote parts of the world
and many expeditions made entirely around the
world.

One of these voyages was undertaken by
Captain Woodes Rogers, a well-known seaman
of the time, and had for its object the circum-
navigation of the globe. Rogers had command of two vessels, the Duke, and the Duchess of Bristol, and was bound first for the
South Seas, thence to the East Indies, and
home again by the way of the Cape of Good
Hope, and there could be no doubt that such
a route offered abundant hope for adventure.
This hope was realized. There were fights
with Spaniards, and adventures with the natives
along the South American coast, from the
Amazon to the La Plata, and the log-book of
the captain was full of valuable descriptions of
the countries visited, and contained many maps
that would be of use to future voyagers. But
the most surprising incident of the voyage occurred while they were yet outbound, and within the waters of the South Sea. The captain

was uncertain of the latitude of the island of Juan Fernandez, and as they wished to make that land, the outlook kept keen watch day and night. But instead of the misty outlines which denoted land, they saw one night a bright fire blazing not far away, and then they grew fearful, thinking that some enemy was near. But in the morning they saw no signs of ships, and as they sighted the island they drew near and sent off a boat to reconnoitre.

But the boat did not return for such a long time that the captain grew anxious and signalled for it, and this at last brought it back to the ship. And then came such a wonder as had never been seen before, though captain and crew had sailed on many a voyage before, for the boat's crew brought with them a creature clothed in goat skins, and of such wild appearance that the captain in his narrative says: "He looked wilder than the goats themselves, and spoke a kind of language that it was difficult to believe was meant for English."

The ship's company crowded around the strange man, who created more astonishment than the discovery of a new kind of animal would have done, and at last succeeded in drawing his story from him.   His name was Alexander Selkirk, and, four years and four months before, he had been marooned or abandoned on that island by the captain of the Cinque Ports, for disobedience and disloyalty.   At first he thought he might soon be rescued and took his fate calmly.   He had a good store of clothes, a gun, some powder and bullets, some tobacco, a hatchet, a knife, a kettle, a Bible, and some mathematical instruments, and for a time was hopeful and comfortable; but as time passed and no ship came in sight, he began to realize his position and was often driven to despair.   Still he tried to make the best of things, and when his powder was gone, he produced fire by rubbing two sticks of pimento together.   He built two huts of pimento or pepper trees, covered them with grass, and lined them with goat skins.   In one of these he slept and the other he occupied during the day.

He lived on crawfish and goat's flesh, which he seasoned with pimento and thus made palatable, though he could never get used to go-ing without salt and bread. He also ate the turnips which grew upon the island, and the seed of which had originally been sown by a sea captain whose ship once touched there. For amusement he wandered over the island and cut his name on the trees, and sometimes, when hard pressed for company, he would dance with the tame kids and cats, singing his own music. The cats, besides being useful as companions, also performed valuable service for Selkirk, in keeping off the rats, which at first showed a disposition to devour his cloth-ing and otherwise molest him. Both cats and rats were descended from ancestors which had originally been left on the island by a passing ship, and to the former and to the tame ani-mals which learned to love him, Selkirk owed all the companionship he had; but they loved him with that faithful love that animals give to their human friends, and their merry company did much to brighten his lonely hours; for dur-ing the four years he was there, only two ships came to anchor off the island.

Both of these ships were Spanish, so that
Selkirk did not claim assistance, fearing that
they would only carry him off to work in the
South American mines. The sailors of one of
the ships, however, caught sight of him as he
was lurking in the bushes, and gave chase.
Selkirk saved himself by climbing a tree, under
which his pursuers passed as they returned
from their fruitless search, and these were the
only human beings that stepped on the island
while he was there.

When his clothes gave out he first made
clothing of goat - skins pinned together by
thongs, though he afterward made a needle of a
nail and ravelled up his stockings for thread.
When his faithful knife wore out he made another of some iron hoofs he found, and for fire
and light he used the pimento wood, which
burned clearly and gave a pleasant odor. On
clear nights he never went to bed till it became
too dark to watch the sea for a ship, and it was
the light from his fire which the men of Captain
Rogers's company had seen the night before
the island was discovered. He became an ex-

pert runner, catching all the goats he required by running them down. Once this accomplishment nearly cost him his life, as a goat he was chasing led him to the bank of a precipice over which he fell, injuring himself seriously. During his stay there, he caught over a thousand goats, the greater number of which he marked on the ear and let go again.

Great was the wonder of the crews and passengers of the Duke and of the Duchess of Bristol on hearing this strange story, which excelled in romance anything ever heard before in real life. Selkirk was their guide over the island, and showed his speed in running by outstripping the best runners in the crew, besides the trained dogs. When the ships sailed he went with them as mate on one of the vessels, which completed their voyage and reached England again in 1711.

In 1712 Captain Woodes Rogers published an account of his adventures, in which he devoted several pages to the episode of Alexander Selkirk. The thick little book, with its plain cover of dark calf-skin, was eagerly read by the public, which delighted in tales of all kinds, and especially those which related to the far-off regions of the world. Selkirk's story was also related in one or two periodicals and papers, so that it was soon generally known in England.

It was this story which De Foe took and, seven years after the publication of Woodes Rogers's Journal, gave to the world under the now famous title of *Robinson Crusoe*. Only the first part of the book was published at first, and it is interesting to know that the name Crusoe was borne by one of De Foe's schoolmates when he was a pupil at Stoke Newington, and studying for the Dissenting ministry. De Foe had his hero remain on the island twenty-eight years, and gave him for companion a trusty and wise dog. And the skill with which he wove the Selkirk episode into a romantic tale of pure fiction was so great, that one who read the story without knowing it to be an invention would think he was reading a true narrative.

De Foe took a common English sailor and in-

vested him with a charm that made him immortal, though he did no deed of valor or chivalry,
and had for his highest aims only the hope of
getting away from the scene of his own adventures. But in spite of this he stands in the
company of the Knights of the Round Table,
and the Canterbury Pilgrims, and the heaven-
bound traveller of Bunyan, and is worthy of the
place because like them he is the creation of
genius.

England went mad over Robinson Crusoe,
and edition after edition failed to satisfy the demand for this marvellous tale, which all could
understand. The working-classes especially
exulted over this hero, who was just like themselves, and who did just the things they would
have done under the same circumstances.
They admired his good sense, his homely invention, his matter-of-fact way of going about
things, and of making the best of things.
When he came to a difficulty they could antici-
pate the manner in which he would deliver himself from it, and if he had done differently they
would have criticised him for a ninny. But he

always did the right thing. He had the inge‐ nuity of the poor and their skill in making ex‐ pedients. He knew how to make one thing do the work of another; he had also the practical patience of his class, which tries one thing after another till something is found to fit the emer‐ gency.

Every farmer reading the book would in his mind see the sailor-brother who perhaps had sailed away never to return. Every farmer's boy, poor in boyish treasures, would know what the loss of the knife meant; every restless soul hemmed in by narrow circumstances, would lead for a time a life so real in that far-off island, that closing the book seemed really like step‐ ping ashore from the vessel that bore Crusoe back to England. Here was a story indeed, because it was not a story but a bit of real life.

And so the English novel was born—a form of prose so different from the romantic prose romances of Arcadia, Utopia, or Atlantis, that it must be placed in a separate class. And a form also since used by some of the greatest writers in English literature. De Foe was the author of many other tales of life, but the story of the desert island is alone the one which has made his name familiar in every quarter of the globe, and upon which his fame as one of England's greatest writers rests. He died in 1731, after a life of such strange changes that it has been said that *Robinson Crusoe* was only the type of his own adventures in the great battle of life, where he was buffeted by fortune and driven hither and thither by a fate that left him at last worn out with the struggle. He was buried in Bunhill Fields, where Bunyan had been laid to rest thirty years before.

The English novel which was thus brought into literature was in one sense of the word already perfect, since no work of fiction has ever yet excelled *Robinson Crusoe*. But the story of the desert island was the story of a man who was separated from his fellow-men, and who lived his life in a place far from England and the influences of English life. For this reason the book does not portray any of those emotions of the heart which control the actions of

15

men who are in constant association with other men, and upon which the English drama was founded. But the eighteenth century was also remarkable for the perfection of the novel, as well as for its birth, and there were five writers who lived during this century whose novels dealt with every-day domestic life, and who by their genius are considered among the greatest, if not the greatest, English novelists.

These men were Samuel Richardson, Henry Fielding, Tobias George Smollett, Laurence Sterne, and Oliver Goldsmith. These men wrote novels of English life as it then existed, and they made character rather than adventure the subject of their books. This was a new thing outside of the drama, and the story of character and conduct in the novel was eagerly read by the same class which a century before had been spell-bound by the story of character and conduct in the drama.

This kind of writing made it possible for every man to imagine himself the hero of a book, for these novels dealt only with the temptations and experiences which are the lot of all, and which do not depend upon adventure or romance for their interest.

By their skill in thus analyzing and painting the human heart, this group of writers won for itself the highest place in the new form of literature, a place which has since been reached only by a very few. They also gave to the novel its permanent place in English literature, and made it accepted as a new force in the world of letters, a force which dealt with the conduct of life, the most important thing in the world, and therefore worthy of the regard of the highest minds. Thus the old story of the ancient minstrel was developed into a form of art which in human interest stands only next to the drama.

Of this group of novelists, Oliver Goldsmith was in point of date the last, and although he wrote but one of the famous novels of the eighteenth century, it was so perfect that it has always been one of the masterpieces of English literature. Goldsmith was born in the village of Pallas, county of Longford, Ireland, in 1728, and was the son of a poor English curate who was trying hard decently to bring up a large family on a small salary. But the home life was happy and healthy in spite of the poverty, and in the little villages where his father was placed at different times, Goldsmith spent a boyhood that was full of pleasant scenes and the memory of which sweetened many after hours. When he was six years old he began his school life in the little village school, and perhaps, if there was any bitter drop in his early life, it came from association with the boys who were his school companions, and who ridiculed his small figure and pock-marked face, his lack of pocket-money, and above all, his amazing stupidity. For all of Goldsmith's boyish brightness went to fun and mischief; in school he was dull and uninterested, and was called a blockhead and dunce, because the lessons which his companions found so easy were to him weary and incomprehensible. But though he was thus looked down upon by his associates, both in the village and afterward at boarding-school, this period of his life seemed to Goldsmith to hold only golden hours. Years afterward, when he was a man struggling with poverty and discouragement, in *The Deserted Village* he describes just such a little village as he must have lived in, and just such a school-master as may have been his teacher; and the picture is so full of sweetness and tender memory that it sounds like a sigh for that lost youth that had fled forever.

Goldsmith's school life ended with a mistake so natural, and yet so comic, that it was used by him as the foundation of one of his best-known comedies. Returning home from boarding-school with a guinea in his pocket, he came at night to a little village and asked the way to the "best house." The person he addressed being a wag, pointed to the mansion of the squire, and thither Goldsmith betook himself, and thinking it was an inn, ordered a room, supper, and a bottle of wine, and invited the squire, the supposed landlord, his wife, and daughter to supper.

Fortunately for Goldsmith, the squire loved a joke, and so the mistake ended pleasantly enough, and with a God-speed from the squire, and the guinea still in his pocket, he went on his way in the morning, all the better off for the adventure. It is this incident which he made the basis of his plot in *She Stoops to Conquer*— a comedy which differed so widely from the sentimental drama of the times that it may be said to have been the foundation of a new school of English plays. In this play Goldsmith turned entirely away from the fashionable plays of the period, and introduced natural characters — the men, women, masters, and servants whom one would find in English middle-class life—and because the plot was so probable, the fun so good-natured, and the characters drawn so true to life, it was recognized at once as a new and valuable contribution to the stage, and is still considered one of the finest examples of English comedy.

Goldsmith entered Trinity College, Dublin, at the age of seventeen, and remained there four years. He was not a good student, and he was in continual trouble because he would neither follow the course of study, nor obey the college rules, and in consequence he was a favorite with none save some other students who like himself, thought more of fun than anything else, and who would leave their lessons any time to play a joke. During this time he knew well what poverty meant, for he had to depend much upon himself, and had many a time to leave off joking and consider where the next meal was to come from. Sometimes he wrote street ballads which brought him in a little money; once he gained a little prize money; somehow he managed to get through college, and as his father was now dead, found himself at twenty-one with his degree in his hand and the world before him, the only friend he could really count upon being an uncle who had helped him through Trinity.

He had not yet decided what should be his calling, and he and his uncle talked much about this serious matter. At last it was thought best for him to enter the ministry, and he presented himself to a certain bishop as an applicant for holy orders. But the bishop did not think Goldsmith would make a good clergyman, and declined to receive him. Then he taught for a while, and getting a little money together, went off to seek his fortune with thirty pounds and a good horse. But he soon came back without horse, or pounds, or fortune, and was glad enough to take fifty pounds from his uncle and go to Dublin to study medicine. Here he remained a year and a half, and then decided to go to Holland in order to carry on his studies more profitably, for Holland was the home of famous physicians. His uncle again furnished money, and for three years Goldsmith lived in Holland, which he left for the purpose of making a tour of Europe on foot. He had one guinea in his pocket, having spent all the rest of his money for tulip-roots—a rare and expensive flower which his uncle had often longed for. Goldsmith despatched the roots to Ireland, and left Leyden happy.

For a year he wandered over Europe, going from place to place mostly on foot, and living probably as the student travellers lived in those days, when even begging for food was not considered a disgrace by the university students, who often spent their vacations in making foot tours of Germany, or France, or Switzerland.

Whether Goldsmith begged, or earned his way by playing on the flute, singing, or doing odd jobs of one kind or another, is not known, but he returned to London in 1756, and settled down there, being twenty-eight years old, without friends, without any profession, and it is likely, not having even a guinea in his possession. He lived in a garret sometimes, sometimes in a better place, and taught, practised medicine, and corrected for the press, and after a while he began writing himself. This, his last choice, remained his permanent one, though it brought little pay and because of his extravagance and hopeless inability to take care of money he was always in debt, and often was kept out of prison only through the kindness of Dr. Johnson and other friends, who loved him and admired his genius, though they declared that he had no common sense.

Although Goldsmith was the author of many works, his most valuable contributions to English letters are the comedy *She Stoops to Conquer* and his novel *The Vicar of Wakefield.* The former is considered one of the best come-

dies in English literature, and the latter is
placed among the most charming of English
novels. He died in 1774, leaving behind him
the memory of a life which injured no man, and
which was brave, honest, and generous to the
end, leaving also to English literature a priceless legacy of two of the finest works of the
eighteenth century.

The Vicar of Wakefield is the story of the
family of a country clergyman, and is one of
the best pictures we have of English country
life at that time. The Vicar, Dr. Primrose,
tells the story of how, after losing all his fortune, he and his family went to live in a farming
community, and of the ups and downs of their
domestic life. The story is told so charmingly,
and with such reality, that in reading it we cannot help believing that we are reading the ver-
itable journal of some worthy minister's daily
life. Nothing happens to these people except
what might happen to any other family in middle-class life, and yet so great is the art of the
book that this little story of home life and simple pleasures holds us as closely as a tale of

romantic adventure. The family consists of the father, mother, two daughters, a grown son, and two little boys. There is also another son who is seeking his fortune abroad. They live in a little thatched cottage of five rooms; a brook winds down the green slope of meadow outside, a lawn and a group of trees add comfort and beauty to the place, and though forced to work for their daily bread, the Vicar and his family have such merry and cheerful spirits that their life reads like an idyl of Arcadia. They go out in the morning and work in the hay-field, the daughters working with their brothers, and perhaps a neighbor or two sharing the labor; at nooning they lie under the trees and listen to the genial Vicar's talk, or recite and sing ballads; in the evening they have a moonlight dance on the lawn, and are in great joy if afterward the pantry is able to furnish some simple refreshment. On Sunday they walk two miles to church to listen to their father's sermon on the blessedness of charity, the beauty of love, the majesty of duty; and the words reach their hearts because they are the same words that they hear from his lips every day. The Vicar in the pulpit is also the father who gives sugar, plums to the little boys for offering to share their bed with a homeless stranger, who counts all men his brothers, and loves the poorest ones the best, and who makes every day's duty necessary and beautiful, because it fits that day and no other.

If the girls are silly at times, and want to wear finer clothes than their circumstances warrant, or to concoct washes for the face and pastes for the hair, the Vicar becomes firm and sternly forbids such frivolity, but soothes their wounded feelings by giving them money to have their fortunes told by the next strolling gypsy. And when the son goes to the market-town to exchange their old horse for a better, and returns only with a gross of green spectacles which a clever rogue has palmed upon him, the father is gently sympathetic, and does not reprove him for his lack of worldly knowledge, and to teach him how to barter goes himself the next time, taking the remaining horse. And when the same clever rogue, under a different disguise, cheats him also by giving him a worthless note in exchange for the horse, the Vicar marvels greatly at the wickedness that could overreach such worldly wisdom as his own.

The book is full of like homely incidents which are treated with such skill that as we read them we find ourselves feeling for the trials of this interesting family as deeply as though they were our own. We are in despair when the Vicar finds he has been cheated or when the crops fail. And when grave trouble comes at last to the household, the undeserved afflictions, the fine fortitude, and the patient resignation of the whole family win our love and respect. The story ends happily, leaving the Vicar and his children well to do and with fine hopes of the future, and we take our leave of them as if they were dear friends; for such indeed they have become.

This picture of English life, where one sees the hawthorn bloom and hears the songs of robins and the murmur of brooks, has only increased its value since Goldsmith first gave it to the world. And while other great novels treat of heroic emotions and deeds, and hold their places in literature not only because of the genius of their authors, but also because of their subjects, this little tale stands on an equal height, because, like an old ballad, it has that feeling which alone reaches the heart, and that simplicity which genius alone can touch to greatest art.

CHAPTER VII.

JONATHAN SWIFT—EIGHTEENTH CENTURY.

Swift was born in 1667, in Dublin, and was thus an Irishman by birth, though of English family. When he was a year old his nurse, who was an Englishwoman, was obliged to return to England, and being very fond of the child she carried him off with her without his mother's knowledge. As he was a very delicate child, the mother feared to risk the voyage back until he was stronger, and consequently he remained nearly three years at his nurse's home in Whitehaven, and was so carefully watched and cared for by the good woman that he came back a comparatively healthy child, while his education had advanced so far that he was able to read any chapter in the Bible.

As his mother was a widow with only a very small income, Swift was again separated from her after two years and sent to Kilkenny School by an uncle, who from that time took charge of the boy. Nothing is known of his school life. When fifteen he entered Trinity College, Dublin, where he remained four years, giving considerable trouble to his tutors because of his disregard for college law, and becoming himself much embittered because of his poverty, which made him dependent upon his uncle for every penny he received. After his college days he spent some time as secretary to a distant relative in England, and during this time was admitted to the church. After the death of this relative he went to Ireland as chaplain to the viceroy, and from this time his career as a public man began. He had already written a religious satire called *The Tale of a Tub*, in which he held up to ridicule the different religious sects of the day, and from this time on his pen was never idle. Nearly all his writings consist of satires directed against the vanities and faults of mankind, or against the politics of the day. And such was his genius that he was able to render great service to the party to which he belonged, even though his own friends feared his cutting words. Swift was a man of unbounded ambition, and aimed at high places in the church and state, but as in both cases he was disappointed, his nature became even more bitter as years went on. The highest point he reached in the church was the appointment of Dean of St. Patrick's, Dublin, in 1713, when he was forty-six years old; and although he performed important service for the state as a writer and politician, he was never rewarded with any post of honor.

Swift wrote an immense number of political pamphlets and letters, but while these show his ability as a writer, they owed their greatness to the day to which they belonged. His greatest work, and one which will always interest mankind, is a profound satire upon human life called the *Travels of Gulliver*, in which a ship-surgeon is supposed to visit unknown countries whose people and customs he compares with those of his own nation, teaching by comparison how small and mean mankind appears when engaged only in selfish interests and ignoble aims.

Gulliver's Travels consists of four narratives of voyages to Liliput, Brobdingnag, and two other countries ; but the last two parts are so full of unpleasant descriptions that they are less read than the others. The two other narratives are as follows :

A ship on its voyage from England to India was wrecked off an unknown coast and all the crew lost, with the exception of Lemuel Gulliver, the surgeon, who found himself tossed on shore late at night, out of sight or sound of any living creature. Being weary and exhausted by the waves, Gulliver decided to make no exploration of the country that night, and so laid himself down to sleep, unconscious whether he was in the midst of friends or foes. Hour after hour he slept on and awoke in the morning with a rested body and a heart full of courage, for he was of a brave disposition and had had many an adventure with barbarous people in unknown seas. But when he attempted to rise he found that he was not able to stir, for while he slept his arms and legs had been firmly fast-

ened to the ground, and as his hair, which was
long and thick, had been also tied down, he
could not even turn his head and could only
look upward, where the sun was blazing high
in the skies. He lay there for a little while,
stunned with his misfortune, and in great wonder as to what kind of people he had fallen
among, feeling almost certain that from their
first act they intended only evil. While conjec-
turing how he might escape out of their hands,
he felt something moving along his left leg, and
presently a little human creature, about six
inches high, came into sight, with bow and arrow
in his hands and a quiver on his back. This
creature was followed by scores of his companions, who swarmed over Gulliver's body much
as a company of ants would swarm over a fallen
log, and he perceived that these people must be
the inhabitants of the land, and that it was to
them he owed his bonds. And with this he
roared out so loudly in astonishment that the
creatures all ran back in fright and fled away.
But as he lay quiet they presently returned.
One of them ventured within sight of Gulli-

ver's eyes and expressed by signs the greatest amazement and admiration, but as their prisoner managed, by struggling with his bonds, to free his left arm and turn his head a little, they once more ran off in terror, and presently Gulliver felt a number of darts pricking his face and hands, and feared that war was declared. The arrows were sharp, and stung him so badly that he could not help groaning aloud, and when he tried again to free himself still another shower of darts fell upon him, almost blinding him; and then he decided it would be better for him to lie quiet while the day lasted and steal away from the country in the night. But as soon as he became quiet the dwarfs gave over shooting, and presently they built a platform which reached up to his ear and upon which one, who seemed to be a chief, mounted and delivered a long speech. Gulliver gathered from his signs and gestures that the dwarf offered him shelter and friendship if he would be peaceable, or war and death if he would not submit; and as he was desirous of being freed from his bonds he signified by signs that he would be peaceable, if they would liberate him and give him something to eat and drink. At this the small creatures seemed rejoiced, and presently hundreds of them appeared bearing baskets of meat and loaves of bread about the size of a bullet. This food Gulliver devoured by the basketful, to the great astonishment of the natives, and making a sign that he wished something to drink, they brought him two hogsheads of wine, each holding about half a pint, which they lifted with great effort upon the platform and rolled forward so that he could reach them with his hand. When he had performed the feat of drinking the entire contents of the two hogsheads the people danced upon his breast with joy, and shouted out their wonder in shrill cries, screaming wildly as he tossed the empty casks into the air, for they had never seen such strength before.

This country into which Gulliver had come was the country of Liliput, and the Liliputians were famous for their skill and ingenuity in carrying on war with their enemies, and in contriving machines for doing their work. They had come to the shore in the morning and had been greatly astounded to find this immense giant asleep in the king's domains, and while some of them stayed to bind and guard him, others had gone to a distant city to see the king and ask his advice. The king immediately ordered a large machine built which would transport the stranger to the capital, and while Gulliver was being refreshed with food and drink, five hundred carpenters and engineers were busy in the king's city making the huge machine he had ordered.

Seeing that Gulliver intended to keep his promise not to break the peace, the dwarfs anointed his wounds with a soothing ointment, and as they had already mixed some drug with the wine he had drunk, their big captive presently fell into a sleep which lasted until the machine for transporting him to the capital arrived. Gulliver was then drawn up to the machine by pulleys, the operation taking three hours. Fifteen hundred horses were attached to the machine, and the procession started on the way to the king's city.

They travelled the rest of the day, and rested at night, Gulliver being guarded by five hundred soldiers who stood ready to shoot him if he stirred. The next day, about noon, they arrived at the city. The king had ordered that the prisoner should be lodged in an ancient temple which stood outside the city gates, and the procession therefore stopped here, and after having his left leg secured by ninety chains, Gulliver was allowed to rise. The astonishment and even terror of the people at seeing this gigantic creature stand on his feet was so great that many of the inhabitants fled in haste. But the king and his courtiers remained, and his majesty approached Gulliver as near as he could force his horse to come, for that animal showed great fear at the sight of such an enormous creature, and the king only kept his seat by the most expert horsemanship. His majesty conversed some time with Gulliver by means of signs, and though he would not promise the prisoner his freedom, Gulliver was made to understand that he should not be harmed if he kept the peace. The king then ordered food and drink brought to him, and Gulliver devoured thirty casks of meat and wine, to the great astonishment of the court.

When the king departed, the common people swarmed around the prisoner like ants, and five or six were so daring as to shoot their arrows at him for sport. But at this the guards seized the offenders and delivered them up to Gulliver to do with as he pleased, for the king had left explicit orders that the prisoner should not be harmed.

Gulliver took the six culprits in his hands and bestowed five of them in his pocket. He then took out his penknife and pretended that he was going to devour the remaining one, and at this the little creature fell into such a fit of terror that his screams could be heard to the outermost edge of the vast crowd which had gathered around, and which numbered hundreds of thousands. But Gulliver meant only to frighten these offenders, and so he presently gave them their freedom and they quickly ran off, while the crowd admired both his strength and kindness, for it was known that even if he had taken their lives the king would have pardoned him, because they were the first offenders. Shortly after this, as Gulliver was tired, he crept into his house and went to sleep, and the crowd dispersed.

Now, at the court great was the wonder and excitement over the man-mountain, as Gulliver was called, for they did not know what to do with him. Some said kill him, and some said keep him prisoner, and no one knew what to do, for they said that even if they killed him they could not get such a great body out of the way, and if they kept him prisoner his enormous appetite would cause a famine, and so they were greatly distressed. But just as they were talking it over an officer arrived and told the court how merciful Gulliver had been to the six soldiers who had shot at him, and this decided the king to let him remain alive for the time anyway. So an imperial edict was issued ordering all the neighboring villages to send in every morning six beeves and forty sheep, together with bread and wine, for the prisoner's use, and six hundred persons were assigned to wait upon him. These servants lived in tents outside the temple and performed any service that Gulliver required. The king also ordered three hundred tailors to make Gulliver a suit of clothes like those worn in that country, and six of the greatest scholars in the kingdom were ordered to teach him the language.

The king himself paid him daily visits and conversed with him, and praised his readiness at learning. But for all this kindness Gulliver was still kept chained to the temple and guarded by soldiers, while his watch, purse, pistols, sword, pencils, snuff-box, pouch of powder, and some bullets which happened to be in his pocket were taken from him for greater safety. Since, with the exception of the pistols and sword, none of the councillors could imagine the use of any of these things, all feared that they were dangerous machines of war. The watch in particular, which was carried off by two men, who bore it between them on a pole, so excited the wonder of the king that he thought from its noise and motion it must be a god.

Numerous were the adventures that Gulliver had in the country of the Liliputians and many were the strange sights he saw. During the first part of his confinement the king ordered a platform built near the temple, upon which all the jugglers and professional tricksters performed wonderful feats.

The cavalry also was exercised before him daily so that the horses might get used to his great stature, and Gulliver even made a plain of his handkerchief by stretching it firmly from four pegs, and upon this plain, which was raised about two feet from the ground, he induced the king to allow certain regiments of cavalry to manœuvre and fight a mock battle, a thing which so amused the king that he ordered it repeated day after day.

At length, when the king became fully assured that Gulliver was of a kind and peaceable nature, he gave him his liberty on the conditions that Gulliver would not leave the country without permission; that he would not enter the city without an express order from the king, so that the people might have two hours' warning to keep within doors, and not be trampled under foot; that the man-mountain should walk only in the high-roads, and never lie down in the meadows or corn-fields; that he should carry a messenger and horse in his pocket once a month for a six-days' journey, if the king desired to send such a messenger to a distant part of the realm, and that if war were declared the man-mountain should fight on the side of the Liliputians.   To these conditions Gulliver consented gladly and was given his liberty.

The first thing that he did was to visit the city, which he had a great desire to see, and he found much entertainment in looking at the tiny palaces and squares and temples, the people keeping within doors all the while for fear of being trampled upon.   And Gulliver declares, in his account of this voyage, that he never had seen anywhere such magnificence and splendor as he saw in the royal palaces of Liliput.

But his liberty was not to be entirely devoted to pleasure, for before long the king's chamberlain came to him and told him that although the kingdom of Liliput seemed so peaceable, there were really grave dangers threatening it. The whole country, he said, was divided into two parties, one of which loved the king and wished him to remain upon the throne, while the other was composed of such bitter enemies that no one knew what measures they might take to show their hatred. The king's party was named *Slamecksan*, meaning low-heeled, and the other party was named *Tramecksan*, meaning high-heeled, from the kind of shoes that they wore, and though the king had only the *Slamecksan* in his employ, the *Tramecksan* were so numerous that the worst fears were entertained by the king as to what they might do.

The chamberlain also said that the kingdom of Liliput was threatened by another people which dwelt in the island of Blefuscu, and that war had then existed for over three years between these kingdoms for the empire of the earth, as the chamberlain, like all the other Liliputians, believed that the whole earth consisted only of the empires of Liliput and Blefuscu, and that Gulliver had dropped from the moon or some other heavenly body.

The chamberlain said that the original cause of all the trouble was very simple. It began in fact with the present king's grandfather, who when he was a boy refused to break an egg in the same manner that eggs had been broken since the beginning of the world. This prince, when a boy, had cut his fingers while trying to open an egg by breaking the larger end, and the emperor, his father, had therefore commanded that thereafter all true and loyal subjects should break the smaller end of their eggs and leave off the ancient practice of breaking the larger ends. And this was the cause of the two rival parties, for some refused to break the egg at the smaller end, saying that the king had no right to interfere with such an ancient custom of the country. The people of Blefuscu sympathized with these rebellious subjects and always welcomed them to their country when they were exiled from Liliput, therefore the present king feared that the *Tramecksan* party would join hands with the Blefuscudians and deprive him of his kingdom. This story was told by the chamberlain with many sighs, and Gulliver immediately promised to aid and serve the king to the utmost of his power, and at this the chamberlain brightened considerably, knowing that the man - mountain was a host in himself.

The kingdom of Blefuscu consisted of a large island which was separated from Liliput by a channel eight hundred yards wide, and the war for this reason was carried on chiefly by the navy. It was evident, therefore, that the greatest blow that could be inflicted upon the Blefuscudians would be to deprive them of their ships, and this Gulliver decided to do. Lying down behind a hillock he was able to get a view of the enemy's ships without being seen, for his presence in Liliput was unknown to the Blefuscudians, and then, finding that the depth of the channel was only six feet at high tide, Gulliver started for Blefuscu, taking with him some iron cables and bars for the purpose of bringing the fleet back if he succeeded in capturing it.

The Blefuscudians stared in horrified wonder when they saw this gigantic creature approaching, and as he neared the ships the terrified seamen sprang into the water and swam shoreward for their lives. Gulliver was thus spared the necessity of fighting, and in a few minutes he had fastened a cable to the prow of each ship and tied all the cables together at the loose ends. During this time thousands of the natives stood on shore and shot poisoned arrows at him, aiming particularly at his eyes, which he protected by putting on his spectacles, and thus escaped without serious harm.

The fifty men-of-war thus tied together formed almost the entire fleet of Blefuscu, and a great wail went up from the shore when Gulliver stepped out into the channel and began to pull at the cables. The ships, however, would not stir, as their anchors held tight, and Gulliver had to step back and cut each of the cables that fastened the anchors with his penknife, receiving about two hundred arrows in his face and hands while about it, and then he began dragging the ships after him. The Blefuscudians could not imagine what the motive of this act could be, for they did not, of course, know that Gulliver was in the employment of the king of the Liliputians, but when they saw their whole fleet of war being drawn toward the enemy's country they set up such a cry of despair that even Gulliver's heart was touched.

The king of Liliput stood ready on shore to receive the fleet, and great honors were paid to Gulliver, who was created a peer of the realm, and, as the Blefuscudians could do nothing without their ships, they sent ambassadors in a few days to sue for peace, and thus the war came to an end without the loss of a single soldier.

Gulliver was able now, by his new position as a nobleman, to do the Blefuscudians a great service, for the king of Liliput, elated with success, desired to invade the island of Blefuscu and with the assistance of Gulliver subdue the country and make it a part of his own kingdom. But Gulliver refused to give his aid to subdue a free people, and for this service the Blefuscudian ambassadors thanked him heartily and invited him to visit their country, where they promised every honor should be paid him. Before long he was glad to avail himself of this invitation, for the king of Liliput was so incensed at Gulliver's refusal to help enslave the Blefuscudians that he speedily began showing his ill-will, and Gulliver was warned by a friend that the king had become his enemy and was determined to put out his eyes so that he would be helpless and at the mercy of the court. This news determined Gulliver to leave Liliput immediately. He therefore sent word to the king that he was going to visit the Blefuscudians, and then hastened across the channel determined never to return. He was received with great honor at Blefuscu, where he remained for several days before his hosts knew the real reason of his visit, for the king of Liliput, not knowing that Gulliver had been told of the design to put out his eyes, supposed that the man-mountain would return in good season and be again in his power. But at last, suspecting something wrong, the king sent a messenger to Blefuscu, demanding that the man-mountain be sent back to him. And as the

king of Blefuscu refused to do this, there would
probably have been another war between the
two countries had not Gulliver discovered a
means of leaving the island and so putting himself out of the power of harm.   As he was walking one day on the sea-shore he saw something
that looked like an overturned boat, and wading
out two or three hundred yards he perceived
that the object was in truth a ship's boat which
had probably been driven shoreward by a tempest.   Gulliver quietly returned to the city and
requested the help of the seamen to bring in this
prize, and then swimming out to it, he was able,
by pushing it and with the aid of cables attached
to some men-of-war, to bring it ashore.   Three
thousand men and twenty of the tallest ships
were needed for this work, and when the boat
was brought to shore the Blefuscudians were
lost in amazement at the sight of a vessel that
could hold at least twenty creatures as big as
the man-mountain.

With the permission of the king Gulliver
hewed down some of the highest trees for oars
and masts, and five hundred workmen made

sails for the boat out of the royal store of linen. Also the king gave three hundred oxen and five hundred sheep, with wine and bread, to provision the boat, and some live sheep and cows for Gulliver to exhibit if he ever reached England again. But the king refused Gulliver permission to carry away even one of the natives, and searched his pockets carefully just before he sailed to see that none were hidden away.

So, with good wishes from his new friends, Gulliver left the curious country of the dwarfs and sailed out into the great ocean and was before long picked up by a home-bound ship, and so came safe to England, where he made much money by exhibiting the tiny sheep and cows as curiosities, and finally sold them to a great nobleman, who could afford such luxuries, for the care of them was very costly. And had it not been for his roving disposition Gulliver might now have settled down comfortably for life ; but this he could not do, because the taste for adventure was so strong that it overbalanced the love of home or friends, and money, and presently he said good - by to his family and was away on another voyage, which was destined to be as full of strange happenings as the first.

On this second voyage the ship in which Gulliver sailed was, like the first, driven far out of its way by a tempest and entered a part of the ocean unknown to any of the company. But spying land they made for it, and seeing on a near approach that it was a green and inviting country, some of the crew went on shore to lay in fresh water and whatever they might find in the way of provisions. Gulliver went along in the boat, prompted by a curiosity to see something of this strange land, and while the crew was busy looking for fresh water he wandered some distance away to make what discoveries he could. But finding nothing of interest to reward him for his walk he returned to the shore and was amazed to see the boat already some distance away and the men rowing hard for the ship, while a human creature of gigantic size was pursuing them. Fortunately for the men, the sea at that point was full of pointed rocks, so that the monster was forced to give over the chase and return to the shore, whereupon Gulliver immediately hurried back out of sight. Taking the first road he saw, he came presently to a high hill, which he climbed in order to get as good a view of the country as possible. And now the most surprising sight met his eye, for he found the whole land as far as he could see under fine cultivation, and saw everywhere marks of civilization, though he had supposed he was in one of those barbarous regions of which he had often heard.

But one thing puzzled him greatly, and that was the strange size of everything he saw. The grass grew twenty feet high, the corn was shaking its golden tassels forty feet above the ground, the hedges reached the height of one hundred and twenty feet, and the trees were so tall that their branches seemed to touch the clouds. This sight put Gulliver into such amazement that he thought for some time he must be back in Liliput dreaming of his own home, whose inhabitants seemed giants compared to the Liliputians. But it was no dream, and he was in the land of giants indeed, as he soon found. Coming down to the level ground he took his way through a corn-field, hoping to find a path that would lead him to some place of safety, but the corn-field only came to an end, where another of the same size began, and between the two, which were separated by a hedge, stood a stile which Gulliver could not mount, for every step was six feet high and the upper stone twenty. He then looked for a gap in the hedge, and while busy about this he saw a huge monster in the shape of a man advancing from the next field. This giant was as tall as a church-steeple, and took ten yards at every step, and mounting the stile he uttered a call so loud that Gulliver thought it was thunder. But he was only calling his men, seven of whom presently came bearing in their hands huge reaping hooks, and immediately began reaping the corn in the field where Gulliver lay concealed.

Gulliver made his way quickly to another part of the field, but here he was forced to remain, for the wind had bent the corn almost down to the ground, and it was impossible to force his way through it.   As he lay there he was horrified to find one of the reapers approaching nearer and nearer, cutting great swathes with every motion of the scythe, and looking so fierce and strong that Gulliver's heart sank within him, and he began to realize how his own strength and size had impressed the tiny Liliputians.   The giant, however, saw nothing but the corn, and fearing that he would be trampled to death, Gulliver raised his voice and screamed out as loud as he could; and at this the reaper paused suddenly in his work, and looking around cautiously, at last observed Gulliver crouching close beside one of his enormous feet.   He stooped and picked him up, and held him close to his face so that he might see him more clearly, and Gulliver took advantage of this to place his hands together in a supplicating position and to beg humbly for his life.

The giant was so astonished to find that this small creature could speak that for a time he could do nothing but stare, but at last he came to his senses, and putting Gulliver inside his coat, ran as swiftly as possible to his master, who was the same person that had come first to the stile.

The master called his men together, and their wonder knew no bounds. Here was a creature who wore clothes, who could talk, and who appeared harmless, and yet who was of such a size that he must belong to a race they had never heard of before. The master placed Gulliver on the ground gently, and he and his men sat round in a circle and watched him gravely, half-tempted to think they were dreaming. Gulliver pulled off his hat and made a bow, then he fell upon his knees and lifting his hands and eyes toward heaven, prayed their mercy in loud tones, and lastly he took out his purse, full of gold, and humbly presented it to the master.

The giants looked at him curiously, thinking him a new kind of animal which had been taught pretty tricks. But the purse of gold they could not understand. Gulliver poured out all the coins into the master's hand, and he gazed upon them as if they were so many grains of sand, having no idea what they were; and at this Gulliver was in despair, knowing not how to treat with people who knew not the value of money.

At last the farmer seemed to comprehend that this midget had a brain and ears to hear with, and he spoke to Gulliver in a voice that sounded like the roaring of a mill; but Gulliver could not understand his speech, for the language was strange to him. Neither could the giant understand Gulliver, though he addressed him in all the languages he knew; and being a man of adventure he knew many; so the two were forced to talk in dumb show like mutes, and for this reason they got on but slowly, and Gulliver could not explain how he came to be walking through the corn-field, and the giant could not fully express his wonder at finding him there.

But after a little while the farmer sent his men back to work again, and spreading his handkerchief upon his hand, he wrapped Gulliver up in it and carried him carefully to the farm-house, and showed him to his wife, who ran away screaming, thinking it was a new kind of mouse, and only became reconciled to his presence when her husband assured her that the strange creature was perfectly harmless.

Very soon she, too, became charmed with the intelligence of such a tiny creature, and when dinner was served she placed Gulliver on the table and gave him some bits of bread and meat from the platter which stood in the centre of the table and which measured twenty-four feet across. Gulliver made her a low bow for thanks, and taking his knife and fork out of his pocket began to eat, to the great delight of the farmer's family, who regarded him much as we should regard a trained monkey. But Gulliver did not find the situation quite so delightful when he attempted to walk across the table to where the master sat; for first the farmer's son seized him between his thumb and finger and held him high in the air, as if he meant to drop him in the pudding-dish; and then the cat came in and jumped into her mistress's lap, and looked at the new arrival as if she were considering how he would taste, and as she was three times as large as an ox Gulliver could not help trembling greatly when he saw her enormous eyes and savage mouth. But he determined to show no fear and walked five or six times right before her, whereupon she drew back and took no further notice of him. Then the dogs came in and stared curiously at him, and as they were of the size of elephants, Gulliver also stared curiously back. Finally the nurse came in, bringing the youngest child, who was a baby, and the baby immediately put out its hands and cried for Gulliver, thinking him a new kind of plaything ; and as this baby always had every-thing it wanted, Gulliver presently found him-self inside its mouth in great danger of being swallowed, and he broke into such terrific roar-ing at this that the baby hastily let go, and Gul-liver dropped out of her mouth and was rescued by the mother, who caught him in her apron, and thus saved him from breaking his neck.

Finally the dinner came to an end and the master went back to his work, leaving Gulliver in charge of the mistress, who put him to bed so that he could take a nap. And being very fatigued, he really did fall into a sleep which lasted two hours, and woke to find himself confronted by two rats the size of mastiffs; but these Gulliver slew with his sword, and this was his last adventure that day, for he was then given in charge of the farmer's daughter, a girl of nine years, who took the tenderest care of the little guest, thinking him far more interesting than any doll she had ever had; and from this time on she protected him from all harm.

Gulliver's life in this world of big things was very curious. His nurse, the farmer's daughter, who was very bright for her age, taught him the language of the country, fitted up a little bed for him out of the baby's cradle, and made such clothing as he needed, so that his stay among these people was very comfortable. Gulliver grew very fond of this child, whom he called Glumdalclitch—which in the language of that country means *little nurse*—and he took care to remember all that she taught him of the manners and courtesies of the country, so that he could amuse his master's guests when they came to see him. For his fame soon spread

abroad, and hundreds came to see the little
creature who ate, spoke, and walked like a human creature, but yet was so small that he
would not make a mouthful for a baby. And
now, the farmer, seeing that Gulliver excited so
much attention, conceived the idea of making
money by showing him off in other villages, and
Glumdalclitch was told to prepare her charge
for exhibition at the next town. The good
child wept sorely at this and begged her father
to let her have Gulliver for her very own, but
this he refused, and she was obliged to accom-
pany her father to town on the next market
day, carrying Gulliver along in a box which had
a little door on one side and gimlet holes for
letting in the air. The party took a room at
one of the inns, and there Gulliver was exhibited to crowds of people who wondered to see
so small a creature eat, drink, speak, drill with
a pike, and flourish a sword, besides doing num·
berless other things. And now his life became
very wearisome notwithstanding the kindness
of his nurse, for his master, spurred on by the
love of money, kept exhibiting him daily, trav-

elling from place to place, till Gulliver was almost worn out, besides being in frequent danger from the curiosity of the crowd, which often
came near trampling on him out of their desire
to get near him, and more often indulged in
jokes at his expense—a school-boy one time
even jeopardizing his life by throwing a hazel-
nut, the size of a pumpkin, at his head.

While they were travelling around in this
way, the news of such a wonder reached the
court, and the queen sent word to the farmer
to bring Gulliver to the palace.   This the farmer was delighted to do, for the constant journeying and performing had worn considerably
upon Gulliver's health, and his master was anxious to make all the money he could, lest his
charge should suddenly die.   When they came
to the court the queen was so delighted with
Gulliver's appearance and accomplishments, that
she offered the farmer a large sum for him.
The farmer thinking that Gulliver would die
shortly, consented to the terms, and it was
agreed that Glumdalclitch should also remain
at court and continue her care of him.   And

so it came about that Gulliver found himself an inmate of the royal palace, and Glumdal-clitch found herself a member of the queen's family, with a governess to carry on her education and a suite of servants at her command.

Gulliver's life at court was easy. The queen grew very fond of him, and delighted to show him off to her royal guests. The king, at first, thought the farmer had deceived his wife by selling her a toy that went by machinery, and he called a council of wise men to decide whether the creature were human or not. The learned men decided that this mite did breathe and think like human kind, and then the king soon came to be interested in his new subject, who could talk about the affairs of life, and seemed for the most part a wise and well-meaning creature. They had many curious talks about England and English customs, and Gulliver related to the king the entire history of England, and told him by what means his native country had grown so rich and powerful. But the king refused to see anything wonderful about the English nation, and said that its history consisted of nothing but a series of wars and bloodshed of every kind, which were due no doubt to the fact that the race was so small and resembled insects rather than human beings.   Then he sighed and said that it was degrading to humanity to think that such insignificant creatures could so imitate the ways of great nations and have their kings and queens, and courts and laws; and the wise men sighed too, and Gulliver could say nothing, though he was much incensed.

But in the main Gulliver's life at the court was free enough from annoyance, though there were many little things that bothered him; for instance, the flies of that country gave him much trouble, and he frequently had to slay them with his sword; and the queen's dwarf, a creature thirty feet high, made all sorts of fun of him, one time even going so far as to drop him in the cream pitcher, where he would have been drowned had not his nurse rescued him. Another time also, when he was left alone in the garden, the gardener's favorite spaniel spying him, picked him up between his teeth and car-

18

ried him carefully to his master's feet. Still another time a monkey seized him and bore him to the roof of the palace, and the servants had to get ladders and rescue him. Such accidents as these could not fail to make Gulliver realize his absurd position in that country, and he longed daily for an opportunity to escape.

But he was such a favorite at court that he was never allowed out of sight, and many weary hours he spent sighing for his native land. In order to while away his time Gulliver took to study, and spent long days in learning to read. A little later he found he could read nicely by mounting up to the open book by means of a step-ladder, and then walking along from one end of the line to the other till he had finished the two pages. By using two hands he could turn the leaves nicely, and when this was accomplished he passed much time in studying the laws and customs of the country, finding therein much wisdom and good sense; so that when he returned to his native country he was able to carry with him quite a number of suggestions for improving and simplifying English laws.

His departure from this strange land was the most curious thing connected with his adventure. It was the custom for the court to travel from place to place, and there had been a strong box prepared for Gulliver to be carried in so that the jolting might not break his bones, or crack his skull. This box was sixteen feet square and twelve feet high, and had a door and two closets. It had a quilted lining, and the door had a lock so that rats and mice might be kept out. It had windows, and was furnished with chairs and tables and a hammock, and on the outside were two handles through which a rope was passed, so that it could be fastened around Glumdalclitch's waist.

One day the queen ordered Glumdalclitch to prepare for a journey, as they were going to a distant place and she could not bear to leave Gulliver behind, for his tricks and accomplishments amused her greatly. He could drive away a fit of the blues by his manner of playing on the piano, which consisted in running up

and down upon a bench placed before the key-
board and striking the keys with two long
sticks. And the misfortunes that he endured
because of his size also amused the queen. So
wherever she went Gulliver must go also.
Glumdalclitch therefore made all things ready,
and in due time a distant palace near the sea-
shore was reached where the court was to
spend a few days.

Gulliver was tired and longed to get a
glimpse of the ocean, which might perhaps give
him a means of escape, so he begged Glumdalclitch to allow a page to carry him down to
the shore so that he might get a breath of the
sea air. To this Glumdalclitch consented, and
when the page had carried him to the shore
Gulliver sat looking seaward a long time, thinking many sad thoughts; for the sea made his
home seem nearer than ever, and yet he knew
not how to reach it. At last, being very weary,
he lay down in the hammock and told the boy
he was going to take a nap. After closing the
window to keep out the cold the page wandered up and down looking for birds' eggs and

shells, and turning a curve, quite lost sight of the box, while Gulliver inside soon fell asleep and dreamed of England. And then a queer thing happened : Gulliver was suddenly rudely awakened by feeling a violent pull at the ring on top of his box, and presently he felt the box being raised first high in the air and then carried forward at an immense speed. Outside his window he saw nothing but clouds and sky, and though he called and called, there was no answer save that overhead he fancied he heard the flapping of wings. This went on for some time, when he heard another noise which sounded like two birds fighting ; then his box swayed two and fro and suddenly began falling with such speed that he almost lost his breath. A great shock came as it struck and plunged through the water, but presently it rose to the surface, and as it was perfectly water-tight, it began floating quietly along. Gulliver now knew that the box had been carried by an eagle which had been attacked by another eagle, and so forced to drop its prey, and he immediately planned a way of escape out of his

difficulties by opening the slide in the top of
his box and letting in air enough to keep him
alive, knowing that if the box kept afloat he
might be picked up by some ship, unless he
starved to death in the meantime. But before
long he heard a grating noise and then felt he
was being towed along, and mounting a chair,
he thrust his handkerchief out of the slide in the
hope of attracting attention. But no notice
was taken of his signal, and he had to remain
quiet till the box was brought to a sudden
standstill. Then a voice called down through
the hole to see if anyone were inside, and Gulliver knew he was saved. He shouted up for
them to lift the lid of the box, and at this he
heard a great shout of laughter and remembered that he was in his own world again,
where men could not lift boxes sixteen feet
square.

But at last his rescuers sawed a hole through
the top of the box and let him out, and Gulliver
was rejoiced to find that he was again in the
company of English sailors, even though they
thought him crazy for a long time because of

his queer talk of the big country he had left, and because he always shouted at the top of his voice, from his habit of talking to people who were sixty feet above him.   And so Gulliver came safe home again and made no more voyages for that time.

In these satires Swift desired to teach the English nation those lessons which every nation must learn before it can follow out the lines of right conduct in its affairs.   Swift must therefore be considered a teacher, though he taught by showing the weakness and pointing out the errors of government, rather than by laying down new principles.

CHAPTER VIII.

HISTORY IN THE EIGHTEENTH CENTURY.

The first bit of history ever written in England was probably some old war-song, which may have been sung a century before it was inscribed on a wooden tablet or a piece of parchment by the ancient bard who thus made himself the oldest English historian. When or by whom this song was given a written form we do not know, but as the history of every people is at first a mere statement of great events, we know that English history must have begun in the same way. Perhaps the old singer was afraid that his song would be lost, for it may be that no younger disciple stood ready to carry it into the future by a similar gift of music; perhaps some great chieftain ordered his favorite battle-lay to be thus preserved, that he might put it beside his chief treasures as an heirloom for his descendants. We do not know. We only know that gradually and slowly the history of England began to be written, in fragments here and there, in the different parts of the country where there were the most battles, perhaps, or where there were the sweetest singers. And from these scattered bits someone, after a time, wrote the first page of real history. If we could see this curious leaf, which centuries ago crumbled away to dust, it might read something like this: On such a day was fought a great battle. On such a day there was a most bloody massacre. On such a day was a great king crowned with a crown that he had won from war-loving enemies. This is all that history meant at first —a simple statement of the principal event of the year, whether it were a victory, a defeat, a famine, or a peace. And such statements were not even called history, and they were never read, for no one read anything, everyone was too busy fighting. But these records served a good purpose, for later on they were incorporated into other records of events that were then happening, so that the past and present were connected by the dates of great events, and this was a great step forward.

These latter records were called chronicles, and as time went on it became quite the fashion to write chronicles. Every old monk or scholar who was not sure he could write anything else, was always certain that he could write a chronicle; and for the sake of variety, and because he did not want his work to read like an old story, the writer would sometimes add much or little to the original statement by putting in some old legend or fable which had never before been written down, but which was generally accepted as truth. And he would also embellish his story of the present by a little description of the place or the personages, and would tell, perhaps, what causes led to such and such events; also, if he were very devout, he might add a pleasant moral, and with homely wisdom point out wherein things might have been done for the better or worse. Thus the chronicle, which was simply a statement of event and date, grew up toward genuine history, the narrative of a nation's life teaching by the story of success and failure, the philosophy or wisdom which should govern the nation's conduct.

Many of these old chronicles, like the first records, lived only long enough to be incorporated into more important accounts, and were then lost, which does not so much matter since their work was done. For, like every other form of literature, history was not the work of any epoch or time, but grew as the nation grew, from small beginnings upward. And at last there came a time when the old chronicles were so carefully preserved in monasteries and schools and the libraries of kings, that they ceased to be totally lost or destroyed by carelessness, and were classed among the most precious possessions of the nation, and from this time on they were guarded so carefully that many of them are still to be found.

Among the old chroniclers who thus laid the foundations of English history we find the name of Gildas, son of one of the British kings who lived in the sixth century, and that of Nennius, another writer of the same period. But the works of these men are so full of legends, myths, and traditions, that it is hard to sift the true from the false. Their names are important only because they stand out from the mist that surrounds these old historians, whose names as a rule are lost. Gildas and Nennius thus represent a class. We can imagine them moving among their people with their heads full of all the wisdom of the time, and their hearts full of piety and religious fervor. And into their books they put a strange mixture that only the ignorance of the time could call history. There were bits of the old Druid lore which could never be held anything but sacred by the Britons, no matter how christianized they became. And there were fragments of fierce battles between Briton and Saxon, which sound like echoes of the old heathen war-chants. And interspersed with these would be a statement of some genuine historic fact, of such importance and of such inestimable value that it shines out from the confusion around it like a ray of pure light. Close beside this would be perhaps an account of some miracle performed by one of the early saints. And this was what history meant in those days.

But later on we come to a true historian in
Bede, who wrote the history of the Anglo
Saxons from their first settlement in England,
and in his work sifted the old chronicles and
tales to such good purpose that he is considered the one authority for the history of that
early period. Bede had the aid of the most
learned men of his country in collecting these
old stories of England, during the time when
the country was divided up into a number of
small kingdoms, each with its own king and
separate history, from the time that the Saxons
had first landed in England and divided the
country up among their great chieftains. And
the work is doubly important because it was
during the latter part of Bede's lifetime, in 828,
that all these little kingdoms were united into
one by Egbert, and the history of England as
one of the great nations of modern times begun.

Bede wrote his history in Latin and called it
"The Ecclesiastical History of the Church,"
because part of his intention was to write the
history of Christianity in England. But it is the
account of the beginning and growth of the

English nation that makes it chiefly valuable, and although the old book is full of traditions that could never have been verified, and has story after story of miracles that could never have happened, yet, after all the defects are considered, there remains enough good to place Bede as the first historian in point of time.

In the next century Alfred the Great translated Bede's history into English, or Anglo-Saxon, which was the language of the people, and about this same time there was begun a curious old record called the *Saxon Chronicle.* This Chronicle related in a brief way the history of the people from the beginning down to Alfred's time, and after his death was continued by successive writers for nearly two hundred and fifty years, during which period the Norman Conquest occurred and the history of England was changed forever by the introduction of a foreign king and nobility, with their love for romance, songs, and tales of all kinds. The Normans brought into England also a fondness for historical narratives, and many books of chronicles were compiled by the scholars of the

day. Among these chronicles the most impor-
tant are those of William of Malmesbury and
Geoffrey of Monmouth, Geoffrey's history be-
ing also famous because it contains the story of
King Arthur and his Knights of the Round
Table, which was then for the first time read in
England.

These old chronicles of the Norman period
are, like the earlier ones, full of myths and
legends, and so little did the historians of that
day realize the importance of the work they
were about that they often wrote their narratives in verse.

This fashion of writing history in verse continued in England long after the Saxon and
Norman races had joined in one, and modern
English was spoken. Up to the sixteenth century the most important events of English history were recorded in poems which were written often by the most learned men of the day.
The old histories in verse and the chronicles
which related the lives of different kings, or the
events of certain reigns, are all that we possess
in the way of historical literature from the time

of Chaucer to Elizabeth. They are quaint and
interesting, and full of the gossip of the time.
When they were not written by the learned, but
by some citizen of leisure or some officer of the
court, who wrote for amusement rather than
anything else, they often contain curious descriptions of the life of the time, which make
them very valuable ; for it is from these old
chronicles that Shakespeare and other dramatists drew their materials for the pictures of
those times which they used in their dramas.
The principal of the old chroniclers are Fabyan,
an alderman and sheriff of London ; Hall, a
judge of one of the city courts ; Daniel, poet-
laureate to Elizabeth ; Drayton, another poet ;
John Stow, a citizen of London, and Hollinshed, the most famous of all the old chroniclers.
All of these belong to the sixteenth century.
It is in these old chronicles that we read descriptions of the pageants, masques, and other
entertainments of those days, and see pictures
of the courtiers dressed in satin and velvet,
wearing velvet shoes embroidered with gold
and silver, and see ladies in robes of gold em-

broidered silk.   In this way, too, we learn that
Queen Elizabeth had three thousand dresses in
her wardrobe, and that once when Henry VIII.
gave a banquet, two hundred different dishes
were served, and his majesty appeared before
his guests dressed in cloth of gold, and surrounded by a company of maskers, all wearing
the costliest costumes.   We also see the other
side of life, and read in these old pages how
bishops and chancellors and monks and common people alike, suffered death at the stake
because of their religion.   So the old stories
are full of the life of those times and invaluable
records of the past.

This century also produced one writer whose
work belongs to the domain of history proper.
This was Sir Walter Raleigh, who began a
history of the world while he was a prisoner in
the Tower of London on a charge of treason.
Only a small part of the work was completed,
but because of its carefulness, its dignity, and,
above all, its purity of style, it is considered one
of the finest examples of English prose, and
makes Raleigh the leader of that group of

writers whose works have made history one of the classic forms of English literature. For a hundred years after the death of Raleigh two men only claim honor as writers of history; but the work of both these men is so important that without it there would be a gap in English history which no later work could fill. Both of these men were active politicians and men of the times, and this gives their work an added value, as they wrote of the events that happened in their own day, and thus transcribed the page of history that was being made right before their eyes.

The first of these was Edward Hyde, Chancellor of England and Earl of Clarendon, who lived during the stirring times of the Revolution which drove the Stuart family from the throne and raised the Puritan party into power, and of the Restoration which brought the exiled Stuarts back again to their inheritance. Clarendon is the historian of one of the great critical periods of English history, and of the fortunes of those two sovereigns of the Stuart race whose romantic story reads like a tale of mediæval life.

He was born in the same year as Milton, and like the great poet, his earliest impressions of life were connected with those grave questions of individual duty and national liberty, civil and religious, which England then was trying so hard to solve. Early in his career Clarendon became an ardent Royalist, supporting the King's party against the Puritan power. And when the Puritans triumphed and the King was executed, Clarendon accompanied the exiled family abroad, and through all their troubles was their faithful friend and counsellor, sharing their privation and poverty, and finding his highest reward in the trust that was reposed in him.

When Cromwell died and the Puritan power fell, Clarendon came back to England with the Stuarts, and for fourteen years was a witness of the events which followed the Restoration, one of which was his own fall from power through the ingratitude of the King. Thus the life of Clarendon is the life of England for nearly seventy of the most momentous years of her national existence. It is this life which Clarendon saw as in a picture, and transcribed in his book called the *History of the Great Rebellion.* In these pages the principal actors of that time stand out from the background of causes and events like great portraits by some master-hand. And although he was a Royalist always, his judgment was never bitter, and we are therefore able to form from his works a very clear idea of the period.   This personal account of the days of the Civil War when Royalist and Puritan turned England into a big battle-ground, where cities were besieged, villages turned into camps, and roar of cannon and beat of drum were heard everywhere, is of priceless value as history, though the work has not the form of a regular history, but reads rather like the memoirs of a private life.

Next to Clarendon in point of time comes Gilbert Burnet, a politician and clergyman, and the author of many works on theology. He wrote a valuable history of the Reformation, but his more popular work is one which was yet unpublished at the time of his death, and which he directed should remain unprinted for six years. This work he called a *History of My*

Own Times, and in its way it is just as important as Clarendon's, for like Clarendon, Burnet
lived during a very important period of English
history. During this period occurred the Second
Revolution, which drove James II., brother of
Charles II., from the country and brought to the
throne his daughter Mary, who was married to
a Protestant prince of Holland, and who was
herself a Protestant; for this time the trouble
was not between the Royalists and the Puritans, but between the Catholic and Protestant
churches, and England was determined on having a Protestant sovereign. For this cause
James II. was deposed, and his son, who was
also a Catholic, was by an act of Parliament
shut off from the succession. This caused
troublous times in England, and everywhere
there were plots and counterplots, and spies and
secret messengers, and no one knew whether the
stranger who came to his house was really a
friend or a secret foe sent to spy upon him.

Burnet was the religious adviser of Mary before she was called to the throne, and he gives
an account of the arrival of her husband's army

in English territory and of the events which followed, together with the causes which led to the Revolution, and a general survey of the times. Like Clarendon's, the work of Burnet took the form of accounts of the different events and transactions of the times, and contains a minute description of scenes which could only have been familiar to a looker-on. Thus both Clarendon and Burnet are valuable historians because of the information they impart, though their works do not belong to the highest order of historical writing.

But the eighteenth century, which gave birth to the novel and the essay, saw history also raised to a fine art, and this was brought about by three of the greatest English historians that have yet appeared. The first of these was David Hume, born in Edinburgh in 1711, and educated in the university of that city. His early writings, which consisted of essays on philosophy and politics, brought him very little fame at the time, though highly appreciated by scholars, and since then universally recognized as of the very highest value; and he was over forty years of age before he began the great work which brought him such immense popularity in his day, and which is still considered one of the finest examples of English prose. This work was the history of England from the accession of the Stuarts to the flight of James II. in 1688. It was the same period which Clarendon and Burnet had made familiar to English readers, and the first volume appeared in 1754. The style of this work was so different from any that had preceded it, that Hume may easily be called the first English writer who made history an art, and revealed the fact that in its form historical literature could be made as perfect as poetry or the novel, and historic events could be treated in such a manner that they would become as interesting to the reader as a romance or tale of adventure.

It is this new sight into the uses of history that gives Hume his highest claim to be ranked with the great historians. Hitherto history had chiefly been a chronicle of events, or a personal account of the period considered. But Hume took the great events of the nation's

life and grouped them skilfully together, and
gave them a place in literature that they had
never had before. He wrote an account of a
battle as one would write a poem, using the
most eloquent language and the most powerful
imagery, till one fairly saw the conflict before
his eyes. He summed up the causes which led
to an event, or the results which followed from
it, in sentences so polished and yet so strong,
that the philosophy of history became as interesting as the study of a character in a romance.
And he drew such a vivid picture of the forces
which controlled events, and of the principal
men of the times, that the period which he
treated appeared like an act in a great drama,
of which the whole national life of England was
the subject.

Hume was the first historian thus to invest
history with that great element called style, or
the manner of doing a thing considered apart
from the thing itself. Not the mere narration
of a historic event, but the manner of narration, must be from this time forth also considered, and this was a priceless gift to English

prose, and raised history to the high level of pure literature.   Henceforth history could not be the recreation of one whose life was given to politics, war, or other business, and who wrote merely as an amusement or after-thought.   But the historian would have to feel that he was not only telling facts, but that he had entered the domain of literature and must prove faithful to the work he had undertaken. At first Hume had the mortification of seeing his volumes unappreciated and neglected, but the newness and beauty of such work soon won a place for it, and one of the greatest trib-utes to his genius lies in the fact that his his-tory became so popular that it was read not only by scholars, but by the people at large. History became fashionable in a good sense, and this was not the least victory to win for a branch of literature that for the most part had hitherto been considered as uninteresting as le-gal documents or papers of state.

Hume afterward added to his work by writ-ing the history of England from the time of the landing of Julius Cæsar down to the accession of the Stuarts. His work, so remarkable for its beauty of style, has one fault so great that it can never be placed among the most perfect examples of historic writing. This is the many inaccuracies which occur in it, and which make it impossible to be relied upon as a perfect statement of truth—a fault which comes from the fact that Hume relied too much upon tradition, and did not search carefully enough for the exact facts. Yet even this error cannot take away from him the honor of being the first writer to win for history the high place that it now holds.

Hume's work for history was carried on by William Robertson, a Scotch Presbyterian minister, who produced three important books, *A History of Scotland, A History of the Reign of Charles V.*, and *A History of the Discovery of America*. Robertson has Hume's faults and beauties in a remarkable degree, and one of his works, *The Discovery of America*, had the added charm of a subject which was forever fascinating to European hearts. America, in the time of Columbus, was deemed a fairy land, a kingdom of romance, a realm of beautiful mystery.   The great Spanish adventurers, Columbus, Pizarro, Cortez, De Leon, were knights of heroic deeds whose stories were unparalleled in history or fiction.   No event in the history of the world was ever so startling and unexpected as the discovery of America, and every circumstance connected with its exploration and settlement was regarded as nothing short of a wonder.

Robertson, with the poetic gift, put himself back into the period when Europe was yet dazed with the splendor of the discovery, and he drew a brilliant, magical picture of those far-off days when Spanish ships sailed away to the sound of music and the solemn chanting of priests, to win honor and fortune for Spain in the new world.

His descriptions of this region of enchantment, of the gorgeous ceremonial with which the Spaniards took possession, of the healthfulness of the climate, luxuriance of the forests, beauty of the thousand kinds of flowers, untold wealth of the mines, and the teachable and humane character of the inhabitants, sounded like a page from Sir John Mandeville or of Marco Polo, but had the added fascination of truth.

Just as in the case of Hume, the success of Robertson's work was largely due to the quality called style, for in many cases he neglected those authorities which would have enabled him to place his statements beyond the reach of question. But there is no doubt that in spite of their defects, these two men did a greater work for history than more careful but less interesting work would have done, for they lifted it from the level of the commonplace to regions of the ideal, and made a subject that had hitherto been considered dry and only of use for the student, fascinating to the general reader and valuable to every lover of literature.

But the perfect historian, one who would combine style with judgment, and a carefulness above suspicion, was also the product of the eighteenth century, and came in the person of Edward Gibbon, who finished a great historical work ten years after the publications of Robertson's last volume. Gibbon was an Englishman, born near London and educated at no one place, as he was so delicate as a child that he was constantly being taken from school to be nursed back to the health that was always forsaking him. But notwithstanding this serious drawback he managed to pick up a good deal of information, and says himself that when he went up to Oxford, at the age of fifteen, he possessed a stock of erudition which might have puzzled a doctor, though he also had a degree of ignorance of which a schoolboy might have been ashamed. About his boyhood there was only one circumstance that indicates the future historian, and that was a fondness for hunting up odd facts of history and a positive genius for taking pains. Nothing was too much trouble if it would only prove a point. Oxford did little for this boy, whose lack of training had not fitted him for the studies he was expected to pursue there, but college life accomplished one thing for him which in the end proved to be the greatest blessing he could have had.

Groping around in the college library, he came upon a book which led him to turn from the

Protestant faith and become a Roman Catholic. And at this his father was so horrified that he promptly took him from Oxford and sent him to Switzerland, to be taught by a tutor whose Protestantism was so strong that it was hoped he would turn the lad back again to the faith of his father.

It was here, at Lausanne, that Gibbon first began that course of systematic study which trained him for the careful duties of a historian, and it was his long residence away from England which so broadened his mind that he was able to take a clear and unprejudiced view of mankind as a whole. To be a perfect historian one must have sympathy without prejudice, and be able to look at a question from many points of view. These things Gibbon acquired while away from England, and thus his debt to foreign travel was great.

He was abroad nearly five years, and came home suddenly because of the war that was then raging in Europe ; and it is a strange freak of fortune to find the young student next employed in drilling a company of militia, of which he was an officer. Gibbon, with the energy that was his great characteristic, put his whole soul and mind into this work. He was determined that his company should be thoroughly drilled, and marching, exercising, and reviewing were conducted with as much spirit as if an enemy were already within the country. He lived in camp and barracks for two years and a half, learning all the minor details of a soldier's life, and studying military tactics from the point of view of a professional.

Yet, he still in quiet moments kept his old love for books, and had even then dreams of writing some historical work. When the militia disbanded, his father, who had desired Gibbon to enter Parliament, but had given up this wish because of Gibbon's dislike to the idea, furnished him with the same amount of money as would have bought his seat in the House of Commons, and with this sum Gibbon started on a tour abroad.

At this time Gibbon was conscious of one thing only in regard to his life's work, and that was that he would write a history. What his subject would be he did not know, for like Milton, many subjects had presented themselves, one after the other, to be rejected for some reason or other. Among these were an account of the Second Crusade, a history of Sir Philip Sidney, one of Sir Walter Raleigh, and one of Edward the Black Prince. But none of them held his mind for very long, and Gibbon started on his foreign travels with a subject for a historical work still undiscovered.

Gibbon visited France and Switzerland, staying a year at Lausanne, and studying hard all the while, and at last he came to Italy. the land of poetry, and to Rome, the city of great deeds. During his stay at Lausanne Gibbon had been busy studying the life of Italy when Rome was mistress of the world. All the old authors were searched through and description after description of the ancient glories of Rome was eagerly studied; and to further familiarize himself with the country he compiled a work on the provinces and towns of ancient Italy and copied some of the old descriptions out in full.

It was then with this book in his hand that

Gibbon traversed the country that was so full of mighty memories, and to him the Italy of the time seemed but an illusion of the day, while the true Italy lived in the ruined temples, the ancient battle-grounds, the famous rivers and mountains, and the cities celebrated for many a bloody siege. It is no wonder, then, that as he neared Rome this impression deepened, and the ghosts of the past seemed to him the only living things, and that the Eternal City itself appeared in all its old splendor, shining from out the mist of the dead centuries with an immortal glory that no time could dim.

In this mood of dreams and fancies Gibbon traversed the streets of Rome, whose ancient temples had long since crumbled to dust, or had been transformed into places of Christian worship. And while in this double world of reality and unreality, the idea of his great work flashed upon him like an inspiration, and with a power that could not be withstood. He has left us a record of this inspiration in a sentence which has become classic. "It was at Rome, on October 15, 1764, as I sat musing amid the ruins of the Capitol, while the bare-footed friars were singing vespers in the temple of Jupiter, that the idea of writing the decline and fall of the city first started to my mind."

Thus his work came to him as in a vision, a subject whose wide scope and magnificent opportunities place it among those chosen by the great poets who have written the immortal epics of the world.

Never had historian chosen such a mighty theme as this, for in the whole history of the world no city had ever such a career as that of Rome, whose empire was so vast, whose power was so great, whose triumphant conquests changed the destiny of every nation she touched, and whose laws and principles of government still form the foundations of every state in Europe. Gibbon was twenty-seven years old when he made the Italian journey, and though he spent years in other employment, the idea of his great work never left him. He began it finally in 1770 in London, and worked on it faithfully for seventeen years, the work including six volumes, and being published under the title, *The Decline and Fall of the Roman Empire.*   In this work nothing is too great or too small to escape his fine sense of what is necessary.   Whether it is the description of a great council, a decisive battle, or the palace of a pleasure-loving monarch, all is done with that judgment which marks the instinct of the true historian, while the work as a whole is elevated and adorned with a style whose magnificence has never been surpassed by any other writer.

The period that Gibbon treated covered thirteen centuries, beginning with the time when the power of Rome was greatest, and ending with the capture of Constantinople by the Turks; for during part of its career the Roman Empire was divided into two great sections, the Eastern Empire, of which Constantinople was the chief city, and the Western, of which Rome was the capital.   And although Rome itself fell in 476 A.D., the Eastern Empire continued for a thousand years longer.   During the time of the Roman Empire occurred some of the most important events in history, such as the rise of

Christianity, the fall of the old heathen religions, the establishment of Mohammedanism, the birth of the modern nations of Europe, and the institution of chivalry and feudalism, the orders which divided nations into great military powers, and by which all lands were held on condition of military service to the king and nobles. These events were the causes which led to the making of the nations of Europe as they now exist, and Gibbon has shown the relation between these causes and effects as only a great philosopher could show it. His great genius for history has been shown by the manner in which he gathered his materials for the work, for he had to depend greatly upon annals and chronicles written in such exaggerated and prejudiced style, that it was very hard to sift poetry from history and truth from fiction. Above all he had to present as living men the dwellers of a past so remote, that they seemed almost like shadows, and to bring his readers into sympathy with the ambitions, desires, hopes, and fears of a people whose national life was entirely different from their own. And this he was also able to do because he had a poet's imagination.   So the *Decline and Fall of the Roman Empire* stands as one of the greatest books ever written.

CHAPTER IX.

Samuel Johnson was born at Lichfield, in Staffordshire, in 1709. His father was a bookseller on a small scale, and Johnson early learned that in his family poverty was something more than a name. He also learned early the lesson which delicate health teaches, as from his birth he was sickly, and suffered so terribly from disease that no one dreamed that he could look forward to a very long life. His father's character was plain, straightforward, and practical; his mother was something of a dreamer, and believed that the disease from which her child suffered could be cured by a touch of the Queen's hand. She therefore carried the three-year-old boy up to London, to be touched by Queen Anne. In spite of her faith, however, the disease remained and Johnson suffered from it all his life. He suffered also from the superstition that he inherited from his mother ; for notwithstanding the wisdom and knowledge that he acquired in later years, he was ruled to such a degree by whimsical superstition that it very often governed his actions.

While a boy he attended the Lichfield grammar school, and in 1728 entered Pembroke College. Here he led a life in which pride and ambition struggled with poverty and misfortune, and because of his fine character gained a noble victory. Johnson was so poor that he could not dress respectably, and his rags excited the ridicule of the mean and the pity of the generous. The ridicule he could bear well enough, knowing well that he was the superior of those who made sport of him. But the pity he could not endure, for his pride was as great as his poverty. He wore his old clothes as proudly as though he desired none other ; and once, when a kind-hearted friend placed a pair of new shoes outside his door, Johnson kicked them away in a fury. Besides his poverty, he was also rough in manner and uncouth in appearance, while the disease from which he suffered caused his face to twitch and his eyes to wink, and gave him a shambling, awkward gait, so that altogether this village lad who had come to Pembroke to learn the classics, cut rather a sorry figure.

But for all that, Pembroke guessed somewhat what manner of boy he was. His independence made his rags seem honorable; his wit won admiration; the amount of knowledge he had picked up was so rare in a lad of his age that it brought him respect, and when it became known that this boy could write compositions in Latin with the ease that other boys played cricket, Johnson ceased to be pitied and was regarded with that share of respect that a college gives a pupil who may in after-days bring it honor and glory. Because of his father's death, Johnson was obliged to leave college without taking his degree, and shortly after he began his career by taking the position of usher in a school, and from this time on for thirty years his life was one of hard work and almost bitter poverty. For, although he attempted to earn his living in a variety of ways, he was successful only in remaining poor. He had a school of his own, wrote for the magazines, and produced some of the finest work of the eighteenth century, but he was over fifty years of age before he knew what it was to be sure of his daily bread. School-teaching failed because he frightened the boys by his fits of sudden temper and by the contortions of his face. Hard work for the periodicals brought him hardly enough to buy bread, and for the great works of his manhood he received very little except fame.

But through all his life Johnson was generous and great-hearted, though the battle of life went strong against him. He was one of Goldsmith's dearest friends, and the one who never failed when Goldsmith was threatened with starvation because of his poverty, or prison because of his debts; and though Johnson was gruff and unceremonious, and was called a bear even by those who loved him, his heart was ever open to those who were poorer than himself, and his brain was ever at the service of those who needed advice or assistance. When he was fifty-three he was granted a pension by the king, and from this time on his life was comparatively easy and happy. He had an admiring crowd of friends who never tired of listening to his conversation, and who were always honored by his attention. He supported a number of old women and men whom he bullied and who humored him to his heart's content, and who regarded him with grateful veneration. Best of all, he had in himself that capacity for friendship that made him give to his friends as tender and faithful a love as that which they gave him.

At the club to which he belonged, and where the greatest men of the day met to chat and converse, Johnson was always the lion of the hour. Everyone listened when he talked, everyone admired his wit and learning, and no one wished to dispute him, even if it had not been dangerous to do so. And so the end of his life was peaceable and pleasant, brightened by the knowledge that his well-earned fame was dear to many hearts, and secure in the belief that he had won from life true honor, and from friendship true regard.   He died in 1795.   His most important works are a series of essays like those of Addison, printed under the titles of the *Rambler* and the *Idler*, a *Dictionary* of the English language, two philosophical poems, a moral tale called *Rasselas*, which he wrote to defray the expenses of his mother's funeral, the *Lives of the English Poets*, and an edition of Shakespeare's works.   He wrote besides many tracts on political and moral questions.

Although Johnson's works do not stand by the side of the greatest in English literature, few other writers ever enjoyed the measure of fame that he received while he lived.   Much of this was due to his immense learning, which made it possible for him to talk or write upon any subject, and much of it was due also to the fact that, although he was not one of the greatest of writers, he was the greatest writer of his time who combined in himself so many different talents.   Add to this his wit, his genius for conversation, his original way of looking at

all subjects, and his splendid strength and simplicity of character, and it is easy to see that
much of his fame was due to the fact that he
was a great man as well as a great writer. And
the fact also that his strength became tenderness when he had to deal with the weaknesses
of his friends, and that his fine mind was always
ruled by his generous heart when brought into
the presence of suffering, explains the unique
leadership he held in that brilliant world of
thought which was so proud to call him king.

The story of Rasselas is as follows:

In the great kingdom of Abyssinia there was
no place so beautiful and peaceful as the Happy
Valley, where dwelt all the royal princes and
princesses till the time came for them to succeed to the throne. This valley was surrounded by lofty mountains so steep that even the
wild animals could not reach their summit, and
the only means of entrance or egress was a dark
cavern which passed under the mountain to the
world outside. The mouth of this cavern was
guarded by heavy gates of iron which could

only be moved by machinery, and was opened only once a year, when the king came to see all his children and remained for eight days, feasting and making merry with the inhabitants and with the retinue which accompanied him.

At such times the dwellers in the valley had the privilege of wishing for anything that they liked, as this was the law of the land, and so, during the king's visit, everyone had everything he desired. The fame of the Happy Valley had spread far and near, and many were desirous of being admitted among its inhabitants. But no one outside of the royal family could be admitted to this valley, unless he proved his superiority in music, dancing, or some other art, or had some gift that would bring additional comfort or happiness to the inhabitants ; and thus it happened that at every visit the king was accompanied by scores of persons who excelled in various arts, and who exerted all their power to please the royal family and thus be admitted to the Happy Valley for life.

All who returned to the world again at the end of the royal visit, told only marvellous stories of the beauty of the valley, and the splendor of the palaces, and the loveliness of the air, and the happy lot of the inhabitants who had every wish gratified, and whose days were spent entirely in pleasure of every kind.

The valley was indeed a beautiful place. Far up their slopes the mountains were covered with verdure and trees, and sent down innumerable brooks and streams whose banks were covered with flowers. The level ground was covered with lawns, gardens, arbors, orchards, and bowers, and pastures where wandered every species of grass-feeding animal. Beautiful lakes were scattered everywhere, inhabited by every kind of fish, and the whole place was musical with the songs of birds from every quarter of the globe. The palaces were most magnificent, and the different rooms were so arranged that one never felt the heat of summer or the cold of winter, but instead, the windows were wide-open always, and the scent of flowers and the songs of birds were as much a part of the indoor as of the outdoor life.

Thus, to outward appearances, the Happy

Valley contained everything of greatest value in the world, and seemed the abode of peaceful content, and as the royal children knew of no other existence, and their teachers told them constantly that the world outside was full of trouble and annoyance, a murmur of discontent was never heard.

And so all went well in the Happy Valley till one day Prince Rasselas, who had reached his twenty-sixth year, awoke with a strange feeling of discontent in his heart. All through the day the amusements of his friends wearied him, and the conversation of his teachers appeared tiresome, and even when he left the palace and went out-doors, the songs of the birds irritated him, the flowers no longer delighted him, the fruits could not tempt him, and in fact nothing in the Happy Valley could please him.

This frightened Rasselas, and he began to seek for the cause of his discontent, and at last he decided that he felt unhappy because he had everything he wished. As soon as he came to this decision he began to wonder if there were not something that he might wish for that he did not know of, and he spent many days in trying to think of some new kind of pleasure. But try as he might, there was nothing that he wished for that was not immediately supplied by his attendants, and at last he gave up in despair and resolved to be forever unhappy, because he could discover no new thing to wish for.

At last one of his teachers reproved him for his discontent, and advised him to return to his companions and share once more their studies and amusements. " Why," said the old man, "are you unhappy when you have everything you want? "

And at this Rasselas no longer concealed the truth, and confessed that he was unhappy only because he had not a single want in the world. The old man was so surprised at this that he could think of nothing to reply for a long time, but at last he told Rasselas that if he had seen the miseries of the outside world he would know how to value the Happy Valley. And thinking he had said a very wise thing, the tutor was much astonished and grieved to hear

Rasselas immediately exclaim that at last he had something to wish for, for, since it was necessary to see the miseries of the world in order to be happy, he should henceforth long constantly to behold them.

For two years Rasselas was quite happy in thinking that at last he had something to wish for, and in dreaming what he should do when he left the Happy Valley. At the end of this time he came suddenly to his senses and began to think how foolish he had been to spend so much precious time in dreaming, and his regret was so deep that for a long time he did nothing but lament his folly. At last, however, he ceased pining over the past and decided to find some means of leaving the valley at once.

But escape seemed impossible. The mountain slopes were searched vainly for concealed apertures, and the iron gates no man could open except by machinery, and after ten months spent in the search, Rasselas decided that he must either remain in the valley or find some means of escape that he had not yet thought of. But through all this time he was happy because he had now a wish which no one could gratify.

Among the dwellers of the Happy Valley was one who was famous for his skill in the mechanical arts. He had invented a wheel which forced the waters of the stream into the highest rooms of the palace, and built a pavilion in which the air was kept cool by artificial showers. In one of the rivulets which ran through a grove he had fixed wheels which put fans in motion for ventilating the grove, and produced music upon instruments of music, and these and other inventions had brought him into great prominence in the Happy Valley. One day, as Rasselas was visiting the workshop of this man, he beheld the design of a sailing chariot, and was told by the master that, wonderful as this invention was by which a chariot could be propelled over the level ground by sails, it was nothing in comparison to another idea he had in his mind, which was the invention of a flying machine by which man could rival the birds of the air in motion, and thus be enabled to journey where he would.

The artisan said that, as man had learned to

swim in the water like a fish, so he might fly
through the air like a bird, and this argument
appeared so reasonable to Rasselas that he
divulged his secret wish to leave the valley, and
received the promise of the artisan to furnish
him with a pair of wings on a certain day, if he
would agree to reveal the secret to no one,
and would not ask him to make wings for anyone but themselves. This Rasselas readily
promised, and now it seemed that there at last
was a chance to escape. But, alas! when after
a year's work, the artisan pronounced the wings
finished, and made a trial flight from a little
promontory, he dropped plump into the lake
like a piece of lead, and Rasselas dragged him
from the water half-dead with terror. And so
all thought of flying from the Happy Valley was
abandoned.

The prince next took into his confidence
Imlac, the philosopher who had visited every
part of the earth, and whose learning was so
immense that he stood alone in the world. He
had lived in the Happy Valley for a long time,
and always said that his varied experiences had

shown him that he alone was happy who kept himself busy with the study of philosophy. Imlac, however, had not entirely lost his love for the world, and he heard the confession of Rasselas with as much pleasure as surprise, and readily consented to assist him out of the valley and to be his guide when they should have reached the outside world.

While Imlac and his pupil were contriving means for their escape, they came one day to some small holes in the side of the mountain dug by a colony of conies which had been driven from their burrows by heavy rains, and as Imlac looked at these holes he immediately conceived the thought that he and the prince might do well to take a hint from the conies and see if they could not dig their way out through the mountains. This was not so impossible as it might seem, as the mountains which surrounded the Happy Valley were of such a shape that their summits overhung the middle slopes, and thus by digging upward through the part that hung over, the prince and Imlac might hope to reach the outer world at last, if they only persevered. Looking earnestly among the bushes they discovered a small cavern, and here they began their mine the next day. The work was slow, as they had to steal time when there was least danger of discovery, but they came to the outside world at last; their secret had been discovered by the Prince's sister Nekayah, who also wished to leave the Happy Valley, and they decided to lose no time but proceed on their journey immediately; and as Nekayah declared she could not leave her companion Pekuah behind, the little party numbered four when all was ready.

The prince and princess, by Imlac's advice, concealed all their jewels among their clothing, and on the first night of the full moon all left the valley, and hurrying through the cavity, came at last to the open side of the mountain.

Imlac desired to take them to the sea-shore, so that they might take ship to a foreign country and thus be out of the way of pursuit; and so they at once began journeying seaward, though they travelled but slowly, as Imlac had to accustom the prince and princess to the sight of strange people who showed no fear in their presence, and who did not prostrate themselves before them as did their subjects in the Happy Valley.

Pekuah, the companion, was able to assist the princess in many useful ways, and travelling in this fashion they came at last to the sea and took passage for Cairo, where could be found travellers and merchants from every part of the earth, and where the prince hoped to study life carefully and at length decide upon a career for himself.

As Imlac took upon him the character of a merchant, their jewels were easily changed into money, which procured them every luxury, and Rasselas and his sister passed for wealthy strangers who were travelling for curiosity, and so their appearance in Cairo excited no surprise or comment.

Rasselas did not doubt that he would soon be able to make a choice of a career, and he spent many hours in imagining his happiness when he should be at last settled in some honorable profession ; and as he thought that happiness could best be studied from the happy, he set himself about finding happy men. But this appeared very difficult. He visited young men who spent their entire time in enjoyment, and philosophers who lectured daily on the vanity of pleasure, and men who said that art or science or the gaining of riches was the chief thing in the world. But though he tried many months, Rasselas could not find anyone who would own that he enjoyed happiness. This puzzled him greatly, for in Cairo was to be found every condition of life that existed. At last he heard of a hermit who lived at a great distance from Cairo, and whose fame for piety had reached every ear, and Rasselas decided that he would visit this holy man and see if he had found the secret of happiness.

The hermit lived in a little dell shaded with palms and made musical by the murmur of a cataract not far away. His dwelling consisted of a cavern which was divided into a number of rooms, and here the travellers were glad to find that everything spoke of peace and happiness. But when they told the hermit that they had come hither to inquire of him how to find happiness, he shook his head, sighed, and after relating the history of his life, said that it was his determination to leave his retreat on the morrow, as his solitude of fifteen years had given him nothing but a desire to see the world once more. Though stunned with surprise, the prince offered to conduct the hermit back to the city with them, and first digging up some treasure hid among the rocks, the hermit joined them, and as they approached the city, greeted it with such expressions of joy that the prince almost feared he had gone mad. Although Rasselas and Nekayah had been disappointed in the hermit, they yet did not despair of finding someone who could tell them the way to happiness. They continued to visit all sorts of people—rich, wise, poor, and ignorant—but no one would admit that he was happy, and the brother and sister at last became discouraged. But just then Imlac said that the only true way to find happiness was by studying the history of the past and comparing it with the present, so as to see wherein those nations which were considered happy differed from those that were unhappy, and he proposed that for the purpose of this study they should all visit the great Pyramids, and learn from those vast monuments of antiquity the secret of happiness.

To this the brother and sister readily consented, and the next day they started for the Pyramids, taking with them camels, tents, and attendants, as they resolved to stay among the Pyramids till they had learned all it was possible to learn from them concerning happiness.

But on the second day of their arrival a sad accident happened, which destroyed all their plans. On this day they had decided to enter the great Pyramid and examine the inner rooms, but as they came to the first entrance, Pekuah, the companion of the princess, drew back trembling, and declared that she should die if she entered a place which she knew was filled with ghosts, and as nothing could drive this thought from her mind they were obliged to leave her behind them.

They passed through the different rooms of

the Pyramid, examining the costly chambers and
marble vaults with great interest, and when
they came to the outer world again Nekayah
had her mind full of the wonders which she
should relate to Pekuah.   But as they approached the tents they found all the attendants filled with terror, for during their absence
a party of Arabs from the desert had galloped
down upon the encampment, seized Pekuah and
two of her maids, and borne them off before the
surprised attendants could interfere.   They had
been driven off by some Turkish horsemen who
had opportunely appeared, and who were then
in pursuit, and the attendants said there was
nothing to do but wait until their return to see
what had been the fate of Pekuah.

The princess was overcome by this sad news,
and when the Turks returned and said that they
had been unable to overtake the Arabs, her
grief knew no bounds.   They returned to
Cairo, and from that day Rasselas and Nekayah forgot all about the pursuit of happiness,
and thought only of recovering Pekuah from
the Arabs, for it was generally believed that

they would restore her if a large ransom were offered.

And in this they were right, for no sooner had the Arab chief discovered, by the richness of her apparel, and the deference of her maids, that Pekuah was a lady of high position, than he became very respectful to her, and ordered all his followers to treat her with the greatest consideration. He bore her to his castle on an island in the river, and except for the fact that she was a prisoner, Pekuah suffered no hardships. The chief was delighted with her knowledge of the world, and spent hours in conversing with her, and as he was also a student of astronomy, he instructed her in the mysteries of the heavens, and the time was in the main filled with pleasant occupations.

Here Pekuah remained many months, during which Rasselas and the princess tried constantly to obtain news of her. Messenger after messenger was sent out to carry on the search, but all returned unsuccessful, and at last Nekayah became so discouraged that she threatened to enter a convent and pass the rest of her life in mourning for Pekuah.

But at last a messenger came in one day, announcing that he had discovered the Arab's retreat, and that Pekuah would be returned upon the payment of a certain sum. This news brought hope again to Nekayah, and the whole party proceeded toward the spot where Pekuah was to be brought. And in a few days the princess had the great happiness of seeing her favorite once more, and they all returned to Cairo.

About this time the party formed the acquaintance of an old astronomer, who was renowned for wisdom and philosophy, but whose mind was so unsettled by long study that he imagined he possessed the power of controlling the laws of nature, and could call up tempests or sunshine at his will. On every other point the astronomer was sane and reasonable, but he persisted in thinking that he had control of the weather. And this affliction seemed so pitiable to the prince's party that they, one and all, set about the kindly task of bringing the old man back to his senses.

With this in view they planned to keep the astronomer constantly occupied with other things, so that he should have no time to think of the weather. They therefore invited him to their house daily, made him share their amusements, and listened with delight to his talk; for he had vast stores of knowledge; and this plan succeeded so well that the old man soon ceased to think continually of the weather, and no longer thought it necessary to regulate the rising and the setting of the sun.

Rasselas and his sister were so rejoiced at the success of their amiable plan, that they experienced the truest pleasure that they had felt since their flight from the Happy Valley, and had they kept on with such works of kindness, it is possible that they might at last have reached the happiness that they were always seeking. But having cured the astronomer, they began again to search for some condition of life which would bring them happiness, and one state after another was discussed and dismissed, until they began to wonder whether any vocation would bring them what they desired. Just as they came to this question the rising of the Nile kept them prisoners within the house, and they spent many days in arguing what life they should choose. Pekuah finally decided that she would like to enter a convent, and pass her life in quiet. The princess thought that she might be happy if she should found a great college for women over which she should preside, and spend her life in conversing with the wise and instructing the young. Rasselas said that he should like to have a little kingdom which he might govern as he pleased, and Imlac and the astronomer decided to make no choice, but to drift along wherever life might lead them. Having at last settled upon what they desired, they began to think of ways of obtaining it. But this they found to be very difficult, and after endless talks and plans they were as far off from their wishes as ever, and when they realized this it seemed so strange to them that they could talk of nothing else for a long time.

They had now been away from Abyssinia a long time, and their search for happiness had been utterly vain.   They had found not one happy person in all their wanderings, and the pursuits and enjoyments of the outside world seemed as tiresome as the monotonous existence of the Happy Valley.   Since this was true, it was clear that they had gained nothing by their journey, and their surprise at this discovery was so great that they could do nothing but talk of it for the rest of the time that they were confined to the house.   And then, since there seemed no use in continuing their travels, they resolved to return to Abyssinia as soon as the Nile subsided, and acknowledge to the friends they had left, that their search for happiness had been all in vain.

CHAPTER X.

The history of England is from the beginning celebrated for the number and popularity of certain heroes, who represented the epochs in which they lived to such a degree that the story of the hero is the story of the times. Thus the history of the earliest ages of England is only to be found in the tales of the old British and Saxon chieftains, as the history of early Christian times in England is preserved in the story of King Arthur and his blameless knights, and the record of Norman influence is found in the exploits of jolly Robin Hood and his merry men.

Every age, in fact, produced its popular hero, the idol of the people and the representative of the times, and around these heroes gradually grew up a literature which pictured the national life, because it was founded upon events which made the nation's history. And no pages in all the story of England's growth are more full of romance and picturesqueness than those which treat of that long warfare between England and Scotland, when the Scots were fighting for their freedom. The early part of the struggle between England and Scotland is often spoken of as the period of Border warfare, because the conflict was carried on chiefly between the clans and families which lived near the boundary lines, and consisted of long years of raiding and guerilla warfare rather than of pitched battles and sieges. These old times are alive with incidents and events of the most romantic nature. Princes and chieftains and leaders, clans and retainers and followers, castles and dungeons and mountain retreats, are the materials which go to make up the history of those days when life meant danger and adventure and sudden turns of fortune, and peace and security seemed impossible dreams. The memory of these times came down to later days, bringing a legacy of traditions sacred

22

to every Scot.   But of these old days there existed no literature and no history, save in the folk-songs which were sung in highland wilds or lowland villages, songs which had been made and sung by the old bards and minstrels who wandered from castle to castle in those troublous days, and whose lays had come down from generation to generation, priceless and sole heirlooms of the past.

There came a time, however, when this far distant period began to possess an interest to scholars and students of literature, and when the old song ceased to be looked upon merely as an old song, and was considered of great value because it was a refrain from those days when the history of the country was being made.   And there grew up a great desire to study the history of that time, so that the dead past might be brought back and its shadowy dwellers once again pass before the eye like living men and women.

In England this desire resulted in the publication of a book by Bishop Percy, called *Reliques of Ancient Poetry*, in which were put together as many of the old songs and ballads as the compiler could find. In this curious and valuable book were grouped together a strange medley of ancient legends gathered from many sources. Some of the ballads had been taken from old manuscript, yellow and worn with time. Others had been jotted down from the lips of some village poet, the last descendant of the old bards. Others still were rudely printed, and had been circulated among the peasant class for hundreds of years. Some were in Highland, some in Lowland, some in English speech of many different counties. Some recorded great battles, and others homely incidents of love and domestic life. But all were full of the life of those distant ages, and brought back the old days with the vividness of a picture.

This interesting book drifted for twenty years among the haunts of book lovers, and won for itself a warm welcome everywhere, and then it fell one day into the hands of a blue-eyed lad who looked and read, and straightway was lost to the present, having wandered back into that golden past which the old poems called up.

This lad was a Scot, by name Walter Scott, and in his veins ran the blood of those old chieftains whose deeds he was reading, for both his father and mother were descended from those ancient historic families whose achievements were the glory of Scottish history. In speaking of his first acquaintance with this book, Scott says that his heart was stirred as with the sound of a trumpet, and perhaps it is not the least glory of the old ballads that they dropped into this boyish mind the seeds which in later years bore such golden harvests for English literature.

Scott was born in 1771 at Edinburgh, but being delicate passed much of his childhood in the country, and here, among the farmer folks, his mind was filled with all those legends and quaint superstitions in which the country people so firmly believed. These impressions sank into his mind, found fruitful soil, grew and flourished, and gave form and color to his imagination in such a degree that when the time came for him to write books, he reproduced the spirit of the old days as no other writer could have done, because it was the same spirit that had influenced him when a child.

Scott was educated in the High School and University of Edinburgh, and was trained for the practice of the law. But as his tastes ran toward literature he found the law little to his liking, and in very early manhood began the translation of German poetry, in which he was quite successful. It was fortunate, however, that he soon discovered that his work for literature must lie in other directions.

With the tastes of his childhood days strong within him, he turned his mind toward the old songs and ballads which made up a large part of Scottish poetry, and he resolved to try and bring into some definite form all the numerous and interesting legends which were woven into the pages of his country's history.

He travelled through the regions celebrated in history, and from cotter and shepherd and farmer, and curious old written songs, he gathered together legends, myths, and old traditions, and became familiar with the scenery and manners of the places where each song or legend had been found. Then he studied, sifted, and edited, and at last bound together in definite form these old bits of history which had been first made by the old harpers and minstrels, and published them in a book called the *Minstrelsy of the Scottish Border*. This book was more than a compilation of old songs, it was the reproduction of a part of the national history, and it won for Scott the honor and recognition that he deserved.

In this work Scott seems to have been searching for the right path in which to work, and the results show that he found that which he sought, for in 1805 he gave to the world an original poem, *The Lay of the Last Minstrel*, which was founded upon the romantic incidents of the old Border warfare. Then came the poems called *Marmion*, founded upon the battle of Flodden Field, in 1513, when James IV. of Scotland was slain and the English gained the victory, the hero Marmion being a fictitious character representing one of the English leaders; *The Lady of the Lake*, founded upon the romantic adventures of Henry V. of Scotland, while wander-

ing in disguise through the western Highlands;
Rokcby, in which the scene is laid directly after
the battle of Marston Moor, where Charles I.
was defeated by the revolutionists; *The Lord
of the Isles*, relating to the stirring days of
Robert Bruce and Scotland's battle for independence; and several minor ones. These
poems were unique in English literature, and
their appearance marked a new epoch.

But great as was his success in these poems,
Scott was really at this period only finding his
way toward his true work. The poems were
splendid pictures of the romantic and chivalrous
ages, and were thrown into those fascinating
metres which appeal to lovers of music and to
the people at large. A passage or description
from one of these poems could almost be
chanted like an old battle hymn, and this lyric
quality added greatly to their popularity.

But still they were pictures of times and
events rather than anything else, and lacked
that human interest which marks the masterpieces of all literature. And Scott's fame, therefore, as one of the great writers of romance does

not rest upon his poems, popular as they were
in his day, but upon his long series of romantic
novels in which is shown such a clear understanding and portrayal of the motives that make
human conduct.   These novels are based upon
incidents in English, Scottish, and Continental
history, or upon domestic life, and in each of
these departments Scott produced a masterpiece.

His first novel was founded upon the attempt
of Charles Edward Stuart, grandson of James
II., to gain the English throne.

In 1745 the young prince, an exile from
England, landed with seven friends on one of
the Hebrides and raised the standard of the
Stuarts.   The throne of England was occupied
by George II., and the English nation, under
the wise direction of the elder Pitt, one of the
greatest statesmen that England has ever
known, was well enough content with its ruling house.   The young Pretender, as the
prince is called in history, had small chance
of gaining the throne; but the Highland
clans rallied to his standard, and in a few

weeks he found himself at the head of six thousand men.

But in spite of the loyalty of the brave Highlanders, Charles Edward was defeated and was obliged to escape to France. But his campaign was so romantic in its nature, and he himself was looked upon as such a hero by his friends, that his attempt to win England was regarded as an adventure of the olden times, when exiled kings won back their inheritance by deeds of personal bravery. This was the last effort of the Stuarts to gain the throne. And with the defeat of Charles Edward the Highlanders ceased to inspire the terror that they had hitherto done. There was even passed an act of Parliament forbidding the clans to wear the tartan, and with this defeat the Highland Scot as a power against the English throne passed out of history. But during the early years of Scott the campaign of the young Pretender was still fresh in the memory of the nation, and the beauty, bravery, and romantic deeds of the prince were among the favorite themes discussed at Scottish firesides. This story Scott wove into his novel which he called *Waverley, or 'Tis Sixty Years Since*, and which he gave to the world in 1814, without appearing as the author.

This novel was received with the same enthusiasm which had greeted his poetry, though few suspected the authorship. And in this work Scott at once reached the highest point of his art. None of the brilliant romances which followed exceeded *Waverley* in magnificent description, stirring adventure, or those peculiarities of human life which make the novels of Scott so dramatic. *Waverley* was followed by a series of stories of such power that they won for the romantic novel one of the highest places in literature.

In *Kenilworth* Scott told the love-story of the Earl of Leicester and the unfortunate Amy Robsart. This picture is one of the most brilliant that Scott has drawn, the story indeed reading like a description by some old chronicler of the pageants for which London was so famous in the days of Elizabeth.

Leicester, the most powerful of Elizabeth's

earls—so great, indeed, that he was looked upon as a possible suitor for her hand—was in love with the beautiful Amy Robsart, daughter of Sir Hugh Robsart, a country baronet. As this great difference in rank could not admit of open courtship their love was kept secret, and Leicester induced Amy to marry him privately, and then carried her to Cumnor Place, one of his country houses, and left her in charge of his dependent, Anthony Foster, who was entirely devoted to Leicester's interests. Before Amy's arrival at Cumnor Place some rooms in the old dwelling had been beautifully fitted up for her reception, as Leicester wished to honor her as far as he could. The walls were hung with velvet and silken drapery, and tapestry from the famous looms of Flanders. There were chairs ornamented with arabesque needlework; and mirrors from Venice; foot-cloths and carpets from Spain; silver sconces which reflected the polish of the wainscoting, made from the foreign woods that had been brought from the West Indies; and a chair of state with a can-opy, cushions, side curtains, and foot-cloth of

velvet embroidered with pearls and surmounted
by two coronets, and beautiful pictures adorn-
ing the walls everywhere. But Amy was not
happy amid these surroundings, whose splendor only dazzled the eyes of the simple country
girl, and left her heart still hungry for Leicester's presence ; for he was away from her almost
constantly, and even when he did come to see
her his visits were stolen, and made at times
when Elizabeth supposed him away from court
on some far different errand.

Thus, even in the first picture of her married
life, there is a shadow cast by the loneliness of
the young wife, which contrasted strangely with
her husband's life at the brilliant court of Elizabeth. This love-story, which begins under
such sad conditions, is made by Scott to form
the centre of a group of brilliant pictures of the
Elizabethan days. From Amy Robsart, in her
lonely state at Cumnor Place we are led to her
father's house, and have a glimpse of the life of
a country gentleman of the sixteenth century.
We see the generous and true-hearted baronet,
lavish in hospitality and with a loyal devotion

to his queen, now bowed under the weight of a great sorrow, and mourning his daughter's absence all the more deeply because he does not know whither she had gone, and supposed in fact that she had fled with Richard Varney, a friend of Leicester's.

Again, we see a picture of one of those country inns where all sorts of people meet to spend the night, and find among these chance acquaintances the typical landlord, Giles Gosling, stout and ruddy and jolly, just such a host as Shakespeare saw many a time on his way from Stratford up to London. Here too is the reckless soldier of fortune who has spent his youth warring in France and Spain and the Netherlands, and who has come back to England without the fortune he hoped to make. Beside him sit the village characters—the mercer, who thinks only of his wares, and listens to stories of life in America and the Indies because they suggest to him fortunes that might be made by trade, and the mechanics who have come to drink ale, and the quiet traveller whose air of distinction sets him apart from the others, and whose courteous comradeship marks him a man of the world. All these meet and chat in the old inn, the purpose of the picture being the introduction of Edmund Tressilian, a former lover of Amy Robsart and her father's dearest friend, who has set out to find her in spite of all the precautions that Leicester has taken.

The inn is in a little village near Cumnor Hall, and through various expedients Tressilian gains access to the house and has an interview with Amy, though he cannot persuade her to return to her father's house. From this point the story rises in dramatic interest, till the highest point is reached in the flight of Amy to Kenilworth Castle, whither the court has gone on a visit to the Earl of Leicester; in this scene Scott brings in a description of those famous entertainments which always occurred at a royal visit. We see Kenilworth in holiday attire, with its portal guarded by warders, whose dress and arms imitated those of the old Britons who were said to have tenanted the castle in the days of King Arthur. At the entrance to the gate stood some of Leicester's retainers, all of gentle birth, forming a double row like a guard of honor through which the queen must pass. These gentlemen carried no arms excepting their swords and daggers, and their dress was the most magnificent that their means allowed; velvet, silk, gold and silver lace, ribbons, feathers, and jewels, served to make their appearance worthy of the eyes of the queen, who demanded always that her attendants should wear the most elegant apparel; and it is interesting to know that among this group Scott has introduced the figure of the gallant and courtly Sir Walter Raleigh, then just rising into fame.

In the twilight of the summer day which Scott describes, the queen and her train of lords and ladies approached Kenilworth and received the homage of the hundreds of country people who thronged the wayside, and among whom may have been the boy Shakespeare, then in his twelfth year. From every tower and battlement of the castle came the sound of drum and trumpet and cannon, and with the salvos of the multitude ringing in her ears, the queen, mounted on a milk-white horse, and preceded by two hundred horsemen carrying lighted torches, passed through the gates of Kenilworth. On the right hand rode Leicester, his dress flashing with gold and jewels, followed by the ladies of the train and the highest-born nobles of the land. From the bridge which led to the entrance tower the queen saw the whole lake illuminated with torches and filled with floating islands upon which rested tritons, nereids, and sea-horses, and in the centre of which stood a masker in the character of the Lady of the Island, who welcomed Elizabeth to Kenilworth, and who claimed to be the famous Lady of the Lake, so familiar to the lovers of the stories of King Arthur and his knights.

With this welcome the queen entered the castle hall, while a blaze of fireworks shooting from the towers overhead announced to the multitude outside that the festivities of the royal visit had begun. The entertainment that followed was on a scale of great magnificence: banquets, masques, and hunting parties succeeded one another, and Kenilworth was turned into a vast hall of pleasure. Persons of all sorts and conditions had flocked to the castle to ply their accustomed professions, and jugglers, players, wandering musicians, and showmen of every description, were to be found within the walls, turning the place for a time into a miniature of the great world of London.

Under cover of one of these companies of travelling showmen, Amy Robsart had come to Kenilworth to beg Leicester to acknowledge her as his wife. Her life at Cumnor Place had become unbearable, and she feared much from the ill-will of Anthony Foster and Richard Varney, the one friend of Leicester who knew of her marriage. So she had stolen away from her prison and had made her way in disguise to Kenilworth, which she entered without revealing herself to anyone. Edmund Tressilian was among the guests present, and through an accident he became aware of her presence in the castle and resolved to guard her from all harm if he could. But this one friend could do very little good in the face of the desperate circumstances which surrounded her. Through a succession of misunderstandings, the queen discovered Amy to be Leicester's wife, and Leicester himself was led to doubt Amy's love for him, and ordered her carried back to Cumnor Place and put to death. After Amy had left the castle, Leicester discovered that she was still true to him, and sent a messenger in haste to forbid the crime. But this messenger did not reach Cumnor Place in time, and Amy was cruelly murdered. This story, which Scott has made so familiar by the pages of *Kenilworth*, was repeated all over England in Shakespeare's day and for many years afterward. Ballads were written upon it, strange and weird experiences were related in connection with it, and Cumnor Place became forever celebrated in English history as the scene in this dark page of Leicester's life. Floating down the centuries it came into the hands of Scott, who has made it immortal and has placed it among the famous love-stories of the world.

In *Ivanhoe* Scott went back to those adventurous times when England was still Norman and Saxon instead of being purely English, and contrasts the life of the Norman conqueror with that of the conquered Saxon. Prince John was ruling in behalf of his brother, Richard *Cœur de Lion*, who had been taken prisoner in Germany while returning from the crusades, and John's well-known wish to set his brother aside and gain the crown for himself, had divided England into two political parties, the one which favored John and the one that still remained faithful to the absent king.

Richard, disguised as the Black Knight, is introduced into the story of Ivanhoe, which besides being a tale of splendid dramatic interest, is a picturesque description of those troublesome days. Besides the character of Richard many strange personages, that represent the social life of the times, are also introduced. Thus we have a glimpse of the order of the Knights Templar, one of the most powerful organizations of the Middle Ages, whose members were sworn to redeem the Holy Sepulchre. We see also some of those Free Companions, or men-at-arms, who drifted through Europe from one country to another, serving in any army that would pay them, and ready for any adventure. We see, too, the Saxon peasant wearing the brass collar which proclaims him a serf and tells the name of his master; and the crusader just returned from the Holy Land; and, as in a picture by Chaucer, the figure of a monk on his way to the rich priory of his order, and beside him a hardy yeoman with his bow of yew. And Robin Hood himself flits through the pages as Locksley, the chivalrous outlaw, side by side with *Cœur de Lion*. Then we have descriptions of tournaments and feasts, and midnight adventures with Robin Hood, and the storming of castles, and banqueting in Saxon halls which were old when the Norman first came to England. And all the persons and incidents are woven together in such a manner that they form a perfect picture of those days, and make at the same time a story of such dramatic interest that it will ever be considered one of Scott's most famous romances.

Scott took his idea of the story from an old English ballad, gathered his materials from old

Anglo-Saxon manuscripts, named his hero *Ivanhoe* from an old rhyme, which stated that *Twing, Wing,* and *Ivanhoe* were three manors which had been lost to their owner because he struck the Black Prince with a racket while playing tennis with him ; and then proceeded to write his first romance which dealt with a remote period.

In the story, Ivanhoe, the son of Cedric, the most powerful of the Saxon earls, has been banished from his father's house because he loves Rowena, a Saxon lady of high birth and his father's ward. Rowena is the promised bride of Athelstane, the last representative of the Saxon kings, and Cedric is determined to bring the match about, even though he knows that Rowena returns Ivanhoe's love. Ivanhoe joins the crusaders and wins laurels in the Holy Land, returning to England about the same time that *Cœur de Lion* appears on the scene in the disguise of the Black Knight. In a tournament that follows, Ivanhoe himself, also in disguise, vanquishes all the great Norman noblemen who have entered the lists, and proclaims Rowena queen of the tournament. But he himself is wounded in the last encounter, and only saved from defeat by the help of the Black Knight. As Ivanhoe falls fainting at Rowena's feet, he is recognized by her and by Cedric, but his father still refuses to acknowledge him.

When Ivanhoe first returned to England, he spent one night at his father's house, disguised as a palmer, and at that time rescued from peril Isaac, a wealthy Jew, who afterward lent him his horse and armor in return for the kindness. Isaac and his daughter Rebecca now came to the relief of the wounded knight, and cared for him, and from this time on the story revolves almost entirely around the beautiful and devoted Jewess. Many strange adventures, possible only to that age, follow. Rebecca is loved by the Templar Bois-Guilbert, who captures her and carries her off to the convent of the Knights Templar. Here she is accused of witchcraft by the Templars, who say that Bois-Guilbert only loves her because she has bewitched him. She is judged guilty, but is allowed to ask for a champion to defend her, according to that curious custom of the age by which a prisoner's innocence or guilt was decided. In some instances, the guilt of a prisoner was proved if he flinched while grasping a red-hot iron ; in others, innocence was allowed if the hand did not burn when passed through flames ; in the case of Rebecca, she would gain her freedom if a knight would come forward in her defence and vanquish the champion chosen by the Order. Ivanhoe proclaimed himself her champion, but on the day of the combat, Bois-Guilbert, the champion of his Order, fell dead at the first shock of the charge, before Ivanhoe could make one fatal stroke. This sudden death from no apparent cause was considered the judgment of God against a knight who had disobeyed the rules of his Order by loving a woman, and Rebecca was pronounced innocent. The story reaches its climax at this point. The marriage of Ivanhoe and Rowena follows, Cedric having been brought to give his consent through the persuasion of Richard, who was again on the throne. The king himself and all the great Norman nobles attended this wedding, and so the book ends with a hint of the peaceful days to come when Norman and Saxon should have mingled together to form the great English nation. Rebecca and her father leave England forever and find refuge in Granada, in Spain, then ruled by the Moors, and the one country in the world where their race might find peace, secure in the knowledge that when the Mohammedan passed his word of honor it was sacred, even though given to a Jew.

In *Ivanhoe*, Scott has introduced some passages of extraordinary power and magnificence. Thus the description of the tournament, with its gorgeous setting of feudal incident, is the finest picture of the days of chivalry to be found in English literature. The lists, filled with fighting knights, the amphitheatre, crowded with beautiful and elegantly dressed ladies, the pages, squires, and yeomen looking on, the jolly followers of Robin Hood shooting for the forester's prize, and the celebrated Knights Templar, famed for their bravery and for their powerful Order all go to make the scene alive with the breath of a past full of that romance and sentiment which has departed forever.

The description of the siege of Torquilstone, Front de Bœuf's castle, is equally powerful, and is made more dramatic by being put into the mouth of Rebecca, who stands in a window overlooking the wall, guarding herself by an old buckler, and reports the progress of the siege to the wounded Ivanhoe. Nowhere is there found a more graphic account of the storming and carrying of a feudal castle, in those days when every nobleman's home was a military fort, manned and guarded for defence to the death.

The trial scene of Rebecca in the hall of the Knights Templar, is still another interesting picture of those dark days when witchcraft, sorcery, and communion with evil spirits were as firmly believed in as the power of the church and the king; and indeed, the whole book is so surrounded by the atmosphere of the times it represents, that it becomes a study of the past as well as a romance, and thus fulfils the true mission of the historical novel.

In *Rob Roy*, Scott again touches Scottish history. Rob Roy belonged to the famous clan of MacGregor, noted for their persistent hatred of the English, for their bravery in battle, and powerful position among the other Highland clans. The name MacGregor had been a terror to English ears for centuries, and even in the reign of Queen Mary there was a commission granted to the most powerful nobles to pursue the clan Gregor with fire and sword, while anyone who offered meat, drink, or clothes to any member of the clan, was made liable to the law. Later on even the name MacGregor was abolished by an act of the crown, and all who bore it were under sentence of death. Death was also promised to any assembly of MacGregors which numbered more than four people, as it was hoped that by this measure the clan would be dispersed.

But the MacGregors laughed at king and parliament and nobles. They kept their rude state secure in their power, and their chief was the only lord they knew. Fire and sword could not reach them, and terrible was the vengeance they wrought on their enemies. It is true that, hunted and hounded as they were, they often met with loss, but scarcely would the loss be known when, from tribe to tribe and chieftain to chieftain, would run the messengers of war summoning the clan to vengeance. And then, starting up like shadows, armed men would fill the hill passes, and the misty Highlands would be alive with the camp-fires of the clan MacGregor. Sure of their chief and of their own devotion, acquainted with every stone and rocky height, careless of death and familiar with danger, they formed a formidable power against the English, and represented in their later days the last remnant of the Scottish spirit which it cost England so much to subdue. But in the course of centuries the power of the MacGregors became weakened, and even the name was seldom heard, as the clan had been forced to take other names to save themselves from death ; their new names they took from the families among which they happened to be scattered, and many of them became known as Drummonds, Campbells, Grahams, Stewarts, and so on, though they were still loyal in their hearts to the name MacGregor.

In the reign of George I., the last important representative of the old clan was Rob Roy MacGregor, who called himself Robert Campbell, and whose exploits and adventures gained him the title of the Scottish Robin Hood. In his retreat at Craig Royston, on the side of Loch Lomond, Rob Roy kept the state and dignity of his ancestors, ruling over his clan and acknowledging no higher authority than his own will. And it was this character that Scott introduced into his romance by that name. In this book Rob Roy, noted for his daring highway robberies, and for his genius in escaping the law, is also made one of the principal agents in what is known as the Rebellion of 1717. This rebellion was the last effort but one of the Stuart family to regain the throne of England. Naturally the Stuart prince looked to the Scottish Highlands for help, and the Earl of Mar responded by setting up the standard of the Stuarts and proclaiming James Stuart king. Rob Roy, as leader of the MacGregor clan

which knew no loyalty save to him, was looked
upon as a powerful ally by the Jacobites, as the
Stuart followers were called, and he figures in
the book as one who might do much to make
the rebellion successful. His secret missions to
Jacobite agents, his dangerous adventures in
behalf of the cause, and his narrow escapes from
death, show well the perils which the Jacobites
endured; and his romantic life as chief of a
daring band of outlaws gives the story such
picturesqueness as belongs only to tales of adventure. Every dale, rock, wood, glen, and harbor of Scotland was known to Rob Roy. His
whistle would gather a band of devoted followers around him at any moment, and his message
of war would summon at a few hours' notice
body after body of men from remote corners of
the Highlands. His name was all the more
dreaded because he seldom met his enemies in
open fight, but depended rather upon sudden
surprises, unexpected ambushes, and other
stratagems for his success.

In Scott's story the love episode centres
around Die Vernon, a daughter of one of the

leading Jacobites, and two of her admirers, one of whom is Rashleigh Osbaldistone, a Jacobite agent. Rob Roy is the friend of Die Vernon and of Ralph Osbaldistone, cousin of Rashleigh, whom she loves, and the devotion and loyalty of the outlaw chieftain form a picturesque background to the love incident.

The wife of Rob Roy, Helen Campbell, is one of Scott's best characters, and the picture of this daughter of the Highlands holding sway at Craig Royston while her husband and sons are away, is full of fine dramatic power. In the end the Jacobites fail through the treachery of Rashleigh and other agents, the lovers are married, and Rob Roy fades back again into the half obscurity which wrapped his romantic career. The book has a powerful interest as showing the methods which attended the famous rebellion, and is invaluable as recording the exploits of the Scottish Robin Hood, pursuing his outlaw life in a century which boasted the civilization and culture of the reign of Queen Anne, and which was famous for its development of English constitutional law. Rob Roy was the last hero of the Scottish Highlands, and his picturesque career is the last link binding the Scotland of to-day with its romantic past. The book is therefore more than a tale of adventure. It is a scene from one of the great dramas of the world's history, closing in shadow as Rob Roy vanishes among the mists of the Highlands, and leaves behind him only a memory like that which lingers around the far-off days of Scotland's national greatness.

In the *Talisman* Scott has taken for his theme a story of the crusaders, with Richard *Cœur de Lion* at their head, fighting in the Holy Land. The book takes its name from a famous talisman which possessed the power of healing, and which cured Richard of a deadly fever. In this story the crown prince of Scotland, in the disguise of the Red Cross knight, journeys to the East to join the Crusaders, meets and fights with the great Mohammedan chieftain Saladin, himself in the disguise of one of his followers, enters the camp of Richard without allowing his station to be known, is made guardian for a night of the royal standard of

England, forsakes his post for an hour at the solicitation of one who claims that a dear friend is in urgent necessity of seeing him, returns to find the standard gone, is sentenced to death by Richard, but has his sentence changed to banishment through the efforts of Saladin, who, in the disguise of a physician, has cured Richard of deadly sickness, and, after a series of romantic and exciting adventures, finally wins back his lost honor and weds the heroine of the story, whose hand had been denied him because of his supposed obscure station in life. Many of those incidents which make the tales of the Crusaders sound like fairy stories figure in this tale, and many of those personages whose names and glory are forever connected with the history of those times. We have the character of Richard, brave and warlike, but often childishly impulsive, opposed to that of the great Saladin, the sultan of the East, and a chivalrous and courtly warrior whose word was as good as a Christian's oath, and whose name inspired such terror in Christian countries that it was used as a spell to frighten children with.

Many curious characters go to make up this picture of the East in the Middle Ages, which represents the character of that credulous and adventurous age when men believed in sorcery, witchcraft, and marvels of all kinds, and when danger and death were reckoned naught in the quest for personal renown and martial glory.

Scott wrote in all twenty-nine romances. Among them we find stories of the Scotch Puritans and English Cavaliers of the seventeenth century, legends of the Border, tales of London when Shakespeare lived there, tales of the Crusaders, and many stories of private and domestic life. In *The Monastery* and *The Abbot* we have the story of Mary, Queen of Scots ; in *Woodstock* a tale of the Civil Wars and the Commonwealth ; in *Quentin Durward*, a tale of the times of Louis XI. of France ; and in *Count Robert of Paris*, another story of the Crusaders. These are among the most famous of the historical romances. *Guy Mannering, The Antiquary*, and *The Heart of Midlothian* are the most famous of the novels of domestic life. In these Scott writes the history of the human

24

heart with as true a hand as that which penned the great deeds of history, and thus connects himself with the great novelists of the eighteenth century and with his successors of the nineteenth, keeping the line of pure English fiction unbroken, while at the same time his romantic novels founded a new school.

The whole series of romances is now known under the name of the Waverley novels. They were all published anonymously, though it was generally believed, even at the time, that Scott was the author. It was not until the Waverley novels had long been given a place among English classics that Scott acknowledged the authorship. He died in 1832.

CHAPTER XI.

In English literature the nineteenth century, called the Victorian age, is so great that it stands next to the age of Elizabeth. It has produced some of the greatest poets and novelists, and is remarkable for its brilliant writers in other departments of literature, such as philosophy, science, history, and the essay. It is also the age of the development of those reviews, magazines, and other periodical literature which do so much toward moulding public thought, and cultivating the popular taste.

The leading historians of this age are George Grote, whose history of Greece is a monument of learning; Henry Hallam, the author of histories of the Middle Ages, of the English Constitution, and of European Literature; Thomas

Babington Macaulay, whose unfinished history of England from the accession of James II., and numerous historical essays, are classic works; Henry Hart Milman, author of a History of Latin Christianity; James Anthony Froude, who has made the Tudor epoch his own; and more recently the learned constitutional historians Freeman, Stubbs, and Gardiner, and the brilliant and popular John Richard Green. These men worked, more or less, in the broad lines that had first been laid down by Gibbon, and their productions are among the finest prose of the Victorian age.

In science the achievements of this century are unparalleled. Within this period Davy has discovered those great laws of chemistry which bind the works of nature together, and brought those subtle and mysterious forces which the old alchemists dreamed of with awe into the realm of pure science. In geology, Lyell has read the history of the earth, and by the print of the fern in the dark layers of coal, or by the presence of the tiny shell in the chalky rock, has followed the wonderful story of the earth's life from the earliest time to the present day.

Faraday and Tyndall have studied the wonders of electricity and heat, and have shown the relationship that exists between the forces of nature and the laws of life. And Darwin, Wallace, and Huxley have gone farther still and have explored the sources of life itself, bringing back from their search such stores of knowledge that the great mysteries of the universe almost seem to stand ready to unfold themselves to the comprehension of man. All these earnest students of nature have put the results of their work into books which form a literature unique in the history of letters, and which of themselves would stamp any literary epoch with greatness.

In philosophy, John Stuart Mill and Herbert Spencer have laid down systems in which are treated the laws that govern thought and the moral nature. They have traced the career of man as a creature of intelligence and reasoning power, and have shown the growth of his mind through all periods of this strange development; from the time when the human race was but little higher than the brute, to the present day, when man has proven himself capable of controlling the mightiest forces of nature. And this story of the intellectual life of man is a contribution to the literature of the nineteenth century worthy of rank with the story of his physical life, as told by Wallace and Darwin.

In the department of the essay, Carlyle, Macaulay, Matthew Arnold, and John Ruskin, have made history, art, and ethics as interesting as romance, while De Quincey and Lamb have given us those unique productions which deal with the virtues and faults of mankind so wisely and sympathetically that they have won a permanent place in English literature. De Quincey is one of the masters of English prose, and his work is a model of elegant style. He produced fourteen volumes of essays and narratives, historical, critical, and humorous, and though many of these are fragmentary, their literary merits are so distinguished that they have procured him a unique place in literature.

Charles Lamb has left in his *Essays of Elia* some of the most charming essays in English literature.   Lamb was distinctly a humorist as well as being a man of the finest sentiment and feeling, and his writings show a mixture of wit, pathos, and fresh, original impressions that has never been equalled.   Lamb lived all his life in London, and found his inspiration in its busy work-a-day life; but it was true inspiration, and the work he produced has a fineness and flavor inseparable from the gift of genius.   Lamb has given to English literature some of the most exquisite pictures of child-life ever produced. The most famous among them are *Dream Children*, the *Child Angel*, and *Rosamund Gray*, creations which he called out from the shadowy world of dream and vision, giving to them a place and name that is loved and cherished by all lovers of literature.

Apart from the great body of miscellaneous writers who have made it remarkable, the century is particularly rich in the possession of some of the greatest writers in fiction and poetry. The most famous writers of fiction, after Scott, are Bulwer, Thackeray, Dickens, and George Eliot, though such names as Jane Austen, George Meredith, and others stand scarcely lower on the roll of distinction.

Bulwer, who was raised to the peerage as Lord Lytton, in recognition of his services to his political party, was born in 1805, the year in which Scott published his first volume of poems. His novels are mainly of two kinds, those founded upon historical events or upon some strange belief in certain hidden laws of nature, and those founded upon incidents of domestic life.

Bulwer's best-known novels of domestic life are *The Caxtons* and *My Novel*, in which he follows the traditions of the English school of novel writing as founded by the great novelists of the eighteenth century. These novels show him at the highest point of his art. *Rienzi*, a story of Italy in the fourteenth century, is one of the finest of Bulwer's historical works. It is a splendid picture of the old Roman days,

which it called back to life, and is full of that
dramatic interest which Bulwer introduced with
such fine effect in his historical novels. *The
Last Days of Pompeii* is founded upon the destruction of Pompeii by the eruption of Vesu-
vius, in the year 79 A.D.   This strange event,
by which one of the most famous Italian cities
was buried for eighteen hundred years, was
made by Bulwer the subject of a story so
thrilling and dramatic, that in reading it one
feels as if he were really wandering back into
the past, which the writer re-created and peopled with forms of life. *Harold* and the *Last
of the Barons* are novels founded upon English
history, and are brilliant pictures of those old
days when England was making its way to
greatness. *Harold* has for its hero the last of
the Saxon kings.   It is a reproduction of that
stormy spirit of the times which witnessed the
Norman conquest and the apparent death of
English liberty, and the character of Harold is
so well drawn that it seems to sum up in itself
all the heroism and despair of that fateful hour
of England's history.   The *Last of the Barons*

has for its hero Warwick, known as the king-maker during the Wars of the Roses, one of the most celebrated characters in English history. Like *Harold*, it is a representative picture of the times it describes, and is marked by the same dramatic force and vigor.

The most famous of Bulwer's novels that deal with the experiences that are called supernatural are *Zanoni* and *A Strange Story*. These stories both reveal Bulwer as a dreamer and a mystic, as well as a student of certain laws of nature which are little understood. The most celebrated of his remaining works are *Eugene Aram* and *Ernest Maltravers*, both of which show his peculiar genius at its best.

Mary Ann Evans, who wrote under the name of George Eliot, is the most celebrated woman in the history of English fiction. Her novels are in every sense novels of character, and are strong studies of the struggle between good and evil which takes place in every human heart. George Eliot found the materials for her books sometimes in the puritanic honesty of middle-class English people, sometimes in the strange and vital individuality which has preserved the Jewish national and race spirit through all the ages that have witnessed the rise and fall of other nations, and sometimes in the pictures of heroism and self-denial which are found in the lives of the mediæval monks; but wherever she turned for inspiration the result was always the same: the story of the human soul in its desires and aspirations, and in this sense her works possess an interest found only in the greatest writers of fiction or of the drama. Her success is all the more remarkable as she never depends upon outside circumstances in producing her effects. The stories of her heroes and heroines resemble more closely the spiritual struggles of Bunyan as described in *Grace Abounding* than anything else in English literature. Indeed, it might be said that George Eliot is Bunyan's literary successor, who has put into the form of fiction the same warfare of the soul that thrills through the pages of *Pilgrim's Progress*. Her best known books are *Adam Bede*, by which she first gained her fame ; *Middlemarch*, a description of English middle-class life, which contains some of the best examples of the development of character ; the *Mill on the Floss*, whose first pages contain a remarkable description of child life ; *Romola*, a study of Italy in the times of the great reformer Savonarola ; *Daniel Deronda*, a picture of modern Hebrew character in its finest form ; and *Silas Marner*, an exquisite little story of an old miser who was won back to manhood by the love of a little child.

Charles Dickens, who among other distinctions is the novelist of child-life, was born at Landport, in Hampshire, in 1812. He was the son of a government clerk, and two years after his birth his family moved to London, and thence to Chatham dockyard, where Dickens began his school life, and where he lived until his tenth year. The father of Dickens was poor and the family life was of the simplest kind, but the home held a little library of good books, *The Vicar of Wakefield*, *Robinson*

Crusoe, some novels of Fielding and Smollett, and the *Tatler, Spectator*, and *Idler* among them, and over these books Dickens pored many an hour. A boy cousin also took him sometimes to the theatre, and once spent much precious vacation time in getting up private theatricals, and this experience, together with the inspiration he received from his reading, prompted Dickens to take to writing himself. So he wrote a play, a tragedy called *The Sultan of India*, and no doubt the production brought much joy to the hearts of him and his boy friends.

This was a happy and careless period of life, but it did not last. The family removed back to London, and as the father was unlucky in business, the burden of poverty grew so heavy that in a few months the father was in prison for debt. The mother went to live with the father in prison, and the family was so poor in friends that Dickens was set to earn his living by covering blacking-pots in a shop. He received six shillings a week for wages, and out of this sum he had to support himself and pay lodgings to

the old lady with whom he lived. Those were
dark days for the ten-year-old boy. The home
was entirely broken up; everything had been
pawned or sold; even the precious books did
not escape the general ruin, and Dickens was
lonely enough and sad enough to have been
made the hero of one of his own stories.

Things brightened a little when he removed
to lodgings near the prison and took breakfast
and supper with the family, at which times they
were waited upon by a small serving-maid whom
Dickens afterward converted into one of his
most celebrated characters. As it was a family
trait to look on the bright side of things, the
prison life was not intolerable, and by and by
better days came and the boy had a couple of
years of school life; then he became office boy
in a lawyer's office, and finally, in his seventeenth
year, he became a reporter, having learned
short-hand in the reading-room of the British
Museum.

His career as a writer of fiction began a few
years later, when he contributed some street
sketches to a paper which was too poor to pay

for them. It was in this magazine, in August, 1837, that Dickens first signed the name "Boz" to his contributions. A year later he was regularly employed to supply a number of these sketches to a newspaper, and received good pay for them. The sketches were well liked by the public, and soon afterward appeared in book-form as *Sketches by Boz*.

This led to an offer from a publishing firm for a series of sketches to illustrate a set of comic drawings they were about to issue, and in March, 1836, Dickens gave to the world the first instalment of the famous *Pickwick Papers*, as he had formed the idea of making his sketches relate the adventures of an imaginary club of Londoners during sundry visits to the country. By the time that the sixth number of *Pickwick* was reached, Dickens was famous. He was twenty-five years old, and the world was ready to welcome him as a new writer of a unique genius. The next year Dickens produced his first regular novel, *Oliver Twist*, which appeared monthly in a magazine called "Bentley's Miscellany," of which Dickens had become the editor. *Oliver Twist* struck a new note in fiction, and gave the pitch to the life-work of the author ; for, from this time on, his genius never wavered in his purpose, which was the portrayal of the life of the lower classes and the righting of social wrongs.

Dickens was the first novelist—with philan-thropic motive, at least—who looked below the surface, and brought to view the human side of the uneducated and often degraded lives of those in the lowest rank of society, and showed that this element had ambitions, hopes, fears, and virtues which differed only in degree from those of the upper classes. In fact, he found that man was always interesting as man quite outside of his surroundings, and he proved the truth of his discovery ; for when he gave these pictures of low life to the world he immediately claimed an audience greater than any novelist had ever had since the days of *Robinson Cru-soe.* *Oliver Twist* deals almost entirely with the criminal classes, and contains the story of a young orphan boy whose lot, by a bitter fate, was joined with that of one of the worst characters in London, the miserable Fagin, who kept a training-school for thieves, and whose custom it was to initiate young boys and girls into all kinds of wickedness. These children, whom he picked up here and there, and kept in his power, were his unhappy slaves, and he was their relent-less task-master. All their comfort in life, their food, shelter, and freedom from blows, depended upon their ability in thieving and other dishonest practices. And the story of Oliver, with its despairing note of pathos, runs through the book, till a happier fortune relieves him from his bondage and brings him to the dawn of better things. But this sad story, which was brought to a happy ending by the art of the novelist, was known to be a picture from life, and the suggestion it brought with it touched the heart with strange power. All who read it knew that even then just such children of sorrow were living their unchildlike lives in the filth and wretchedness of London streets, and thus *Oliver Twist* stood for much more than a powerful and tragic story by a new and popular writer. It was in reality the introduction to polite society

25

of a world lying close beside its own, but whose misery and degradation made its inhabitants seem like aliens. Who could think of childhood as wicked, scheming, depraved, and shorn of all the innocence which makes it divine? Yet this was what *Oliver Twist* showed, and the world was forced to think that somehow and somewhere there was a cruel wrong to be righted by those whose happier fate had placed them in pleasanter paths.

In his next novel, *Nicholas Nickleby*, Dickens did more than lay bare the evils of the criminal class, which were the more easily exposed because they were the results of open wrong-doing by people who made no pretence of goodness. In *Nicholas Nickleby* he attacked that class which, while being openly respectable, still treats the unguarded helplessness of childhood in a way that leads to results both physically and morally degrading. In this book he indicts that class of cheap schoolmasters whose schools were only abodes of misery for the unhappy pupils. Here Dickens attacked a very grave social wrong, but he did it in his own way and

used his own weapon, that of good-natured sar-
casm and broad humor, which disarms hostility
and makes of ridicule a two-edged sword. If
half the picture were true, these schools for children of the respectable poor must have been
very prisons for their miserable victims. The
masters were dishonest, mean, and cruel, the
fare was wretched and insufficient, the discipline
aimed only to break the spirit and develop
craven heartedness, cheating, and lying. In
Nicholas Nickleby the character Smike, the unfortunate and unhappy, is made to represent the
victims of this demoralizing system. Smike is
a most powerful example of the miserable children whose only idea of home was found in these
schools. He is wretched, ill-treated, starved,
and his moral nature dragged into depths of
abject slavery. Because of his utter helplessness, utter innocence, and the undeserved misery
of his fate, Smike stands as one of the most
pathetic of Dickens's pictures of unhappy childhood.

In *Dombey and Son*, Dickens has given us
another view of child life, and shown us how a

child may be poor in other things than money
or home and friends. Little Paul Dombey is
the only son of his father, who has such a desire
to perpetuate his fame and achievements in life,
that as soon as the child is born his name is
joined with that of his father over the door of
the great warehouse where the business is carried on. Henceforth it is "Dombey and Son,"
and the poor little junior partner is one of
Dickens's best loved and most pathetic characters. He is simple-hearted, affectionate, and
cares only to be loved, but his father wishes
him to become a prosperous business man, a
duplicate in fact of his pompous self, and so the
battle of life begins early for little Paul. He is
taught only that he must grow up and be a man
like his father, and that to obtain a partnership
in the firm is the greatest ambition in life.
When he is five years old his father talks to
him as if he were grown, and is horrified if the
child shows a fondness for anything childlike.
At six he is sent to school to learn Latin and
Greek, and mathematics, and the creed that his
father is the greatest man in the world. No

pains are spared, no money is withheld to make
this child a fit heir to the Dombey greatness.
But little Paul could not live up to this expecta-
tion. At six years of age he still persisted in
remaining a child, with the ambitions and lik-
ings of a child, and thought more of the stories
his sister told him as he sat on her knee than
of all the glory that should come to him as heir
of the Dombey name. Yet, still he wished to
please his father whom he loved, and tried to
master the hard lessons in grammar and mathematics when his mind was full of visions of the
dream-world of childhood instead, and the trees
and winds were whispering the secrets that only childhood knows, and when the great sea
moaned out its sad stories that darkened his
eyes with tears, and brought to him hints of
other worlds than his own ; even sometimes of
that world farthest away of all, where dwelt the
mother who had drifted away from life when
little Paul was born.

And so somehow, between this conflict of
what he wanted and what his father thought
best for him, little Paul himself found the bur-

den of life too hard for his little weak shoulders. And one day he slipped it off, and went away to that beautiful world of his dreams of which the sea had often sung to him, and found his mother waiting for him with eyes of love, and left behind him only his poor little wasted body to remind his father that the firm "Dombey and Son" had ever existed. It is a sad story of misunderstood childhood, and shows Dickens in one of his most poetic moods, one in which he grasped the depth and significance of a child's heart as few poets are capable of doing.

One of the most popular of Dickens's books is *David Copperfield*, which is written in the form of an autobiography, and which is supposed to contain many reminiscences of the author's own life. In this book occur some of the most famous of the Dickens characters. David Copperfield himself worked in a factory at ten years of age, just as Dickens did, and his unhappy life in the company of his rude companions at his work reveals what Dickens might have suffered himself when he was a lad employed in pasting blacking-pots. Here too comes in the famous Peggotty, friend and nurse of David's childhood, whose tales charmed his childish ears, and whose love was the one bright spot in his life after his mother's death, when he was set to earn his own living. The visit of David to the boat-house where lived Peggotty's brother and her niece, "little Em'ly," and her nephew, Ham, is full of the quaint, homely fascination so irresistible to children. What delight to live in a boat which is a real boat, though moored fast so that it cannot drift off and drown one in the night! How blissful to hear the waves beat and the winds blow against the sides, and to recall all of Peggotty's most blood-curdling tales, and yet to know that one is snug and warm, and Peggotty herself just outside the door busy about some act of kindness. And then the walks upon the beach with "little Em'ly," and their talks about all the wonders of life, under the light of the solemn stars which the children feared yet loved. It is a pretty picture, and the reader of Dickens lingers over it lovingly, feeling that this bit of child romance is too sweet and pure ever to fade away into the region of forget-fulness.

In this book, too, are the Micawbers, with whom David lives while working in the factory after his mother's death. They are always out of luck, they are eternally in debt, but, neverthe·less, they smile serenely in the hope of better days. David shares their joys and sorrows, and their suppers when they have any. He lends them money out of his paltry wages, car-ries their teaspoons to the pawnbroker's, and is as sure as they are that a bright future awaits this remarkable family. It is pleasant to know that when David Copperfield had grown to be a rising young author, with the prospect of a happy life before him, the Micawbers really did come into the good fortune that they had so confidently expected, that Mr. Micawber paid all his old and numerous debts, and that like the people in a fairy story they were happy for-evermore.

In *Bleak House*, one of his greatest works, Dickens deals with the long and cruel delays of the law in settling up estates. The chancery suits, as they were called, were a great blot upon the administration of the law, and often whole estates were swallowed up in the expenses caused by years of delay, and not a penny would be left for the rightful heirs. In his book Dickens took the imaginary case of " Jarndyce and Jarndyce " to illustrate the injustice of this system, and the story is an eloquent protest against such wrong. Besides this idea, the story contains one of the most powerful tragedies of domestic life, and brings in incidentally a number of the most famous of the characters of Dickens. Among these is poor Jo, the little street Arab, who has no home, no friends, no happiness in life, and whose only knowledge of the civilization of which the English nation boasts comes from the policemen, who are continually telling him to " move on " when his weary little body seeks refuge in some doorway. The story of poor Jo is one of the saddest, because it is one of the most truthful, that Dickens ever told. Anyone familiar with London streets could see the original of this poor little hero, ragged, starved, utterly friendless and alone, and who never knows what human sympathy means until he lies dying. Then, indeed, the kind-hearted young surgeon who attends him redeems the world for Jo and makes it seem a place not wholly bad, though even then there has been so little good in his life that the child is very willing to close his eyes and leave it behind him forever.

Among his other works Dickens produced a series of tales from year to year, called the Christmas Stories. The first of these, *A Christmas Carol*, appeared in 1843, and for a number of years one story of this kind appeared every year. The most celebrated of the Christmas stories besides the *Christmas Carol* are *The Cricket on the Hearth* and *The Chimes*. In these stories Dickens did much more than give to the world novel and interesting tales of domestic life. He really introduced a new and beautiful spirit of Christmastide which taught its own sweet lesson of peace and goodwill. And that this was needed was shown by the wave of Christmas cheer which began to sweep over the land, and which makes the English Christmas the happy, jolly, merry time of loving and giving that it was in the old days of Father Christmas, King Misrule, and the other saints whom the Puritans of Milton's day tried in vain to dethrone. In the *Christmas Carol* comes the character of Tiny Tim, the little cripple, whose father is clerk in a counting-house with just enough salary to keep his family from starvation. But poor as they were, there was always a little family feast on Christmas-day, and the description of this holiday when Tiny Tim rides home from church on his father's back, and of the roast goose and plum pudding and general joy which followed, shows Dickens in one of his most sympathetic moods. It is a story full of cheer and happy suggestion ; and the story of the miser Scrooge, who is won back to his better nature by a dream in which his selfishness and miserliness are seen in their true light, and who thenceforth becomes an ideal friend to the poor, is one of Dickens's happiest conceptions. From that Christmas-day Scrooge is a different man. His friends know it, and his business acquaintances, and the nephew whom he has always snubbed because he was poor, and the clerks whose salaries he raises. And as one of these clerks was Bob Cratchitt, Tiny Tim's father, there was unlimited rejoicing in that family, and Tiny Tim well expressed their joy and thankfulness when he said, " God bless us, every one," in honor of the never-to-be-forgotten day.

The most celebrated perhaps of all Dickens's child characters is that of little Nell in *The Old Curiosity Shop*. Little Nell is the granddaughter of the keeper of a little shop where all sorts of odd and curious things may be found for sale. The picture of the fair, blue-eyed, delicate child standing among the suits of rusty mail, odd china figures, and fantastic carvings in wood, iron, and ivory, is very striking. It at once makes the character seem far off and unreal, as if belonging to another world than that of workaday London, and this atmosphere surrounds little Nell to the end. She is a being of another sphere from that in which her companions live, and her life only touches theirs as a beautiful and holy influence, which they but dimly feel and cannot understand. Little Nell was happy enough with her grandfather, until the old man took to gambling in the hope of winning a great fortune, and then all her troubles began. Night after night the grandfather went to gambling dens and lost all the money he could get from his poor little business or by borrowing, until at last the little shop lost all its wares, the household furniture was pawned, and there was nothing left in the world for the child and her grandfather save the love which still lay between them, and which no loss could impair. Then leaving London and all its false hopes and bitter disappointments far behind, they started out to seek a new home in a new place, walking everywhere, for they had no money. And then Little Nell learned many things of life. She learned first that London, with its miles of streets and thick black, smoky air, was only a tiny part of the great world outside, and that this new world had delights which even the richest of London folk could not have. Here were fair skies, and green trees, and gay flowers which she might pick and call her very own. Here were quiet rivers where little boats glided to and fro as if the world were taking a holiday. And as they walked through this quiet and peaceful world her grandfather was as happy as she, so that life seemed very good and beautiful to her. They wandered miles and miles from London, and had many strange experiences. They were often weary, sometimes hungry, but never unhappy, and their love for each other was like a bright star even in their darkest hours. Other wanderers overtook them and joined their fortunes to theirs for a little while, and this seemed but natural, for it appeared as if the whole world had gone gypsying. Sometimes they were in danger from association with bad men who tried to work them evil. Once Little Nell became assistant to the renowned Mrs. Jarley, who travelled through the country exhibiting her collection of wax figures to village folk and young ladies' schools. And again they were entertained by a kindly schoolmaster, whose little home seemed a paradise to these homeless ones. The best of it all was that Little Nell never went back to the horrors of London. Her little wandering feet brought her after awhile to a little sleepy village whose pavements were worn with time, and where a ruined church and neglected grave-yard filled the air with memories of far-away days. Beyond the village lay fields, and woods, and pastures with wide spaces of sky above them, making the village itself seem more shad-owy and sleepy still. And here Little Nell folded her hands together one day, after some weeks of pleasant rest, and shut her eyes to all earthly sight, as a flower might close its petals, and they laid her in the shade of the little church which she had learned to love, and where she slept so peacefully after her long journey that all who loved her could only be glad that she had found this rest at last.

The most celebrated of Dickens's other books are *Martin Chuzzlewit*, a story of American life, *A Tale of Two Cities*, a story founded on the French Revolution, *Great Expectations*, and *Barnaby Rudge*. Dickens was also the foun·

der and editor of a magazine called *All the Year Round.*

The great fault of Dickens lay in his habit of exaggeration. Nearly every character that he touched was thus either slightly caricatured or slightly idealized from its natural type, a fault which mars his art throughout. In this he differs from, and is a lesser artist than his contemporaries George Eliot and Thackeray, whose characters will exist for all time as types of mankind. But though Dickens was seldom the perfect artist, his genius was so great that he easily holds his place as one of the masters of modern fiction; and his devotion to his work and the consecration of his talents to the uplifting of his unfortunate fellow-men must forever stamp him as one of the greatest humanitarians as well as one of the most popular writers in English literature.

William Makepeace Thackeray, the greatest English novelist of the nineteenth century, was born at Calcutta, India, in 1811. When he was seven years old he was sent to England and became a pupil at the famous Charterhouse school, which he ever afterward loved. Here he showed a fondness for drawing, and amused himself and his fellow - students by making caricatures of the persons and events connected with their school life. After he entered Cambridge he became the editor of a weekly paper called the *Snob*, published by the students, and contributed to one of the numbers a parody on the poem for which Tennyson, a fellow-student, had received a prize from the university.

His connection with the *Snob*, however, meant nothing more to Thackeray than the fun of the moment, as he had planned to become an artist, thinking that his power lay in that direction, and he left Cambridge without taking his degree, and went abroad to study art. He travelled over Europe, seeing many of the great cities, studying in Paris and Rome, visiting the great German poet Goethe at Weimar, and filling his portfolios with sketches and caricatures of all the quaint, odd, and interesting things that came in his way. Pictures he did not

26

paint. He was always intending to do it, but the time for beginning was always delayed. During these years, however, when it seemed doubtful if he would ever settle down to serious work of any kind, Thackeray was laying up stores of priceless knowledge. He was a born student of human nature, and this contact with men and things was the best education he could have had. His keen gaze saw men as they were, while his broad and generous heart could also measure accurately the conditions and circumstances which made them so, and thus he was able to sum up their worth honestly and truthfully.

While, therefore, he thought he was studying art, he was really studying human nature with the directness and skill with which a physician studies the human body. When a man finds his greatest pleasure in analyzing and tracing the motives that prompt men's actions, and the results that spring therefrom, and when he feels tolerably sure that he can read the story of the human heart as one reads a tale from a book, he does not become a painter.

He becomes a writer. Thackeray became a novelist.

He began in a very humble way, and his inborn love of fun prompted him at first to enter the field of literature rather as a witty humorist than anything else. He published in a magazine two stories of Irish life, *Barry Lyndon* and *The Great Hoggarty Diamond*. These stories, which appeared over the name of Michael Angelo Titmarsh, together with some burlesques, art criticisms, and humorous sketches, introduced Thackeray to the public as a new writer, but no one dreamed that the greatest novelist since Fielding had appeared.

Thackeray's literary career was one of honor and success, and the reputation which soon came to him grew brighter and brighter as the years went on. His greatest novels are *Vanity Fair*, the publication of which placed him among the greatest English novelists, *Pendennis*, *Henry Esmond*, and *The Newcomes*, though he wrote a number of novels of lesser importance, as well as sketches, ballads, and the charming fairy story, *The Rose and the*

Ring, which show the same careful touch that distinguishes his masterpieces.

Thackeray dealt with the conditions of city life, and with the life of the middle and upper classes. He describes chiefly that world whose dwellers have been born to the heritage of refinement, education, and position in life, and thus his art is in striking contrast to that of Dickens, who found his characters in the lower walks of society. Thackeray looked below the surface of education, refinement, and gentle birth, and found that the motives which governed the life of the upper world did not greatly differ from those which influenced the lower class, and that the heart of polite society was little, if any, nobler than that which beat in the breast of the uneducated masses. There was the same cruelty of selfishness, the same moral weakness, the same yielding to, rather than conquering, untoward circumstances; of course there were heroes in this upper world, but then there were also heroes in the lower. His studies made him a teacher, and beneath all his brilliant pictures of life one sees a hand that guides to higher things. And in his teaching Thackeray used that most powerful weapon of all, satire. But it was not the satire of Swift, pointed with ire and weighted with bitterness ; it was the satire of the friend who sees the remedy with the disease, and finds the best foe of evil in that principle of good which is eternal in the human heart. Thackeray's satire therefore is genial and healthful, with a ring of hopefulness in it. This, with his inexhaustible humor, his keen insight, and broad humanity, make up his character as a novelist.

CHAPTER XII.

The nineteenth century, great as it is in prose, is quite as great in poetry, and has produced a long list of famous verse writers. The poets of this century fall naturally into groups according to the period in which they lived, the first group including the poets Byron, Shelley, and Keats, whose genius alone would have made the century remarkable ; the second group includes the men who are known as the Lake Poets, and to the third belong the poets of the latter part of the century.

Byron was born in London on the 22d of January, 1788, but spent his early childhood in Aberdeen, where he and his mother lived almost in poverty. Under other conditions, this life, far away from the strife of the great world, might have been a time of happy growth for the future poet; but from his birth Byron was the victim of unhappy circumstances. His mother was a woman of violent and ungovernable temper, and at one moment she would caress the child passionately, while the next might witness one of those fierce struggles of temper between mother and son which, even in those early years, darkened and embittered the home life. They were poor, too, and their poverty was considered a reproach by both mother and son, while a slight lameness caused Byron such agonies of mental suffering that there is no doubt his whole nature was warped by brooding over this defect. Thus from the first Byron's soul was clouded by false ideas of life, and outward conditions were allowed to hinder all healthy growth.

When he was eleven years of age he inherited the title and estates of his grand-uncle, Lord Byron, and this change of fortune took him and his mother back to England and to Newstead Abbey, the family seat, not far away from famous Sherwood Forest.   In this district, ringing still with the echoes of the early notes of English song, Byron spent perhaps the happiest hours of his life.   The stress of poverty was removed, his school-days at Dulwich and Harrow were, on the whole, pleasantly passed, and above all it was the period when the first hint of the poet's gift came to him, though the verses he then wrote showed little trace of the genius which developed later.

From Harrow he went to Cambridge, in his fourteenth year, and two years afterward published his first volume of poems, a collection of verses such as any clever, poetic boy might have written.   They would hardly deserve mention, except from the fact that they were criticised so severely by the " Edinburgh Review " that Byron, in a passion of revenge, wrote in their defence a furious satire called *English Bards and Scotch Reviewers*.   It was this satire which first brought him into popular notice, and which first showed his mastery in versification, and his keen and subtle wit.   This event, too, first showed Byron his own power, and it is not unlikely that it decided him to choose a literary career.

After leaving Cambridge, Byron went abroad and made a long tour of countries then but little known to English society. He visited Greece, Turkey, and other countries of the East, and his impressions of these remote places were given to the world in a series of brilliant poems which took the public by storm. These poems were tales of people and countries whose history was as full of picturesque incident as that of Scotland, and Byron, by the power of his genius, carried the romantic poem to a height never reached by any other English poet. Scott had awakened a love for romantic poetry, and was, indeed, the founder of the new school which won its way so quickly to favor. But Byron crowned the work of Scott with a genius so splendid that it is his name which shines above every other in the department of poetical romance.

He returned to England from the East and for a time found himself the lion of the day, but domestic trouble soon drove him abroad again, and from that time his life was spent in foreign lands, Switzerland and Italy being his favorite haunts. The history and scenery of these countries he immortalized in a series of poems that are unique in English literature.

Byron's life during all these years was wild and lawless, so that the world was constantly divided in its opinions of him, some excusing his faults because of his great genius, and others blaming him all the more severely because his splendid talent was so often lost and misdirected by his foolish life.

Later on his love of adventure and his great power of sympathy led him to adopt the cause of the Greeks, who were then struggling with Turkey for their independence. Byron threw his life and fortune into their service. He became the idol of the Greek army, and by his practical skill aided the Greek commanders in bringing their troops into fine military order. But the unhealthy climate soon affected his health, and three months after his arrival in Greece he died at Missolonghi, of marsh fever, at the age of thirty-six. The Greek patriots

mourned for him as for one of their own chieftains, and his name will ever be associated
with the cause of Greek liberty.

Among the principal poems of Byron are
*Childe Harold, Don Juan, The Giaour, The
Bride of Abydos, Manfred, The Prisoner of
Chillon, The Siege of Corinth, Mazeppa,* and
Cain, though the list is so long that it is hard
to choose from. Besides his long poems he
also left some exquisite lyrics, among them
the beautiful *Hebrew Melodies,* which are so
touched with pathetic reminiscence that they
sound like a refrain echoing from the long-past
days of Jerusalem's glory.

Childe Harold, Byron's longest poem except
one, and the one which brought him greatest
fame in his life, is a descriptive poem of the different places visited by Byron during his life
on the Continent. In this poem Byron brought
in the manners and customs of the people as
well as some of the important events of their
history. His magnificent powers of description, the newness of the subject, and the romantic charm of the old stories so seized upon

his English readers that *Childe Harold* became to them a living person, and the places thus described — the battle-field of Waterloo, the castles of the Rhine, the Swiss lakes and mountains, the wooded slopes of the Apennines, the Bridge of Sighs, and the Coliseum—were hereafter forever associated with the name of Byron.

In *The Prisoner of Chillon* Byron tells an old story, from the times when Switzerland was fighting for her liberty.   One of the greatest of the Swiss patriots was Bonnivard, who was imprisoned for three years in the Château of Chillon, and Byron, with the poet's skill, arrays before us in the poem all the incidents of that dreadful period; so that we see again the gloomy dungeon far beneath the level of the lake, the damp walls, the barred windows, the columns rising like shadows through the dusk, and the prisoner, chained and helpless, living to see all his companions die one by one before his eyes.

The Giaour, The Bride of Abydos, The Siege of Corinth, and *The Corsair*, are tales from Turkish life and are among the best of Byron's poems. *Mazeppa* is the story of a young page who, for his daring in loving a lady of higher rank than his own, was lashed to the back of his horse and driven from his country into the land of his enemies, who finally rescued him and became his friends. *Manfred*, a dramatic poem, is a story founded upon one of those legends of the Alps in which the hero, Manfred, holds communication with the unseen spirits, which are supposed to lead him at last to his death. *Cain* is a dramatic poem founded upon the Bible story of Cain and Abel, and thrown into the form of one of the old mystery plays. Like *Manfred*, it is one of the most powerful of all of Byron's productions.

Percy Bysshe Shelley, the eldest son of Sir Timothy Shelley, was born at Field Place, Sussex, in 1792. Unlike that of Byron, his childhood was happy and healthy, and in his comfortable country home, with the companion-ship of his sisters, the boy led a pleasant life up to his eighth year. But when he entered the great public school at Eton, Shelley began that struggle with life which never ended until his death, and in which his best time and strength were wasted. For Shelley, like Byron, refused to acknowledge any higher authority than his own will, and claimed that each man should lead his own life as seemed best to him, without regard to all the laws of the state or society.

And his first quarrel with the world came at Eton, where he refused to fag. Fagging had always been a pet institution at Eton, and the pupils regarded fagging and being fagged with the greatest veneration. But Shelley pronounced it brutal and refused to submit to it, and this unheard-of independence at once brought him into trouble. His school-fellows began persecuting him as only school-boys could, and Shelley suffered as only a high-minded, sensitive boy could suffer from their brutal jokes and malicious tyranny. But he remained the victor morally, and perhaps it was this experience in his school life which developed so strongly in him the hatred of authority and law.

At Oxford, Shelley kept up the same spirit of opposition to all established customs, and it is not strange to find that he was at last expelled with the reputation of one whose views of life were dangerous to his fellow-students, and whose peculiarities—such as refusing all food but dry bread for days together, throwing stones, sailing paper boats, and other childish amusements—showed perhaps that his mind was not altogether right. Shelley was then seventeen years old, and his expulsion from Oxford was really his entrance into the world, as he never returned again to his father's house and five years after went to live in Italy. During the last part of his college life he published a volume of poems, but this collection gave no hint of his great genius. And the next work that he did, a long poem called *Queen Mab*, was printed only for private circulation.

But almost immediately after this Shelley began his real work for English literature by the composition of poem after poem of such beauty and power that he must ever stand among the greatest of English poets.

As in the case of Byron, the poetry of Shelley suffered from his unusual views of life, and from the troubles that came from holding such views. But unlike Byron, Shelley did not always put himself into his poems and draw pictures of his own sufferings. Instead, he wrote poems which showed his heroes suffering from the unjust laws of the state, or religion, or custom, and in which he endeavored to picture a state of happiness which would follow the making of newer and better laws.

All of Shelley's long poems, *Queen Mab*, the *Revolt of Islam*, *Hellas*, *Alastor*, the *Witch of Atlas* and *Prometheus Unbound*, were written in revolt against what he considered the shams of society. And with the exception of *Prometheus Unbound*, none of them rank among his finest work, though all have parts of exquisite beauty and perfection.

In *Prometheus Unbound* Shelley reached the highest point of his art, for it was a great subject treated by a master hand. For though it was written in the same spirit which prompted the others, the idea here was one which has appealed to the best minds in all ages. In the old Greek myth, Prometheus, the light-bearer, who gave to man the priceless gift of fire, was represented as bound by adamantine chains to the rocky mountains of Caucasus, as a punishment for his sin against the great gods who wished to keep mankind in helpless slavery. And this story, with its mystical suggestion of self-sacrifice for the sake of truth, is one which the poets of all ages have loved to dwell upon. Æschylus, the greatest of the old Greek dramatists, put it in immortal verse. And to Shelley, whose heart was ever tossed by doubt and unrest, the strong, beautiful thought was the means of one of his greatest inspirations.

In his poem he represents Prometheus as freed from his fetters by the power of Truth, and a victor over the deities who chained him. The poem was written in the dramatic form, and in it Shelley showed such mastery over sublime and beautiful imagery, and invested the character of Prometheus with such heroic grandeur, that the *Prometheus Unbound* took rank with many critics as the greatest poem that had

27

appeared since the *Paradise Lost*. But though *Prometheus Unbound* is the grandest creation of Shelley's genius, it is by his minor poems that he is best known to most readers.

In these poems Shelley seems to have loosened his restless spirit from the wearying cares of earth, to let it soar upward and find rest in the great heart of nature. So exquisite are they, that they seem but transcriptions of the varying, beautiful moods and expressions of the outer world, and they rank among the most perfect lyrics in the English tongue.

In *To a Skylark, The Cloud, The Sensitive Plant, Ode to the West Wind*, and other lyrics, we have the very spirit of melody, motion, and power transmuted into the poet's song. And it is these minor poems which show Shelley the companion and lover of nature, who understands her changing moods, her different voices, and her divine teachings. Here he is the true poet, uplifting and inspiring, and it is in this department that his genius wrought its greatest work for English literature, and that he becomes in so great measure the inspiration of the great poets who succeeded him.

One of the last written of his poems is also one of the best, the elegy called *Adonais*, on the death of the poet Keats. In this poem the lament is so tender, the pathos so sincere, and the melody so exquisite, that Shelley seems to have culled the most perfect flower of his song to immortalize the memory of his brother-poet. In form it is one of the finest elegies in English literature, and in view of the sad fate of Keats, it is perhaps the one held nearest the hearts of all lovers of English verse.

At the age of thirty, a few months after the completion of *Adonais*, Shelley was drowned in the Gulf of Spezzia while sailing with a friend from Leghorn. His body was burned in the presence of Lord Byron and other English friends, and the ashes were then carried to Rome and deposited in the Protestant cemetery, which contains also the grave of Keats.

When Byron was eight and Shelley four years of age, a child was born in the family of a groom living in Moorfields, London, who was destined to share in their honor of creating a new poetic literature for England. This was John Keats, of whose childhood little is known except that it was in the main happy and comfortable, though his family was poor, and he was but one of several children to be provided for. We know, indeed, that Keats had a loving mother to guide his early years, and that he returned her affection with a passionate love far beyond that shown by most children. And we know that the little home, with its humble surroundings, so guarded and cherished the ideal of family love that the future poet ever kept its memory in his heart as one of the most beautiful gifts that life had brought him. But beyond this, up to his fifteenth year, very little is known about Keats's early life.

But that matters little, for Keats came into the world with one of those natures that seem to be independent of all outward circumstances. He was an idealist, and a dreamer of dreams; one who lived always in a world of his own, and peopled it with thoughts and fancies that had no place in the life around him.   And in this beautiful world of unreality he grew and flourished, and did not know that he missed anything that wealth or position might have brought. And yet, if there were ever anything strange about genius, it would be strange to find this child of the poor, humbly bred, and far removed from the great world of literature and art, destined above all the other poets of England to weave into its literature those immortal forms of beauty which gave to it a grace never possessed before.

For Keats is the poet of beauty always. The whole world to him was a vision such as was revealed to the old Greeks, who placed beauty above every other thing, and he is in this way connected more closely with the first great poets of the world than any other writer. In Shelley's poetry one feels that the poet sought refuge in the ideal to free himself from the disappointments of the actual world.   In Keats one is made to feel that there is but one world, the world of beauty, and that this with its divine meanings is the true abode of man.   This sentiment is so much a part of him that he is often thought of as belonging as much to the antique Greek world of art as to the present day.

Keats became a poet very young, and when only eighteen published a volume of verses. This volume, however, brought him into no notice, and, indeed, except for its promise of better things, does not indicate the great genius of the author. But a year later he brought out another volume, and though this collection showed the presence of a new poet in England, it was the hostile criticism it received which first brought Keats widely into public notice. In this second volume was incorporated the poem *Endymion*, one of the best known of Keats's poems, and the one which attracted such harsh censure that its history has become a part of English literature.

Endymion is the story of the love of the goddess Diana for the shepherd youth Endymion, as told in the old Greek myths, and into the retelling of it Keats put all the fire and force of a nature just awakened to the knowledge of

its own gifts; so that the story became new, as
if he had brought back to life the very forms
and scenes which had become a part of Grecian
mythology thousands of years before. And this
Keats could do, because that old world did exist
for him, and he lived in it, and thought in it, and
wrought in it as the old Greeks themselves had
done. And so his poem had life and vigor and
reality, and this is what gives it its place as a
new creation in art, even though its beauty is
marred by faults.

But to the England of 1819 *Endymion* appeared as the folly of an obscure boy who
thought that fine language and picturesque description could pass for live poetry. *The Quar-
terly Review*, one of the leading critical journals,
attacked the poem in a bitter article that noticed
only the blemishes, and passed quite over the
spirit which set the poem apart from anything
of its kind that had yet appeared; and this un-
fair criticism was almost the first notice that the
literary world received of the advent of the new
poet.

To Keats himself the unjust criticism brought

such a shock as he was little able to endure, for his health had been poor for a long time, and thus the blow was much harder to bear. But in spite of the faults to be found in this volume, and of the hostility of the powerful critics who attacked it, its publication gained Keats some friends among those who were well suited to judge of its merits, and who saw in it the promise of a true poet.

Two years afterward, in his twenty-fifth year, Keats published his third and last book of poems, in which his genius seems to have reached its full flower. It is these last poems which give Keats a unique place among the greatest English poets, and which show us how great a loss to English literature was his early death. Among these poems are *The Eve of St. Agnes*, a love poem remarkable for its rich coloring, *Lamia, Isabella, or the Pot of Basil,* six great odes, and the fragment called *Hyperion*. If Keats did not attain his highest point in *Hyperion*, he showed in it his greatest promise, though it is unfinished and is indeed but a small portion of what was to have been a long poem. In this poem Keats intended to relate the story of the Titan, Hyperion, and his war with and victory over the sun-god, Apollo, as related in the Greek myth. The story was only begun by Keats in the fragment that he has left, but we are able to judge from this what the remainder might have been. *Hyperion* is characterized by such strength and nobility that it is easy to see in it the marks of highest genius, and had Keats lived it is more than probable that English literature would have been enriched by another great epic.

In his lyric poems Keats ranks with the greatest of English poets. His *Ode to a Nightingale* and *Ode on a Grecian Urn*, are particularly celebrated for their exquisite melody and insight, and indeed all his odes are so touched by the unique charm of his genius that it seems almost as if here he stood alone. And this is true of almost every poem in the volume last published by Keats. And as this volume was the crowning of his work as a poet, we can see how Keats has come to be regarded as the poet above all others who has infused into English literature the spirit of the old Greeks. Keats not only added to English literature his own beautiful work, but he has been one of the greatest influences in the development of later English poets.

The greatest poets since his day have turned to him for inspiration, and his own spirit has so diffused itself through the works of his successors that he may be said to have left an impression upon English verse which can never fade away, and which is as immortal as his own immortal poems. But while Keats was thus giving to the world these flowers of song, his life was most miserable and unhappy, for he was burdened with care and striving with a wearing disease. So there will ever hang about these last poems the sadness of his life, bringing back with subtle pathos the picture of the young poet singing his songs so bravely while the beauty of this world was fading from his sight. The last months of his life were spent in Italy, whither he had gone in search of health. His friend, Joseph Severn, a young artist of great promise, accompanied him on this journey, and it was his devotion which brought the only ray of light into the last days of the young poet. Severn was poor too, like Keats, and the two had many a bitter struggle with poverty, even in that last painful illness. But through it all Severn was ever the thoughtful, care-taking, loving brother who sought to make his love a shield between his friend and the dark shadows which clouded him. There is, in all literature, no picture so touching as that which shows us Severn in his devotion to the young poet who lay dying, disappointed in every earthly wish, and with the bitter remembrance that even his work had not yet won any place in the world.

"Write on my tomb-stone—'Here lies one whose name was writ in water'"—he said to Severn in the gloom of those last days. And this was done, and may be still read on the stone that marks the grave. But Severn lived to see this bitter prophecy quite blotted out by the fame which crowned his friend's name, and which placed him among the best loved of English poets.

These three poets, Byron, Shelley, and Keats, with a fourth, Walter Savage Landor, one of the greatest of English poets and whose work is also deeply imbued with the Greek spirit, form the first group of the nineteenth century poets. The next group was composed of men who were very closely connected by the ties of friendship. And because the foremost of the group spent most of his life in the English lake district, it was called the Lake School. This group of poets did not form a new school of poetry, for although they were connected by social ties, and by their sympathy with the religious and political reforms which were then attracting the attention of Europe, their work differed so widely that hardly a trace of the influence of one mind upon another can be discovered.

Wordsworth, the founder of the school, and one of the greatest of England's poets, was born at Cockermouth, Cumberlandshire, in 1770, and it is his poetry particularly which has conferred lasting fame upon the English lake region. From his earliest years, when he was at school at Hawkshead, in the most beautiful part of Lancashire, to the end of his life, Wordsworth was the lover and apostle of the world of nature in a sense that no other English poet has ever been. Other poets have sung the beauty of the outside world, for all great English poets were lovers of nature, but to Wordsworth seemed to belong an insight and comprehension which set him apart from the rest. Chaucer brings before us the beauties of nature with a dewy sense of freshness that seems a part of the beauty itself, and from this old singer down to the present day poets have interpreted the varying moods and graces of the natural world with loving sight and tender touch. But Wordsworth not only saw the external beauty which dazzled his brother poets, and felt the subtle charm which rang through the murmur of the brook, or the song of the lark high in the sky, he saw and felt something deeper. And reading his poems one goes beyond the outside beauty, ever changing and evanescent, and feels that spiritual beauty, the beauty of the soul, which remains always, and is the heart of all other true beauty.

Thus Wordsworth in his poems seems not only to love and admire nature, but to commune with her, to take from her her thoughts and meanings, and it is this communion translated into verse which gives him a place beyond that of any other poet of nature.

Wordsworth's first work was the publication, in 1793, of two poems, called *An Evening Walk* and *Descriptive Sketches*—the latter being the record of a walking tour in the Alps. Very little notice was taken of these poems, though it is said that Coleridge, who was then at Cambridge, saw in them some promise of the great genius afterward developed. But six years later Wordsworth produced, in conjunction with Coleridge, a little book called *Lyrical Ballads*, in which were four or five poems which distinctly marked the appearance of a new poet.

Lyrical Ballads was published with the object of obtaining enough money for a trip abroad, and immediately after its publication

Wordsworth and Coleridge went to Germany for a short tour. It was after his return from this journey that Wordsworth settled permanently in the lake district, and that he and his friends received the name of the Lake Poets.

From this time on Wordsworth settled himself to a purely literary career, and his long and uneventful life gave him opportunity to bring his art to its highest point. His longest poem is *The Excursion*, an unfinished philosophical epic ; his *Ode on Intimations of Immortality* is perhaps the grandest ode in the English tongue, and a composition that places Wordsworth next to Milton in sublimity of thought, though his *Ode to Duty* has been set even higher by some critics.

In his other poems he touches almost every phase of country life. In the simplicity of his style Wordsworth differed widely from the poets who preceded him. He cared nothing for the romantic and beautiful imagery of Byron, Shelley, or Keats, and it was his great desire to found a school of poetry which should be based upon the truth and simplicity of natural feeling rather than upon unusual experiences or heroic passions.

It is the indication of his great genius that he succeeded in doing this, and that later poets have been glad to learn from him his art of raising the common things of life to heights unattained before. Wordsworth's work suffers greatly from his seeming inability to choose his subject. Everything seemed to him worthy of poetry, and thus he produced a vast quantity of work which has no poetic value, and which mars his work as a whole. But he must be ranked, in spite of these defects, by what he really accomplished for great poetry, and thus it is easy to place him among the greatest of English poets.

Wordsworth's serene and happy life, consecrated to a beautiful art, came to a close in 1850, in his eighty-first year.

Coleridge, the friend of Wordsworth, shared with him the honor of making the Lake School famous. In the *Lyrical Ballads*, which the two friends published together, the best and longest poem was by Coleridge, and although he was then but twenty-five years of age, and produced an immense amount of work afterward, this poem has always been regarded as his best. It was called *The Ancient Mariner*, and was a weird story of shipwreck and disaster thrown into the old English ballad form.

The story is supposed to be related by an old sailor, one of the unfortunate crew, and this endows it with a reality and homeliness that make its fantastic wildness seem natural and common. In this poem the superstitions of the sea, the unlikeness of its life to any other existence, and the awful loneliness of the surviving mariner among his dead companions, are pictured with a fidelity that brings them before us as an actual experience. And it showed the power of Coleridge's genius that he could produce this effect in spite of the mystical atmosphere in which he clothed this poem, in which occur such strange visions of the unearthly and supernatural that one cannot tell whether the hero was possessed by some spirit of evil or whether he really did see things hidden from the natural visions of man. The poem is also

28

one of the best examples of Coleridge's ex-
quisitely melodious touch, the metre being so
perfect that the poem sounds like music.

There can be no greater contrast than that
between the poetry of Wordsworth and Coleridge. The one was the poet of nature, who
saw and interpreted the soul of the visible
world ; the other was the poet of the imagination, as no poet has ever been before.
To other poets came dreams of heavenly or
earthly beauty for their inspiration or interpretation, but Coleridge seemed rather to dream
of dreams. His poetry is so unreal, so full of
elusive mystery, so fantastic and grotesque,
that it seems as if he had woven into it the
very web and tissue of which dreams are made.
Indeed, one of his most perfect poems, *Kubla
Khan*, he said always was merely a transcription of a dream. Some one came and woke
him as he slept, and the dream was broken off;
the part that remained in his memory he wrote
out, making *Kubla Khan* a unique poem in the
language. *Christabel*, another beautiful poem,
has the same wild charm. It is the story of a

young girl who is supposed to be under the influence and control of a witch, and the mingling of reality and unreality is so subtle that they melt together as one dream fades and mingles with another.

It is the poems of this class which set Coleridge apart from all other English poets, and give him that individuality which belongs only to the highest genius. Outside of these productions, however, Coleridge produced some exquisite lyrics and love poems, and some odes of wonderful melody and richness. He also made a masterly translation of *Wallenstein*, the great trilogy of the German poet Schiller, and wrote an original tragedy called *Remorse*, which contains some beautiful examples of pure description, though it lacks dramatic power.

But outside of his poetry Coleridge accomplished a wonderful amount in the field of prose. Besides being a poet he was one of the most subtle and original thinkers that England has ever known. His mind seemed to embrace all subjects, and nothing seemed foreign to his universal grasp. Philosophy, theology, and literature interested him equally, and if he had been less of a dreamer, and more of a worker, one cannot say where his achievements might have stopped. As it is, Coleridge always impresses his admirers as being himself greater than anything he produced, an instance in which genius seemed to take possession of its object rather than to be possessed by it.

Coleridge's prose works consist of several volumes of talks, essays, sermons, and criticisms, and show the immense range of his powers, and the reason for the great influence he exerted upon his contemporaries and successors. He was the first great thinker to introduce the German philosophy and literature into England, and the first great critic to analyze the plays of Shakespeare, and point out the laws which govern the works of the Elizabethan drama, and it is to him that English literature owes some of the best work of the men who found in Coleridge that suggestive inspiration which distinguishes him above all other writers.

Coleridge was born in Devonshire in 1772, and was educated at Christ's Hospital and Cambridge. He travelled abroad, and was at one time so deeply interested in socialism that he formed a plan of establishing in America a model republic which should teach ideal democracy to all the world. This, however, was never accomplished, as neither he nor Southey, the two principal leaders, had any money to carry out their plans.

Coleridge spent most of his days in quiet uneventfulness, admired and loved by the students and literary followers who considered him their guide and teacher, and happy in his half-dream-like life. He died in 1834.

The poet Southey was, next to Wordsworth and Coleridge, the most famous of the Lake School of poets. But though Southey produced an immense quantity of poetry, he was lacking in the true inspiration which marks the lasting works of genius. Southey was famous in his day, and was such a diligent worker that he produced one hundred and nine volumes of writings. Among these were several long poems, *Thalaba ; or, The Destroyer*, a poem of Arabian adventure, and *The Curse of Ke-*

hama, a story of Hindu mythology, being the best known. He also translated innumerable stories from the Spanish and Portuguese, and from mediæval legends. His works all show great learning, but perhaps his *Life of Nelson*, the famous English naval hero, is the only one that approaches perfection of style. Southey is read by students and lovers of poetry, but his work lacks the vital force which would appeal to the general reader. Nevertheless, because of his friendship and intimacy with Wordsworth and Coleridge, and the position he held in his own day, his name will forever be connected with the genius of the Lake School.

Later nineteenth century poetry has well realized the fair promise of the beginning.

Among the poets of this period may be mentioned Matthew Arnold, whose poetry is marked by such deep intellectual insight and feeling; William Morris, whose *Earthly Paradise* is an echo from the pre-Shakespearean verse; Dante Gabriel Rossetti, in whose ballads and sonnets one sees the fire of genius mingled with the quaint romanticism of the days of chivalry, and Algernon Charles Swinburne, whose *Atalanta in Calydon* connects him with Keats, and so back to the poetry of Greece, and whose lyric quality and rhythmic felicities are unique.

All of these poets have a charm and vitality not possessed by any other group of minor poets in any age, and they have produced work of such a high order of merit, indeed, that they can only be called minor when compared to the few great poets who stand beyond and above all comparison.

Among the later poets also stands Robert Browning, whose genius reaches to the greatest heights, and who must ever stand among the greatest of English poets.   Browning's verse is marked by such depth of thought and insight into the human soul, and by such dramatic intensity and power, that it forms a class by itself.   His poems are largely poems of the soul, dealing with those subtle problems and questions that only the greatest genius could un-

ravel or indicate the solution of. His most famous poems are *Paracelsus*, the story of the
famous old alchemist who lived in the sixteenth century; *Sordello*, an Italian poet of the
Middle Ages; the dramatic poems *Pippa Passes*,
Colombe's Birthday, and *In a Balcony;* two acting plays, *Lucia*, and *A Blot on the 'Scutcheon*,
and *The Ring and the Book*, a poem of Italian
crime in which the story is repeated eleven
times, in as many different ways by the different
actors in the scene.

But Browning's shorter poems also ring with
deepest poetic feeling, and in fact, whatever he
touched left his hand bearing upon it the seal
of the master. His great defect as a poet
is the ruggedness of his verse, which is often
strained and uncouth, and which seldom possess-
es the melodic sweetness which thrills through
the lines of other great poets. But great as this
defect is, it is so overshadowed by his genius
that in thinking of Browning one thinks only of
the wide grasp and fine touch which make him
one of the greatest of England's poets.

Browning was born in 1812, in the neighborhood of London, and died in Venice in 1890. He married Elizabeth Barrett, and Mrs. Browning is the woman poet whose *Sonnets from the Portuguese* are among the most beautiful sonnets in the English language, whose long narrative poem *Aurora Leigh* is a masterpiece, and whose minor poems show a depth of feeling and pathos inseparable from true poetic genius.

In the early part of the century a little child, standing beneath the swaying trees that shaded the lawn of the old rectory where he lived, said to one near him, " I hear a voice in the wind." This was the first line of poetry ever made by Alfred Tennyson, one of England's greatest singers, and whose work, with that of Robert Browning, fitly crowns the poetry of the nineteenth century.

Tennyson was born in 1809, in Lincolnshire, and was the son of a clergyman. He began publishing poems at the age of eighteen, but it was not until three years later that he produced anything that indicated his great genius. At this time, however, he published a little book called *Poems, Chiefly Lyrical,* which, though it received little notice from the public, contained some verse marked clearly by that indefinable thing called promise, and his literary career may be said to date from that time.

Tennyson's most celebrated long poems are *The Princess, Maud, In Memoriam, Enoch Arden, Locksley Hall, The Northern Farmer, Idylls of the King.* But besides these he has written shorter poems of such exquisiteness that they can only best be described by the word Tennysonian, a word that stands for that rare combination of faultless melody and color which this poet has introduced into English poetry.

The Princess is the story of a young prince who left his father's kingdom, and travelled far southward in search of the fair princess who had been his betrothed from childhood. No one at his father's court knew of the journey, and the young prince and his two companions travelled in disguise, as they had no hope that the princess would receive them when they reached her dominions. For the princess, when she became of age, had refused to marry, and had built a

great Palace of Learning over which she pre-
sided with great dignity, and in which she
taught that marriage was not a thing to be considered by any woman of courage or brains.
And all the noble maidens who were her pupils
listened to this teaching with great respect and
admiration, and none of them ever dreamed of
lovers, but all passed their days in studying geometry and science, and in visions of what a
beautiful place the world would be if women
ruled all the affairs of life, and there were no
men anywhere.

But the prince could not bear to give up the
beautiful princess whom he had loved from
childhood, so he started out to seek her like a
knight of old, choosing danger and perhaps
death rather than the loss of her.   And when he
and his friends reached her palace, they found
entrance much more easily than they had hoped,
for in their disguise the princess took them for
three maidens who had come to study with her,
and so welcomed them cordially.   But this de-
ception could not long be kept up, and when
it became known who the three new students

were, there was great commotion in the Palace of Learning, and the prince was only saved from death by the arrival of his father's army, which fought for him in the great battle that followed. Yet he was wounded almost unto death in spite of his brave defenders, and the old king, his father, wept bitter tears, fearing that he would have to return to his country alone, and leave his son behind him in the grave. And this might have happened, had not the princess suddenly found that, notwithstanding her devotion to learning and her scorn of men, she was very much in love with the young prince. This surprisingly happy change, of course, made the prince give up all thought of dying, and so the story came to a glad end.

The Princess has an atmosphere of mediæval life, in which the modern problem of woman's position in the world would seem strangely out of place, but for the great art shown in the composition. The poem is beautified by a number of Tennyson's most exquisite songs, and shows throughout the touch of the master's hand.

Enoch Arden is the story of a sailor who was

shipwrecked, and absent from home for many years, returning to find that he had been looked upon as dead, and that his children had learned to call the friend of his youth father. This is one of the most pathetic of Tennyson's poems, and the picture of the returned husband, keeping his identity unknown, so that he might spare his wife and children, is so strongly and poetically drawn that it appeals at once to the heart.

The Northern Farmer is a transcription of the homely life of a North Country woman, touched with a poetic grace that lifts it out of the commonplace and suggests the homespun genius of Burns.

In Memoriam is an elegy on the death of Tennyson's friend, Arthur Hallam. It is not one poem, but rather a series of short poems in which the great subjects of life are discussed. The immortality of the soul, the meaning of life and death, the relation between God and man, and the uses of friendship, love, sorrow, and death are here made the themes of some of the noblest philosophical verse that England has yet seen. Tennyson was seventeen years in composing this poem, which represents at once his highest art and intellectual grasp.

In the series of poems the *Idylls of the King*, Tennyson has retold the Arthurian legends with a power and beauty that makes them seem new. The old legends, as collected by Mallory in the fifteenth century, have all the mediæval charm and simplicity that marks the pre-Spenserian poetry. Mallory tells the stories as the old monks told their tales of saints and legends of the fathers, with the directness of utter faith, and in the language of the common people who heard them. And these qualities connect them so closely with the old English poetry that they seem like old songs thrown into the language of prose. But Tennyson took some of the prose narratives and clothed them with such richness of thought and description that it is as if one saw the old picture of Mallory set with jewels and glowing in the radiance of unfamiliar light.

In these *Idylls* Tennyson relates the coming of Arthur to his kingdom and the adventures of his most famous knights of the Round Table,

ending the series with an account of the last
battle and death of the hero-king. One of the
most interesting of the Idylls is that of *Gareth
and Lynette*. Gareth was the son of one of
the old kings and the news of Arthur's heroic
deeds and the glory of his court had filled his
heart with longing to go to Camelot and become one of the famous knights. But as he
had two brothers already at court, his mother
refused him permission to go, and when she was
at last overcome by his entreaties, she said that
he might go if he would promise her to serve in
the king's kitchen for a year, thinking that this
hard provision would keep him at home. But
Gareth, since he could go in no other way, said
that he would accept the condition, as all service
to the king was honorable and worthy of one
who desired to be a knight. So he clothed
himself as a serving-man, and with two old servants took his way to Camelot, whose distant
towers shone like an enchanted city though all
the weariness of the long way. But when
they entered the famous city, which had been
built long ago to the music of harps played by

fairy kings and queens, they felt well repaid for all their trouble, for the great hall of the king shone like the splendor of the sun and the knights stood goodly and tall and strong, like trees of the forest, and the king himself, the fairest and greatest among them, looked like one whom all must serve gladly, whether life or death might come from it.

Then Gareth, keeping his promise, begged of the king that he might serve in the kitchen for a year, and this the king granted, and none of the knights wondered at the request save the great Launcelot, for they did not see beneath the disguise, but Launcelot saw, and wondered that so noble a youth should crave such a boon. So Gareth served faithfully for a month, and kept his secret well. But at the end of that time his mother's heart could no longer stand the thought of such indignity, and she released him from his vow and sent word to King Arthur that it was her son who served in his kitchen. And then Arthur yielded to Gareth's request to be sent on some mission, as was the fashion of knights; and when there came to the court a fair maid who had wrongs to be righted, Gareth came forward and begged that the quest should be his, and every one marvelled when the king granted the boon, and the maid Lynette turned from Gareth in scorn and called him a kitchen knave, and begged that Launcelot might be her deliverer. But this the king would not grant, and Gareth and Lynette started out together. Through all the perils and dangers of the way she scorned him, though he fought her battles and gained victory over the knight of the Morning Star and the Brotherhood of Day and Night, and after each victory she would taunt him and say that he was a knave of the kitchen and no true knight. And Gareth bore all her revilings silently, saying only that his deeds would answer her words.

And so at last Lynette, won by his courage and knightly gentleness, began to look upon him with favor, and scorned him no longer, and when the quest was won she became his wife, caring not that he was lord of a great realm, but cherishing always the thought of his perfect manliness and stainless knighthood.

In the Idyll *Launcelot and Elaine* Tennyson tells the story of Elaine, the lily maid of Astolat, who loved Launcelot so well that she could only die when she found he had no love to give her back. This poem, which shows us Elaine up in the tower guessing the devices on Launcelot's shield, caring for him through his illness, confessing her hopeless love for him, and then dead, floating down the river to Launcelot in the lily-decked barge, is one of the most beautiful of all the Idylls. It is full of sweet regret and tender pathos, and justly ranks as one of the most perfect of Tennyson's poems.

In *Merlin and Vivien* the poet tells how the great enchanter Merlin yielded to the wiles of the wicked Vivien, and told her all the secret of his art. *Geraint and Enid* is the story of the trial of Enid's faith by her husband, who bade her follow him through the world and never speak to him, no matter what danger might come, and tells how at last she proved her utter love and faithfulness.

The Holy Grail is the story of the search for the Holy Grail, the golden cup from which

Christ drank at the Last Supper.   Many of the
knights started on this quest, but save the
pure-hearted Galahad no knight might see it,
and he saw it only dimly, floating before him
in the moonlight, gleaming across the wide
wastes of moor and bog, shining through the
dusk of old forests, or kindling the sky with
new and unearthly radiance, but always at a
distance, until at last it led him across a bridge
whose piers stretched far out into the great
sea ; and then in a mystic vision he saw the
Heavenly City and the Holy Grail passing out
of sight into the wonder of heaven, its trailing
glory falling rose-red upon the sea, and then
fading to darkness.

Many were the knights who followed this
holy adventure, and of those who left the hall
of the Round Table more than one lost his
life in the vain search, so that from that day
the number of Arthur's knights was lessened
as no war or quest had ever lessened it before,
leaving a sadness in the king's heart that no
after-time could soothe.   In this poem Tennyson has caught the old mystical feeling which

thrilled through the spiritual life of the mediæval monks who spent their days and nights in
dreams all ecstasies of devotion. He has also
given the note of pure religious fervor which
characterized these men, and made their lives
consistent and beautiful, and thus its spiritual
beauty adds another grace to this exquisite
Idyll.

The Idylls close with the *Passing of Arthur*,
which contains the account of the last battle
fought by the king against the traitor Modred,
who was striving for the kingdom. The duel
with Modred, whom Arthur slays, and the death
of the king from a wound he himself received
form the chief incidents of this poem, which is
marked by such grandeur of style that it is
unique among the Idylls. The description of
Arthur lying in the faintness of death upon
the silent battle-field, where all his knights
save one lie dead, is unparalleled in English
verse. The picture is so powerfully drawn,
and so full of the atmospheric effect, that the
scene is brought before our eyes even more
perfectly than it could have been produced by

a painter's brush; while the rhythmic beat of the lines, the weird, melodic ebb and flow sounding like the sea surge, runs through the verse like a fitting accompaniment to the scene of action. And so we get our last glimpse of Arthur dying by the winter sea, attended only by the faithful Bedivere. And first Bedivere throws Excalibur, which no man save Arthur may wield, into the lake, and then bears the king down to the water side, and gives him in charge of the black-robed queens who have come to bear him to the shadowy vales of Avalon. There, far beyond the reach of mortal sight, he may be healed of his wounds, and come again to earth to inaugurate a new order of noble knights, who shall wage war against all unmanliness and sin, so the legend runs, a legend which held the peasant mind for many centuries, during which the story of Arthur's glorious life and mysterious passing was universally accepted as truth.

Besides these long poems, Tennyson has produced a large number of minor poems of such beauty that they alone would mark him as one of England's noblest poets. Added to the exquisite quality of his verse, which has made him loved by the poets who delight to call him master, there is a charm that appeals to all who love beauty of any kind. It is this which has made Tennyson one of the most popular poets that have ever lived. His poetry is known and loved wherever the English language is spoken, and the sound of it is familiar to many to whom other poets are but sealed books. In this respect Tennyson enjoys a fame shared only by those great song writers whose ballads have become a part of the soul of English literature. It is rare to find a great poet known as familiarly as the folk-songs of a people are known, but this high distinction belongs to Tennyson, whose influence upon the popular taste has been so ennobling and vast that one cannot well compute the debt that is owed him.